‖‖‖‖‖‖‖‖‖‖‖‖‖‖‖‖‖‖‖‖‖
⟡ **W9-AUA-033**

Dark Power

Power.

Up, up he swirled, using the heavily charged air.

Patience.

He had acted too soon. After so long, so long that he had almost forgotten it himself to hear the sound of his name on another's tongue. Iyeeeee! He screamed it aloud, used the voice of the wind.

He shuddered. His need was overpowering. So firm, so supple, the flesh that had been his, had been denied him for time immemorial. Up, up he whirled, exhilaration racing through him although frustration gnawed within. So close.

He was not yet strong enough. In unfulfillment he cried aloud, his voice, the voice of the thunder, roaring over the island, sweeping over the sea.

Patience, a voice counseled within him, remnant of earlier, craftier days.

Power. It would come to him. All he had to do was wait. Time was now a friend.

PATCIE'S PAPERBACK
BOOK EXCHANGE
256 E. GRAND AVE.
FOX LAKE, IL   312-587-0503

THE BEST IN BONE CHILLING TERROR
FROM PINNACLE BOOKS!

Blood-curdling new blockbusters by horror's premier masters of the macabre! Heart-stopping tales of terror by the most exciting new names in fright fiction! Pinnacle's the place where sensational shivers live!

FEAST   (17-103-7, $4.50)
by Graham Masterton
Le Reposir in the quiet little town of Allen's Corners wasn't interested in restaurant critic Charlie McLean's patronage. But Charlie's son, Martin, with his tender youth, was just what the secluded New England eatery had in mind!
"THE LIVING INHERITOR TO THE REALM OF EDGAR ALLEN POE"
— SAN FRANCISCO CHRONICLE

LIFEBLOOD   (17-110-X, $3.95)
by Lee Duigon
The yuppie bedroom community of Millboro, New Jersey is just the place for Dr. Winslow Emerson. For Emerson is no ordinary doctor, but a creature of terrifying legend with a hideous hunger . . . And Millboro is the perfect feeding ground!

GHOUL'S   (17-119-3, $3.95)
by Edward Lee
The terrified residents of Tylersville, Maryland, have been blaming psychopaths, werewolves and vampires for the tidal wave of horror and death that has deluged their town. But policeman Kurt Morris is about to uncover the truth . . . and the truth is much, much worse!

Available wherever paperbacks are sold, or order direct from the Publisher. Send cover price plus 50¢ per copy for mailing and handling to Pinnacle Books, Dept. 17-213, 475 Park Avenue South, New York, N.Y. 10016. Residents of New York, New Jersey and Pennsylvania must include sales tax. DO NOT SEND CASH.

THE SHAPECHANGER

Elizabeth Ergas

PINNACLE BOOKS
WINDSOR PUBLISHING CORP.

Pinnacle Books

are published by

Windsor Publishing Corp.
475 Park Avenue South
New York, NY 10016

Copyright © 1989 by Elizabeth L. Ergas

All rights reserved. No part of this book may be reproduced
in any form or by any means without the prior written consent
of the publisher, excepting brief quotes used in reviews.

First printing: May, 1989

Printed in the United States of America

To my two best friends

—my husband, Leonard Ergas
whose counsel, patience and belief sustained me

—my mother, Beatrice Pines
whose faith and love encouraged me

and

To the memory of my father, George Pines
the inspiration for all my creative endeavors

PROLOGUE

AUGUST, 1932

The daub of crimson shone like a jewel on the tip of the knife. Lothar Voss stared at it, then transferred his gaze upward. He could feel the excitement begin, deep within him. He let it build, let it grow until it vibrated throughout his body. Ever so faintly he began to tremble. The last stroke, the final plunge, and it would be over.

It had been hard, this summer of loneliness, frustration and . . . tragedy. But he would not think of that now, would not spoil this penultimate moment.

Now. Now is the time. His brain signaled his hand and the knife descended. A deft stroke, a curl of his wrist, and it was done. Lothar Voss dropped the knife onto a paint-smeared cloth and stepped back to survey the completed picture for the first time. There could be no doubt. The trembling of his body, by now almost uncontrollable, confirmed what he had suspected for

7

some time. This painting was more than his best work—it was a masterpiece.

Margaret, he had to get Margaret. He needed to share this moment. His triumph needed a witness. Not that his wife would, or could, understand the true depth of his achievement. His genius. Genius. Yes. He liked the shape of that word.

The fresh air came as a shock after the studio with its familiar, comforting smells. He inhaled deeply, forcing clear, pine-scented air into lungs more used to the acrid fumes of solvents and turpentine. A hint of chill drifted off the ocean, through the thick stand of trees, a sharp reminder that summer ended sooner in northern Maine than it did elsewhere. No matter. They could leave now that he had finished. That should make Margaret happy. He frowned, wondered briefly if anything would ever make Margaret happy again. No, not now. He did not want to think of flesh, perfect in shape and form, a mirror of his own youth, a flowering of his seed. His son. His perfect son. His perfect dead son.

Guilt flickered on the edge of his mind. Ruthlessly he rejected it, as he did anything that interfered with his creative drive. Ordinary people had to adjust their lives to his. Margaret knew this, had known it from the beginning. There had been no reason, no real reason, to change after . . . *My son, my son, it would not have brought you back.*

He should not have to entertain these thoughts, not now, in his moment of glory. Lately, though, every time he looked at Margaret, saw those sad, grief-haunted eyes, he knew they were covering resentment. She resented him, as much as whatever she blamed for the tragedy. The accident. Well, there was no going back; there could be no resurrection of their dead. This day would be a new start. He guessed he owed her that much.

He set off at a half-walk half-run, all his enthusiasm and excitement returning in a rush. He began to make plans, estimating how long it would take the painting to dry sufficiently to enable him to pack it. The small canvases, done earlier in the summer, mere exercises really, would present no problem. They could be exhibited alongside his masterpiece, the stepping stones to genius. Absorbed in this pleasurable daydream, he tripped over a boulder and was propelled forward by his own momentum, but he managed to save himself from a nasty fall by grabbing a low-lying branch of a tall white spruce. The tree's needles, stiff and sharp, bit deeply into his hands. With an oath he jerked them free, staring in horror at tiny dots of blood where the needles had penetrated his skin. The sight of blood, especially his own, caused a sick roiling in his stomach. He wrenched his eyes from the wounds, fighting off faintness and nausea.

The house was just up ahead, past the stand of spruce and evergreens that gave such cool shade even on the hottest days. He reached it in no time, was about to go inside for first aid, when the sound of his wife's voice drifted to him, coming from the clearing on the southeast side. He and Margaret were alone on the island. Curiosity overcame the pain in his hands. A chilling thought stopped him cold. What if Margaret had slipped quietly over the edge of sanity?

He began to move again, forcing himself to turn the corner, to discover whatever awaited him in the clearing. He could barely hear her now, her voice low, indistinct, merely a susurration repeating yes, yes, oh yes over and over again, reverberating in his brain.

Lothar gathered his courage and stepped around the corner of the house. Gone was his mental vision of an incoherent, babbling Margaret as the reality that replaced it almost made him gibber. His astonishment quickly turned to numbness, as his eyes filled with the picture before him, his artist's perceptions registering each detail with excruciating clarity.

Margaret was lying in the grass on her back, her legs spread wide in abandon, her arms outflung. She was naked, save for the man astride her. Her hands were rhythmically squeezing clumps of grass, opening and closing, following the tempo of the man's thrusts, as he rode her with something akin to frenzy. As Lothar watched, completely paralyzed, Margaret locked her arms and legs about the man, reaching down to cup his buttocks with her hands from which long blades of grass dangled. At her urging the man gentled his pace, settling into a steady pattern of deep thrusting and slow withdrawal.

Lothar's numbness receded, his emotions seesawing from disbelief, to rage, to a cold, stark fury. *Whore* his mind screamed, while a small, rational, detached part of him recognized something vaguely familiar about the man pounding into his wife. The shape of the head, the jut of the hip. Madness. Here he stood cataloguing details while his wife cuckolded him under the open sky. He would never know if he had made a sound, finally venting the primal scream of rage which pushed him from within, or if it was his shadow, falling on her face as he approached, which alerted her to his presence. Her eyes opened wider, recognition contorting her features into a mask of stunned disbelief.

"Lothar!"

It was a shout, a plea, a denial.

His artist's eye continued to note details. Margaret's face froze, leaving its prettiness hideously distorted. The man lifted himself off her, levering onto his elbows, producing a wet, sucking sound as his chest slowly separated from hers. Lothar could not tear his eyes from the sight of his wife's breasts heaving with passion. An hysterical laugh bubbled in his throat, quickly aborted as the man, obscenely still joined to Margaret, still buried deep within her flesh, slowly began to turn his head.

Ear, cheekbone, nose, lips, chin: the profile emerged, tantalizingly slowly, as if the man knew what Lothar was thinking, was torturing him with this last, maddening act. An elaborate obscene joke. Friend? Enemy? Once seen, never forgotten; familiar, well-known; yet totally, frighteningly, alien. Margaret lay like cold, gray, lifeless sculptor's putty beneath the man, a forgotten pawn in this game they were playing, a game in which Lothar knew neither the rules nor the play, but the result of which he was just beginning to suspect. A hand, his own, reached out and grabbed the other's shoulder, forcing the play, turning him about. It was then that he recognized him, saw and knew immediately the full face revealed. He was grinning, widely, as if enjoying some cosmic joke. The familiarity was explained, even the unsureness, the hesitancy.

Lothar Voss stared long and hard at the face of madness.

He was looking at himself.

CHAPTER ONE

JUNE, 1989

It took them the better part of three days to reach Puffin Landing. It had not been an easy trip. The closer they got to Maine the more nervous Chip became, withdrawing into himself for long periods. Kate did most of the driving, discovering early on that introspection and traffic safety were not compatible. Then there had been the added problem of their mostly-Irish setter, Natty Bumppo, who was less than an ideal traveler, disgracing himself once in Connecticut and then again in Massachusetts.

They left New York on Monday, stopping frequently to sightsee. Kate regarded it as a minivacation, a blissful interlude away from housekeeping and daily cares. For Chip it was merely a postponement. Now it was Wednesday, and with mixed feelings Kate spotted a sign indicating Puffin Landing was five miles ahead. She glanced sideways at Chip, who had insisted on taking the wheel after their lunch stop. Probably some male instinct to show he was in control. The thought amused her and she turned her head to hide her amusement from him. Chip had been noticeably short on humor lately, another byproduct of the grant. Or, rather, The Grant, as she was coming to think of it.

They emerged from a wooded stretch into bright sunshine, the road narrowing from two lanes down to one. The small seacoast village, tenaciously hugging the rock-strewn shore, was dazzlingly white and clean in the afternoon sun. Through the open windows they could smell the sea.

Chip drove sedately down the main street, obediently slowing and then stopping as the village's single traffic light went from yellow to red. They were the only car on the road. An elderly woman, with finger-waved white hair and wearing a flowered cotton dress, painfully shuffled across the street. She disappeared into the dim interior of a pharmacy-newspaper-sundries store, but not before turning and giving their rented hatchback a thorough inspection.

"She did that on purpose. I swear it. She deliberately waited until we were close and then she punched the walk button." Chip shook his head ruefully and gave Kate one of those quirky smiles which always tugged at her heart.

"Of course she did. I saw her. It's probably a game she plays with strangers."

"Some game." They were moving again, idling slowly, Chip frowning at each house and building they passed. "Can you catch an address, it looks like we're running out of the business district." They reached the end of the street. Chip pulled over onto the shoulder and stopped. "This is ridiculous, anyway. They could have mailed us the keys to the house. I'm sure the island isn't too difficult to find."

"I'm sure it isn't, Chip, but for one thing, we don't know who has been hired to take us out there, and for another, we must make arrangements about the car. Then, there's the mail, the—"

"Okay. Okay. Spare me the list." Chip snorted. "You'd think they would have the Police Department right out where everyone can see it."

They were looking for the police, or rather, Sheriff Daniel Sheridan, who held the keys to the house on Smoke Island. He had also undertaken to make all the arrangements pertaining to their residency. Wilma Thompson, Chip's agent, had been in touch with him and had been uncharacteristically impressed.

"It's a small place, hon. There's probably no need for a visible police presence. How about that gas station?" Kate pointed ahead.

"Again? Kate, really—Argh." Chip exaggeratedly massaged his rib cage where Kate had given him a none-too-gentle poke.

"There are other uses one can make of a service station," she said primly. "Shall we?"

There was no one about when they pulled into the two-island station moments later. Clanking metallic noises came from the side of the building where there were three service bays, two with their overhead doors pulled down. The third had a car up on a lift, two men working under it while a third sat on an empty crate and watched.

Chip backed the car up, maneuvering until they were near the occupied bay. None of the men even glanced their way. "Desperate for business," he observed out of the side of his mouth. When it became obvious he would have to take the initiative, he shut the engine off. Immediately the car filled with the cries of gulls, the piercing noise seeming to swell in volume inside the confined space.

Kate watched as Chip walked around the car and headed for the service area. As always, she admired his tall, spare frame, the easy grace with which he moved. He could have been an athlete, had in fact been interested in track in college, but dropped it when it interfered with his studio time. Everything in Chip's life had to accommodate his art. Everything. She understood this; had always understood it.

"That the new artist feller, come to live out at th' island?"

Kate jumped, the gravelly voice taking her unaware. "Why yes," she replied, recognizing the questioner as the man supervising the work. A quick glance confirmed it, the crate was now unoccupied.

The man chuckled, seeing the direction of her glance. "I kin still move, fast an' quiet like, iffinit pleases me." He thrust his grizzled head close to hers, grinning widely, baring a mouth almost completely devoid of teeth.

Kate recoiled, jerking her head farther inside the car. The stranger followed, uncaring of her unease. His eyes, sharp under a screen of thick, bushy brows, missed nothing, traveling over her features, down her body and then moving on to probe and catalogue the interior of the car.

Kate inched sideways, wishing Chip would hurry back. The man's wheezing breath almost drowned out the raucous cries of the gulls. Kate consoled herself with the thought that he was probably harmless, a local character. Besides which, nothing could happen to her here, in broad daylight, with her husband within earshot. Uneasily she remembered an incident on Lexington Avenue this past winter. It had been in all the papers, a kind of splashy this-could-happen-to-you article. A woman was waiting for her husband in a parked car when a man just got in and drove off with her. She had been raped and beaten, then thrown out in a deserted area. All because her husband had to stop for cigarettes. Or had he also stopped for directions?

Now she was being fanciful, letting her imagination run away with her. No one was going to make a victim of her. Not in the city, and not here, where that sort of thing was surely uncommon. Not if she could help it. But the fact remained that a decidedly unsavory character was altogether too close to her. To be on the safe side, she gradually worked her left hand up to the steering column and as unobtrusively as possible removed the ignition key, palming it, ready to throw it out the window at the first sign of trouble. Natty Bumppo snoozed peacefully in the back seat, as usual completely worthless as a guard dog.

"You the missus?"

Kate nodded, quickly quelling the absurd urge to show him her plain gold wedding band as proof. She wished Chip would return. She could not see him anymore, either the old man was blocking her view or he had disappeared into the interior of the service bay. How long could it take to get directions to the Police Department?

"Any children, missus?"

"No, no children." She wasn't sure, but she thought that relief flared briefly on the old man's seamed face. Ridiculous. He was only being nosy. Small town life, as advertised.

"Pretty." He reached out and touched her thick, sable-dark hair.

Kate exercised all her willpower not to flinch. He is harmless, there is nothing to worry about. She let the thought run through her mind, repeating it silently over and over, like a mantra, childishly hoping belief could will reality.

"Thank you." She stifled the urge to giggle. Good manners triumphed even under a threat of violence. With her peripheral vision she caught sight of Chip. The old man either read her eyes or sensed Chip's nearness, for suddenly his face changed, taking on an urgent expression. Emboldened by Chip's imminent arrival, Kate retreated farther into the car, hoping to discourage him. Her ploy backfired, for he bent low and thrust himself inside, after her, bringing his weathered, leathery face within inches of hers.

"Listen, missus," he growled, alarming Kate even more, "listen hard. Go not to yon island. He waits for you." Once again he fingered Kate's hair, letting a silky strand run through his gnarled fingers.

Kate could hear Chip's footsteps now. He was almost to the car. She forced herself to sit still.

The old man heard him too. His manner became more hurried, his speech more staccato. "Listen, missus. Go away. Go home. Death waits there. Death . . . and more."

Kate shivered, afraid despite her best intentions. The

18

old man was so intense. She had no doubt he believed what he said.

"Kate? What the—?" There was a note of alarm in Chip's voice.

Kate heard his rapid approach but could not tear her gaze from the mesmerizing eyes of the old man. He fascinated and repulsed her.

"Listen, missus," he said again, "listen to Old Nate." Urgency distorted his lined features. He withdrew as Chip's shadow loomed over the car. With amazing agility he scuttled back toward the service area.

"What was that all about?" Chip climbed into the car and slammed the door, rousing Natty Bumppo from his doggy dream.

"I . . . I'm not sure." Kate hesitated, trying to sort out her thoughts.

"The damnedest thing just happened."

"What?" Mentally she shrugged. What she had to tell him could wait. Nothing had happened. Not really. The old man was probably sun-touched. "Where's the Police Department? Did we miss it back there?"

"Yes and no. Where the hell's the key?" Chip pawed impatiently through his pockets.

Belatedly Kate realized she still clutched it in her hand. Silently she gave it to Chip, who jammed it into the ignition, apparently uninterested in why she was holding it. The engine whined and then caught. Chip threw it in gear and steered them toward the road. As they rolled past the service bay two coveralled figures emerged. One had a large wrench in his begrimed hand. He raised it, as if pointing the way, but to Kate it looked more like a defiant gesture, maybe even a

19

threatening one. She glanced sideways at Chip and noticed his hands gripped the steering wheel with unnecessary force. His knuckles were white.

"Chip—?"

"Did you see that? God, what a strange experience." He gunned the engine and they shot forward onto the blacktop, turning right, away from the main street. They were traveling at a good speed, heedless of any village limits. Chip glanced frequently into the rearview mirror.

Kate turned and saw what he was looking at. Three figures, unnaturally still, stood on the shoulder of the road watching them. They looked sinister in spite of the distance dwindling their size.

"Where are we going?" Kate fought to keep her voice steady. Chip's agitation, coupled with her own unsettling experience, was making her nervous again.

"We're going to Daniel Sheridan's house. It seems the sheriff doesn't set up shop in the village until July, when the tourists arrive. That character with the wrench gave me directions." His voice changed, becoming higher, more nasal. " 'Down the road, 'bout two-, mebbe three-tenths a'mile, road forks. Take the right hand all aways down to th'water. Can't miss it. Ain't nothing much a'else down that ways.' " He shook his sandy head. "Jeesus. What a character, Kate, you can't imagine."

"I think I might have some idea," she replied dryly. Now was the time to tell him about the old man's warning, but perversely, she could not get the words out. Deep in thought, she realized Chip was talking, had been, in fact, for several moments.

". . . and when I mentioned that we were headed for the island, he clammed up and turned surly."

Kate jerked abruptly out of her reverie. "He . . . he what?"

"Weren't you listening?" Annoyance warred with exasperation as Chip glanced at her.

"Yes, of course I was." This was too much like the old man's dramatically delivered message to be coincidental.

"There's the fork. At least he didn't lie." Chip steered right and they followed the winding road, now little more than a wider-than-normal single lane. "Look for a white clapboard house with green trim."

"Chip, what do you think it was? Back there. The reason for his unfriendliness."

"Dunno." There it was again, Chip's version of a Down East accent.

"Seriously."

"Oh, probably nothing more than a touch of xenophobia, is all. Seriously, Kate, that must be it. Why, these people are so insular that they regard anyone living at least ten miles away as a foreigner. They're afraid of outsiders. Afraid we'll corrupt them, maybe marry their daughters. City slickers never have been popular with country folk, historically speaking, of course."

"Of course." Kate let Chip's foolery persuade her into a happier frame of mind. The old man became nothing more than what she had thought he was originally—a local character. She had magnified the incident out of all proportion. She was tired, tense from the long drive.

She almost convinced herself.

The road wound in an easterly direction. Occasionally they caught a glimpse of the sea, only to lose sight of it again. They passed two houses, one white with yellow trim, the other yellow with brown trim. Neither spoke, each, perhaps, unwilling to give voice to the thought they shared. They were not welcome in Puffin Landing.

Minutes later they found the right house. A sign at the foot of the driveway announced "Daniel Sheridan—General Contractor." On the bottom, in smaller letters, almost as an afterthought, it read "Sheriff" with an arrow pointing to the back of the house. Chip pulled the car to the side of the drive and shut off the engine. Bird cries again filled the car, high soprano voices supported by the unmistakable low register of heavy surf pounding ceaselessly against rock. Natty Bumppo poked his sleek rust-colored head out of Kate's window, his ears lifted as if he were trying to identify these strange new sounds.

They got out of the car and walked around to the back of the house, following a dirt path that ended at a door set three steps up into a glass-enclosed porch. A sign tacked to the door invited one to enter. Chip pushed and it opened easily. "Just like New York," he observed, and went on in.

Kate lingered outside for a moment, enjoying the fresh salt-tinged air, the warm rays of the sun, unfiltered by air pollution. The dog barked excitedly at gulls and arctic terns as they wheeled and glided in a cerulean sky, swooping low in graceful dives to scoop silvery fish out of the water. Their cries filled the air, their voices high, thin, wailing. A Greek chorus. A Greek chorus moaning a minor-key lament behind a crazed Medea. Why did they all have such wounded, tear-drowned eyes? The children. Oooooh the dead children. Kate shivered, horrified at the image. The old man had mentioned children. The view suddenly lost its charm. She called sharply to the dog and fled after Chip.

It was cool and slightly damp inside. The room was an office, with a scarred walnut desk and two scratched metal file cabinets taking up most of the space. The other furniture, two chairs, a sofa and a table, looked as if they came from a garage sale, or straight out of an attic. Even a dusty red geranium looked second-hand, its clay pot cracked. Kate gravitated toward the table which held a coffee maker, a pitcher of lemonade and a dish of chocolate chip cookies covered with a clear plastic wrap. A clipboard and pad was next to the cookies.

"Well, he's not here." Chip's voice had a nervous edge to it.

Kate glanced at him, surprised by his tone. "Perhaps he's back in the house. We should call out," she suggested placidly.

"Here, read this. I found it on the clipboard. What a way to run a business."

Chip thrust a piece of paper into her hands and went to stare out the window. Kate shrugged and read the brief note. Daniel Sheridan was at the Malone place, putting in new windows. He estimated his return around three o'clock. By her watch that was only about ten minutes away. "We're not in New York now," she said mildly, "things are done differently here."

Chip snorted. "And if he were out busting up a drug ring would he leave a note, 'Down at dock waiting to arrest international gang of heroin smugglers. Back as soon as ship comes in.' ''

"I take it that was not a question." Kate helped herself to a cookie and took a bite, surprised to discover they were home baked. "Maybe his wife is at home, Chip. The cookies are still warm."

"He's not married."

"Oh? How do you know?"

"My friend at the garage told me. Before he learned I was going to be his neighbor." Chip rapidly lost patience with the conversation. "Look, Kate, that island out there. The closest one. Do you think that's Smoke Island?" He sounded nervous again.

"Could be, hon, but I don't see any house. Or a studio. There are so many islands. Strange, I didn't expect that."

"It's called New England's drowned coast. It was formed during the last Ice Age. That, out there, was a mountain range." Chip waved his arm, encompassing the breathtaking view commanded by the window. Outside, past a short, grassy verge, stretched the seemingly limitless sweep of sea and sky, peppered by areas of land, some furred by trees, others mere juts of granite rising from the restless waves. "The weight of the ice cap pushed the mountains under the ocean. The islands are the summits, resurfaced when the glacier retreated." Chip broke off, almost as if embarrassed by his knowledge.

"Been doing a little research, huh fella," Kate teased.

"Never hurts," he admitted, shrugging modestly. "Besides, I wanted to learn a little something about the island that some day is going to be known as the place where my true genius flowered.''

''Humble, aren't we?''

''Honest.''

''That's better,'' she commented, noting his voice completely lacked any of the earlier nervousness.

''What's better?''

''My secret. Now, what shall we do, wait or go back into town and do some grocery shopping? I don't expect to find a Gristede's on every other island.''

''Hardly. You're not in New York now,'' he teased, happy to see she liked being reminded of a different way of life as little as he had, short moments before.

''*Touché.*'' The sound of a heavy engine outside alerted her that any decision had been taken out of their hands. Unless someone had come to report skullduggery amongst the lobster pots, Daniel Sheridan was back.

CHAPTER TWO

Sheriff Daniel Sheridan came as a complete surprise to Kate. If asked, outright, what she had expected, she probably would have admitted to envisioning the stereotypical picture of the small town law enforcement officer. Rod Steiger before Sidney Poitier came to town in *In the Heat of the Night,* complete with beer belly, small beady eyes and narrow mind.

The reality—several inches over six feet, trim athletic build, no older than the midthirties—let the screen door bang shut behind him and took off a sweat-stained New York Yankees baseball cap to reveal gleaming blue-black hair curled in damp disarray. He was dressed in denims and a work shirt, the sleeves rolled up displaying well-muscled arms baked walnut brown by the sun.

They shook hands all around. It amused Kate that he gave them both a thorough scrutiny. His dress might be casual, but the man was all business. For a fleeting instant, as her hand was gripped firmly by his large, callused one, she thought she saw something flicker deep in his eyes. It could have been surprise, or even recognition. Whatever, it was gone as fast as it had come, leaving Kate to wonder if she only imagined it. First the old man at the service station and now this. To cover her confusion she bent down to pet Natty Bumppo, who was leaning heavily against her legs.

"That's a fine looking dog you have there." The sheriff reached down and scratched the setter behind his long, silky ears, thereby earning a look of slavish adoration. "What's his name?"

"Natty Bumppo." It was Kate who answered, since Chip had gone to stand at the window, completely disassociating himself from them. He appeared fascinated with a telescope mounted on a sturdy-looking tripod.

"Ah. The Leatherstocking himself." A grin of wry amusement lit Daniel Sheridan's bronzed features. "Good boy. Good scout." A tug on the dog's ears and the plumed tail thumped enthusiastically against the plank floor. "Named for the Pathfinder, I presume?"

"The only path that dog can find is the one leading to his bowl." The nervous edge was back in Chip's voice. He had turned his back on the window and was glaring at them from across the room. His eyes slid quickly away from the frown on his wife's face and came to rest on the sheriff. "If it's not too much trouble, Chief, I'd like the keys to the house now. My wife and I would like to get settled out there before it gets dark."

"No problem." Seemingly in no hurry, the sheriff straightened up from his crouched position, first giving his new friend a few good thumps on the flank. His laconic movements completely belied the sharp look he threw Chip. "Most people around here call me Daniel," he said mildly. "There's little call for me in my official capacity. A few rowdy drunks come Saturday nights. That and all the problems tourists can have about covers it." He paused and regarded Chip steadily, his dark gaze challenging him. When he spoke again there was a thread of steel in his voice. "Or perhaps you were referring to something else?"

Kate looked from one to the other, perplexed by the sharp question. A subliminal current passed between the two men, charging the air like the few hushed moments before the violence of a sudden summer storm. She saw Chip start to shake his head in negation, although she caught a gleam of understanding as it flashed across his face. If she had seen it, so had the sheriff. Before she could even begin to understand what was happening she heard Chip laugh, trying to diffuse the tension.

"Like what?" he challenged, striving for and just missing an air of nonchalance.

"Like my Indian blood, for instance." The tall sheriff shrugged, as if indifferent, but his eyes continued to bore into Chip's. "I thought for sure your artist's eye would note the lines, here and here." Briefly his hand touched his high cheekbones and then brushed past his widely spaced eyes. "The coloring too is a dead giveaway, I'd think. No matter, though." He let it drop, apparently satisfied with the point he had made. He ambled over to the scarred desk and withdrew a ring of keys that he threw onto the desk top. "The keys to the house. In case you wish to lock up."

"You mean it's open now. Anybody could walk right

28

in?'' Chip was becoming belligerent again, something he used frequently to hide his insecurity. The look he threw Kate was eloquent. What were they doing here, wasting time?

"Anybody could walk right in, as you say, but so far nobody has. The island has never been disturbed."

Kate wondered at his strange choice of words. Almost as if the island was sentient, was capable of being disturbed. It was probably a regional colloquialism. She pushed the peculiar phrase to the back of her mind as she listened to the sheriff talk about the home which was to be theirs for the coming months.

"As you know, I have been in touch with Wilma Thompson ever since the beginning of May. By the way, let me be the first in Puffin Landing to congratulate you on winning the Voss Grant. It's quite an accomplishment, I'm told."

Chip's face flushed with pleasure at this praise, and he nodded his head in acknowledgment of the compliment. Forgotten for the moment was the strange antipathy which had marked the first moments between the two men.

The atmosphere grew perceptibly warmer.

"Everything is ready out on the island." The sheriff spoke directly to Kate. "Henry and I have been working to get things in shape since the end of winter when the trustees of the estate first notified me that there would be a recipient of the grant this year. Not that we knew then who it would be, you understand." A quick smile animated her face, and he smiled in return.

"Henry?"

"Henry Packer. He's a general handyman who acts as caretaker for the Voss property. The island's main-

29

tained all year long, although as far as anyone can remember, it's never been used during the winter months. Winters can be mighty tough around here, especially on a small island."

Kate's gaze went automatically to the glass wall that offered the magnificent view of the island-studded bay. She tried to imagine a slate gray vista, icebound waters bordered by snow-encrusted land, weighed down under a steely sky. It was a bleak prospect. "I can imagine," she said softly.

"It has its own special beauty," the sheriff said just as softly, as if he could see the picture in her mind. "A dangerous beauty, but then, a touch of danger only serves to enhance its attraction. But that's not what I wanted to tell you." He busied himself shuffling through the papers on his desk, not looking up until he located the one he wanted. "I knew I had it here somewhere. This is a list of the improvements made to the property and the new appliances installed at the house. The big thing is the generator. It's new and running perfectly. The trustees had no faith in the old one. Not after so many years. I think you'll be pleased with the others," he said, handing the list to Kate. "Everything is in working order."

She ran her eyes down the page, happy to note the list included a new freezer. She could stock up on supplies and be fairly self-sufficient. As she scanned the page she kept one ear on the sheriff, who was telling Chip that Henry Packer took care of all repairs and maintenance, including the yard work, albeit by an irregular schedule. The sheriff's next words, though, came as a surprise, a rather upsetting surprise.

"What did you say?" Surely she had misunderstood.

"There is no telephone, and no mail delivery."

She had heard correctly. "But . . . we'll be completely cut off."

"You didn't know?"

"No. Wilma omitted to mention it."

With relief she saw there was no look of male condescension on the sheriff's face. No poor-little-woman-lost-without-a-phone-stuck-to-her-ear slyness lurked behind his eyes. Chip studiously avoided looking at her, a sure sign he knew all along. Kate felt a moment's anger, anger at his selfishness, but almost at once suppressed it. It would do no good. As always. Perhaps he would change. Surely now, with the recognition the grant assured, he would settle down once he started work. Only the anticipation made him nervous. Deep down, though, Kate feared she was only fooling herself. Chip would never change. If he did, if he lost that childish, selfish streak, might he not also lose that which gave him his unique talent? In any event, there was nothing she could do about it now. They were here for the duration, and she would just have to make the best of it.

She looked up to see something akin to sympathy flash across Daniel Sheridan's face. She felt suddenly ashamed for letting a stranger have a glimpse of her private thoughts. Not only a stranger, but a professional trained to read what people sought to conceal.

"You won't be completely cut off, Mrs. Windsor. We've got a signal system, using flags, that works well enough. I'll check every day," he promised, indicating the telescope Chip found so fascinating. "Believe me, it will be all right," he added gently, noting the worried frown creasing her forehead. "And as for your mail, I can arrange a box for you, or you could do it yourself today, before you leave, if you like. Bess Perkins runs the Post Office out of the back of the general store. You probably passed it on your way through town."

"Yes, I remember it. Thank you, Sheriff, I think I will arrange it today. And please call me Kate."

"A pleasure, Kate. And it's Daniel, remember?" A smile took any sting out of the reference to the previous tension. Only Kate appreciated this nicety, for Chip was busy with thoughts of his own.

"Perkins. Any relation to the thin, dark fellow with a surly expression who works at the gas station?"

"Walt's her husband, and he owns the station. Why? What happened?" Daniel Sheridan was totally alert now, his voice official, demanding a response.

"Nothing happened. Not in the way you mean. The man was rude, is all. Downright unfriendly the second he learned who we were." Chip obliged, but his own tone was barely civil. "And that old character, bothering my wife—"

"Nate? Was it Old Nate who bothered you?"

"No. Yes. He said his name was Nate. Old Nate."

"Yes?" His voice was gentle, but nonetheless insistent on an answer.

"He didn't bother me. He just wanted to . . . to warn me." Kate pushed the words out in a rush, feeling flustered and silly to admit that a harmless old man had had such a profound effect on her.

"Warn you?" Chip threw her an incredulous look then turned all his pent-up frustration onto the sheriff.

"Now look here, Chief, I don't know what kind of town you run here, but if—"

Sheridan held up his hand and Chip stopped in mid-sentence. Showing no sign that he was bothered by Chip's outburst, he calmly regarded Kate, urging her to finish. "He warned you, you say. About what?"

"The island. Smoke Island. He said . . . he said to go home. Death was waiting on the island. Death . . . and more."

"My God, Kate, that's unbelievable!" Chip exploded. "Why didn't you tell me then. I would have—"

"You would have what, Mr. Windsor?" The question effectively silenced Chip. Sheridan turned to Kate, his features softening at the distress evident on her face. "There's more, isn't there? Try to remember. If you put it all out in the open it won't eat at you."

Kate nodded, acknowledging that he was right. She did feel better. But still, she could hear the old man's gravelly voice, low and insistent, prickling the hairs on her nape, saying . . . saying what? In her mind's eye she saw again the seamed face, the features contorted by urgency and by something else. Some powerful emotion. With a start she realized what she had been denying ever since the incident. The old man was afraid, really afraid, both for himself as well as for her. His fear had been very real and very personal. All of a sudden she remembered what he said. She looked into the sheriff's clear, calm gaze and said: "Go not to yon island. He waits for you."

"I see."

"Well, I don't. A bunch of senile mumbo jumbo.

33

Claptrap. The old man just wanted to frighten you, Kate, and obviously, he succeeded. Probably just having a little fun at your expense.'' Chip stared at Kate, daring her to raise an objection to their going to the island. Apparently reassured by what he saw in her face, he allowed a smile to cover his own features, perfectly willing to be reasonable since he felt assured of having his own way. ''Come on, honey,'' he cajoled, ''admit that was what it was. Just the locals scaring the city folks. They probably had it all planned ever since they learned we were coming.''

''But they couldn't have known we would stop there.''

''Really, Kate. If it hadn't been them, it would have been someone else. Maybe even the ch—, uh, the sheriff, here.'' He laughed, to show he was only kidding.

''That's one explanation, certainly.''

''You see, Kate, Sheridan here agrees with me. Now, how about we get started, before it's too late?''

Daniel Sheridan turned to Kate and addressed his remarks to her, apparently heedless of Chip's fulminating impatience. ''Old Nate is, as you've already surmised, the 'local character.' He has never, ever, harmed a soul. This I know, personally. You have nothing to fear from him, I promise you.''

''Yes, I thought as much.'' Kate saw and accepted the reassurance. ''But why—?''

''Why would he try to frighten you? Who knows? Your husband is right when he says that local people, especially in towns and villages as small as Puffin Landing, are wont to have a little fun at the expense of visitors.''

''But you don't believe that, do you?''

"No, no I don't." A big hand raked through his dark hair, further disrupting any semblance of order. "Look, there's a simple explanation for this. This entire area is steeped in legend, some of it true, verifiable, some of it manufactured, a good story to tell the tourists. Indians lived here long before it was settled by the Anglos. The Indians also had their legends, passed down from generation to generation. Some of their legends have mixed with those of the white settlers. Old Nate spends his time listening to other people. He probably has absorbed more of the lore of these parts than any other living being. Take the name of this village, for one. Puffin Landing. Means those cute little sea parrots can be found here. Right? No, not in living memory. They all upped and left, deserted us, for an inhospitable rocky island just off the coast. The reasons for this change of venue are locked up in those tiny feathered craniums, but that doesn't stop the stories that 'explain' it. Not by a long shot, it doesn't."

He hesitated momentarily, then went on, though it was plain he chose his words carefully. "A lot of the stories have to do with the islands. So, given some accidents that have happened on or near Smoke Island, and the fact that it has been uninhabited for over twenty-five years, there was bound to be stories about it. And that's probably what Old Nate was warning you about."

"I see."

"Good." He beamed at her.

Kate felt like the good little pupil who has just found the unimportant square root of some number. There was something, though, that the sheriff was not saying. Something he knew, knew consciously, but deliberately

35

CHAPTER THREE

Two hours later she stood with Chip on the narrow dock of Smoke Island. They watched Norman Day, the teenager who ferried them over, depart. Their belongings were piled about them, including the groceries Kate purchased in Puffin Landing's general store. Natty Bumppo, no better in a boat than in a car, lay disconsolately between them, his nose tucked into his paws.

"That kid is fired, the next time I see him, and that's a promise." Chip glared angrily at the boat's foaming wake, noisily slapping against the salt-seasoned gray boards of the dock.

Kate made consoling noises and involuntarily took a step closer to him. Smoke Island loomed above, appearing inhospitable and somehow, darkly menacing. They had to climb a set of steep stairs, and that prospect, in the fast-gathering darkness, was not at all appealing. The steps were hewn out of the island's granite core, and at the bottom, were moist from sea spray. They looked slippery and dangerous. "Well, shall we?"

Chip stared at her uncomprehendingly, and Kate felt impatience rise within her. It had been a trying day—more than trying, disturbing—and all she wanted was something to eat and a place to lay her head. A long soak in a hot tub would also be nice. Conscious she had to provide all three things for herself—there were no more motels and restaurants—she tried to keep her voice on an even keel as she explained what should have been obvious.

"We've got to start right away." She waved her hand over the piles of luggage and the cartons strewn along the length of the dock. "We're losing the light, and it's going to take several trips to haul this stuff up there. And," she paused for emphasis, "we don't know how far the house is from the top. We might have quite a walk."

"Damn that kid. He was supposed to do this."

"I know, but the fact is, he didn't. That leaves thee and me." Thoughtfully she gazed over the water, noting that the boat containing the reluctant Norman Day was now only a smudge on the near horizon. Closer in, a bank of fog appeared to be bearing in their direction. "Chip, did you notice that he *tried* to get out of the boat and help?"

"No, I didn't. The lazy, no good—"

"Okay. Okay. I get your drift. But I still think he tried. I wonder why he couldn't."

"Ingrown selfishness. Spoiled kid. Thinks he's got us by the short hairs. Well, next time I see him—"

"Chip. Please. I don't think we've got much time left."

"Okay, lead on, MacDuff. What should I take first?"

Kate bit back the comment that he should be able to

figure *something* out for himself. She pointed to the dog, who was trying to make himself invisible behind a carton of groceries. "We can't leave him here," she stated practically, "and we both know he'll never go up those stairs under his own power."

Chip groaned but obediently captured the reluctant Natty Bumppo, who, once secure in his arms, started to lick his face enthusiastically, thereby impeding progress and making the ascent up the stone steps even more dangerous. Kate followed close behind, carrying a bag of groceries.

The house was easy to find and not too far from the stone steps, situated in a stand of tall firs at the terminus of a narrow, dirt-packed path. They turned on lights just inside the door and deposited the setter on the floor and the bag of groceries on a chair.

"Well, at least the lights work around here."

Kate sighed at Chip's aggrieved tone. He was in one of his difficult moods. Not now, please, she silently pleaded, knowing she did not have the strength to cope with both a strange house and her husband's temperament.

"Of course they do, Chip. The sheriff did say that the generator was new and that everything worked."

"The sheriff said? Well, the sheriff also hired that kid, and he sure as hell didn't work."

Kate chose to ignore the remark, unwilling to fight. Briefly she wondered why Chip, indifferent to most people, was so antagonistic toward Daniel Sheridan. Deliberately she pushed the problem to the back of her mind. There were things to do. Hastily she shooed the dog farther down the hall. "We've got to go back now, even though I'd like to explore." Chip wisely did not comment. Norman Day's name did not pass his lips. Without further ado they shut the door on the unhappy setter and hurried back to the dock.

The job of transferring their belongings up the steps did not take as long as Kate had feared. She breathed a sigh of relief when she looked over the cliff edge and saw the top of Chip's sandy head rising for the last time out of the pooled darkness below. "Thank God," she breathed. "I didn't realize it could get so dark."

"Yeah. Life without neon. Ain't it grand." He selected two of the bags containing groceries and motioned with his head for Kate to do the same. "Might as well get these inside first." He started down the path without waiting. In seconds he was swallowed up by darkness, as if he had never been.

Kate stood without moving, letting the night surround her. It was dark, darker than it should be, given the hour. Looking up she saw there were few stars. The sky was pewter, marbled with streaks of dirty white. A wind came off the water, carrying the strong smell of brine. It ruffled the branches of the trees, creating a chitinous squeaking sound as thousands of sharp needles brushed against each other. The wind had a voice of its own, thin and reedy, otherworldly.

Kate suddenly felt very vulnerable, very alone. Hastily she picked up the nearest suitcase and ran stumblingly down the path. Once away from the steps it got even darker, the tall trees, their branches locked, towered overhead, creating a leafy, impenetrable arch. Inky shapes teased her, making her think she was not alone. The suitcase was heavy, weighing down her arm and forcing her to slow her pace. A rustling came from behind and Kate swung about, painfully bumping her shin with the bag as her own momentum gave it a life of its own. With a decidedly unladylike oath she dropped the bag and bent to massage her ankle. Something cold and wet pressed itself into the small of her back, precisely in the spot where her shirt had hiked up out of the waistband of her slacks, baring a few inches of naked skin. With a cry of alarm she pitched forward, uncontrollable terror squeezing rational thought from her brain.

"Kate. Kate, where are you?"

The sound of Chip's voice, impatient and cranky, turned her world around a hundred and eighty degrees again. The path was merely dark, not threatening, the shadows were just that and no more, and the cold, wet thing in her back was Natty Bumppo's nose, eagerly soliciting a love pat. Kate gladly complied with this request, using the few moments it took to try to salvage her composure.

"God, Kate, where have you been?" Chip had managed to find a flashlight, that he played before him like a blind man's cane.

"I bumped my shin. I guess the suitcase was too heavy." Easier to admit to that than to try to explain her deviation from rational thought into mindless terror. No longer alone she now felt more than a little silly. The city girl would have to learn a new way of life. "Where did you find the flashlight?"

"In the kitchen. There were two of them, plus a lantern. Here." Chip thrust one of the flashlights into her hand and picked up the suitcase. "I'll take this one back. Why don't you get the rest of the groceries. The other stuff can wait for morning. It's been a long day, hon."

"But . . . but we can't just leave it there. All our stuff, right out in the open."

"Why not? What's going to happen to it?"

Chip was reasonableness itself; in fact, he was being a bit too reasonable. Sudden understanding came, followed by swift, tension-caused anger. The rush of adrenaline which had pumped through her veins when she had felt besieged now deserted her, leaving a dull lethargy in its wake. "It's the studio, isn't it? You just can't wait for morning, can you?"

"Kate, hon, try to understand."

"I do. I do. But this island is larger than I thought, and you don't know the way. You could get lost . . . or worse."

"Nonsense." Chip was all brisk reassurance, content with her implicit compliance. "There are paths here, I'll just follow them. You can hear the surf long before you get near the edge. Besides which, you'll do better without me. I'd only get in the way. You know I'm hopeless in a kitchen."

Kate bit back the retort which rose to her lips. Now was neither the time nor the place to have a marital spat about selfishness. Perhaps it was she who was being the selfish one. She knew how important this was to Chip. Maybe he could relax, lose some of his pent-up tension, if he went to the studio right now. Standing on tiptoe she gave him a firm kiss then turned him about and gave him a farewell pat on the behind, football style. He threw her a grin over his shoulder, his face wearing that innocent-little-boy look which never failed to move her. She wondered if he were aware of its effect, then immediately rejected the thought as unworthy.

Natty Bumppo danced between them, comically torn by this unexpected decision. "Stay. Stay with Kate." Chip put him out of his misery with a firm command and then was gone, once again abandoning Kate to the night.

She wasted no further time, quickly returning to the steps and beginning only the first of many trips between them and the house. She was constitutionally unable to leave the task undone, a trait Chip well knew. The flashlight made all the difference, banishing shadows to their proper perspectives and giving her her own space. Wispy tendrils of fog curled about the trees, bringing with them a dank clamminess. After several forays against this new phenomenon, Natty Bumppo stayed close to her, rarely straying farther than her heels.

Kate left everything piled just inside the door. She had earned a long, relaxing bath. Time later to choose a bedroom, organize the kitchen, and make a light dinner. The house looked and smelled clean and fresh. Henry Packer had done a marvelous job. A large, old-fashioned bathroom on the second floor had an enormous claw-footed tub squatting grandly in the middle of the room. Kate looked no further.

Twenty minutes later she was luxuriating neck deep in foamy suds. She had let the water run very hot at first, misting the mirrors. The fog had thickened outside, and now it pressed against the windows. Kate had the sensation of floating in a private, secret world. She relaxed, welcoming the gradual easing of tension and tightness from her body. Natty Bumppo lay dozing on the bath mat.

She let her mind wander, without discipline, an old trick when she was trying to avoid something. Two thick candles stood on the vanity, not a reassuring sight. She supposed she should learn about the generator; there really was very little which had to be done. It was an unsettling thought for someone used to activity. Tomorrow she would unpack, maybe even set up her typewriter. In anticipation of many idle hours she had contracted with an agency to type term papers and manuscripts. Although they no longer were hurting for money, with both the grant and her own teaching job, anything extra would not be unwelcome.

As she soaked, Kate listened to the sounds the old house was making. In time she would grow used to them, probably not even hear them after a while, but right now every groan, every rustle, every creak seemed alarming. This thought skirted too close to the ones she was trying to avoid, so she hastily switched mental gears, summoning the image of Daniel Sheridan to banish them. The sheriff, thus conjured, did much to settle her anxiety. Kate recalled his reassuring manner, the way he reduced her fears without belittling them. She wondered why such an attractive man remained single, then realized he might have been married once. She knew next to nothing about him, after all. Except that he had been considerate to her . . . and antagonistic to Chip. Had it only been pride in his Indian blood, his heritage, which had sparked the hostility? Or had it been something else?

Natty Bumppo growled low in his throat, distracting her from her thoughts. From her supine position Kate watched him tilt his sleek head, listening. He appeared puzzled, his hunter's eyes wildly roving the steamy room, looking for something. His behavior was alarming. She splashed to an upright position, her skin

44

puckering in the cool air. The bath water had grown tepid while she lay dreaming. The setter growled again and bared his teeth, something he rarely did. "Easy boy, easy. Chip. Is that you?" In the stillness her voice had a high, thin edge. "Chip, answer me, I'm upstairs," she called. There was no response. The dog faced the window now, his body rigid, his teeth bared, a constant low-timbred growl issuing from his taut throat.

Thoroughly alarmed, Kate stood up and forced her legs leaden with fright to climb over the high side of the tub. All kinds of horrible thoughts raced through her head. Stupid to call out like that, targeting herself. If it were Chip he would have answered by now. She listened, straining to hear the sounds that she feared, listening with every fiber of her being for a shuffle, a stealthy step upon a stair, some clue that would tell her of another's presence. There was nothing; at least there was nothing that had not been there before. This thought did nothing to calm her. There could have been someone in the house all along, someone concealed, waiting, watching, *spying* on her.

The island has never been disturbed. Strange words. Kate could hear them clearly in her head, hear the deep, reassuring voice of Daniel Sheridan. He had sounded so sure of himself, so convincing.

"The island has never been disturbed." It was a whisper, a verbal totem to protect herself. It had no effect, neither on herself nor on the dog, who still stood in an alert stance, his body straining toward the fog-blind window.

She had left her robe on a wicker stool by the door. She willed herself to move, anxious to cover her nakedness. Her eyes caught movement. She stopped, rigid, her heart slamming into her chest at a greatly accelerated rate, answering the sudden surge of adrenaline which fright had sent pulsing through her veins for the second time that night. The movement stopped with her. In relief she realized it was nothing more than a mirror, steam-fogged and deceptive. She was drawn toward it, almost against her will. This is madness, a voice whispered in her mind, cover your naked flesh and find a place to hide.

There was something wrong with the image. Something subtle, but nevertheless wrong. Kate peered at it, fearful and yet fascinated, unable to stop herself. The image was dim, as if viewed through a cataract. There was her tall, slim body, her skin faintly glowing, pink and healthy from the water. The features, what she could see of them, had her shape, the large eyes, long, thin nose, soft sensuous lips, framed by the wings of her long, dark hair, softly gleaming as it fell in straight cascades down her back. *The hair.* Kate began to shiver. The shivering grew stronger and stronger, until her entire body vibrated, like a bow which has just kissed an arrow good-bye. With trembling hands she reached up and felt her own hair, securely pinned in a knot on the top of her head. There was no answering motion in the mirror. Feeling faint she leaned forward and wiped it with her hand, trying to erase the impossible.

Averting her eyes she bent and picked up her robe, belting it tightly about her slim waist. Her movements were purposeful, as if by ordering her muscles to obey her commands she could restore things to their rightful order. She fully intended to leave the room without looking in the glass again, but curiosity overcame superstitious fear. The mirror, when challenged, produced her image faithfully, true to her flushed cheeks, her too-bright eyes and her upswept hair. At the doorway she turned to look into the room, but whatever strangeness had inhabited it was no longer there. She turned off the light and went downstairs to wait for Chip, Natty Bumppo faithfully trotting after her.

Later that night she sat on the edge of their bed giving her long, dark, straight hair a vigorous brushing as she listened to Chip enthuse over what he had found in the studio. She was not really listening to him, not for content, but for the security which his familiar voice brought. She had not told him what had happened. She knew he would not believe her. He would have a dozen explanations. He would remind her of her gullible nature. He would point out that she was tired, overtired really. He would cite tension, blame eyestrain from driving. He would even, knowing him as she did, hint delicately at "woman trouble," as if premenstrual tension could be the culprit when all else failed. He would tell her nothing she had not thought of herself, therefore she had chosen to keep the incident to herself. Maybe it was a twist in time, a vision of Kate-in-the-future, rather than a reflection of Kate-in-the-here-and-now.

Chip came and stood over her, his shadow completely enveloping her slender body. "Beautiful," he breathed, his fingers picking up several strands of silky hair.

His words and the action were echoes in her mind. The old man, Nate, had said and done the very same things that afternoon. Kate could feel Chip tug gently as he wound the long strands through his fingers. The long strands. She barely managed to repress a shudder as she pictured other long strands of hair—those rippling down the back of the woman in the mirror. The stranger, the unKate in the mirror. Bemused, she looked down at the thick mass of her hair. It gleamed a lustrous blue-tinged black in the soft candle glow. Chip had insisted on lighting the candles for their first evening, and she had not had the heart to protest, although she would have preferred more light and less shadow.

"Just beautiful," he repeated, removing the hairbrush from her hand. He picked her up and moved her to the center of the bed.

"Chip?"

"What?" His voice was muffled, as he was busy nuzzling her neck.

"You won't let anything happen to me, will you? You'll protect me, watch over me, won't you?"

Chip moved over her, completely covering her body with his own. In the dim light his hazel eyes were unreadable. A lock of his thick sandy hair had fallen over his forehead, creating a shadow which emphasized the curve in his nose, legacy of a childhood fight. "Will I ever," he replied, and promptly proceeded to show her she had his undivided attention.

At the foot of the bed Natty Bumppo lay on an oval braided rug. His eyes were glued to the windows. There was nothing to see; nothing but the fog, thick and impenetrable, blindly returning his stare.

* * *

48

He was dreaming, drifting with the river of time. He was not asleep, was no longer capable of it; nevertheless, he dreamed. The dream was fashioned of bits of memory, interwoven with fantasy. It was good, the dream. As always. Without it, eternity yawned.

He dreamed undisturbed, alone in his universe, master of it, his pulse the pulse of life itself. As he dreamed the daylight faded, giving way to murky twilight. He took no notice. The dream held him in thrall.

She was in the dream. Again. She turned toward him, dusky skin bathed a rosy hue by the light of the fire's dancing flames, long black hair shining to rival the raven's wing. She smiled, a secret smile, her lips parted slightly, a moist portal to delight. The fire's flames were reflected in her eyes, mirroring the passion banked deep within her, the passion which waited to erupt and pour like molten lava out of its dark, confining prison. He trembled with longing, setting the trees aquiver, producing a thin, keening wail as thousands of needles gave voice to his desire. It was not enough. With the skill born of long practice he captured the voice of the wind, playing it through the swaying branches until it sang in minor key, counterpoint to the leaves. He prolonged it, knowing what was to come, knowing it would be better for waiting.

A sound intruded. He paused, confused; he knew the sound did not belong.

There, it came again.

He was no longer alone!

Stunned, he separated himself from the dream. It could wait. It had moved with him, flowing with the current of time, different yet the same, unchanging yet constantly new, his eternal companion. It had come with him from the past: the past was the present; the present was the future; the future was now. The dream waited in the future.

He was weak; he had spread himself thin, lulled by the pattern of countless days gone by. It had been so long. He trembled, this time not from remembered passion, but with the promise of something new. Gradually he became more aware, more able to help himself. Still wrapped in shreds of dream, he fought to emerge.

The world was dark, the sun no longer warmed the earth. A bolt of excitement shot through him, dispersing the last vestige of fantasy. He had not been disturbed after the light had faded for a very long time.

Awake now, every sense tingling, he probed his world. There was no doubt. He was no longer alone. The noises separated, became two—no, three— different sources. Two were strong, definite. The third was weak. A child?

A fever of impatience consumed him, making him clumsy, impeding his efforts to get moving, to start the search. He looked about wildly, trying to decide what to use, what to take, what would be best. Tendrils of fog, wispy advance fingers of the denser bank, wound sinuously about the island's edge, smudging the sharp outlines of rock and tree with a filmy white veil. With glee he clasped those seeking fingers, pulling them toward him, until he was cloaked entirely in the swirling mist. Silently he glided forth. The house drew him, a lighted beacon stabbing the shrouded dark. Billowing in his dank disguise he covered each square of light, looking inward, finding nothing until he surged upwards. There his search ended. Pressed against the clear glass barrier, trapping the streaming light, he shivered in thick clouds of vapor. Within, a glimpse of dewy skin; supple, glistening limbs; dark, gleaming hair. Disbelieving, he stared . . . and thought he was dreaming still.

CHAPTER FOUR

Kate sat on a sun-warmed rock atop the cliff that was Smoke Island's highest point watching Natty Bumppo sniff a patch of beach pea, his rust nose clashing harshly with the pinkish-lavender flowers. He was no more than three feet away, had not been farther ever since they had come to the island, two weeks ago. He lifted his head and turned soulful eyes toward her. "I'm right here, boy, carry on," she assured him, watching affectionately as he went back to his investigation of the tightly clustered flowers. There was a thoughtful expression on her face. If only the dog could talk . . .

She transferred her gaze to the small area of sandy beach below where the surf roared as it washed over the jutting rocks in the small protected cove that provided the island's only safe swimming waters. She never tired of the sight, finding a curious comfort in the never-ending spectacle. Every day she came here to check the signal system and also because she needed the exercise that the walk gave her after a morning spent at the typewriter.

The routine of her life on the island was pleasant, if a bit lonely, except, sometimes, for no discernible reason, she felt disquieted. Like now.

There was a change in the atmosphere, a minute shifting in the very atoms of the air. Kate spun around. There was no one there. Nothing. Only the woods, dark and silent and faintly menacing. The sensation intensified. They were alone on the island, she and Chip and Natty Bumppo, but often, like now, she could not shake the feeling that she was being watched. It was silly, but still the feeling persisted. It was quiet, too quiet for her taste. It amused her that she could miss all the noise and hustle of the city. "Honk honk," she said, and laughed at the look on the setter's face. "Sounds more like a goose than a taxicab, doesn't it? Maybe it'll improve with practice. What do you think?"

The dog ignored her, not running up, plumy tail waving in excitement, as he normally would when directly addressed. He was staring at something beyond her, his eyes fixed unwaveringly on it.

Kate spun around so fast that her long hair whipped stingingly across her face. Again, there was no one, nothing, there but the piney woods, that dark, quiet place. It smelled of dampness, and she always had the uneasy feeling that mold and fungus were growing, multiplying madly, crazily, against all the laws of nature, just out of sight beneath the thick carpet of dry, brown needles.

"Easy, boy. Easy." The setter did not respond. Goose bumps pebbled her skin, mute evidence of her body's instinctive reaction to—to what? Nothing had changed, it was still quiet, peaceful.

Natty Bumppo began to back up, slowly, carefully placing one foot behind the other as if he were walking a circus high wire without a safety net. He started to growl, low in his throat. Kate's thoughts flew back to the first night on the island, something she had refused to think about ever since she had almost convinced herself that what she had seen in the mirror was a fatigue-induced hallucination. The dog was acting much the same way now as he had that first foggy night. He stopped, his body rigid, set in a hunter's stance, the keening, eerie growl now issuing steadily from his throat.

Kate felt her own throat tighten in fear, but although logic and common sense were on her side, reminding her that Smoke Island had a total population of three—two adults, one dog—she could not convince her trembling body that there was no menace. There is nothing there, her mind whispered, but it was talking to sinew and muscles made jellylike by dread.

Out of the corner of her eye she perceived movement. Her breath caught in her chest. The dog stopped his keening growl and started to whimper. A yellow butterfly fluttered out of the shade and into the sunlight, looping drunkenly in wide circles before setting out on a seemingly suicidal course straight for Natty Bumppo's gaping jaws. The setter's ears lay back flat against his sleek head, his long tail pointed downward, as rigid and unmoving as the rest of him. His whimpering ceased, replaced by an awful broken panting sound.

Seeing her beloved Natty so besieged broke Kate's

54

own fear. She whirled around, ready to do battle with whatever threatened them. There was nothing there. The woods looked just as they always did, its darkness broken by shafts of thin sunlight filtering down through the layers of leaves. Kate turned and looked back at the dog. He was still rigid with fear, his flanks heaving spasmodically. The yellow butterfly had ceased to flutter erratically and was moving purposefully toward him. It picked up speed as it went, until it resembled a miniature, yellow guided missile. It flew directly in front of him and then hovered before his face. Kate had the wild notion that it was engaging him in some kind of animal showdown. Then, with a lazy flap of its fragile wings, it propelled itself off and was quickly lost to sight in the tall clumps of tough seaside goldenrod that grew thickly along the cliff's edge.

The atmosphere lightened. She looked at the setter and saw that his body was relaxed, no longer crouched in that rigid, mindless posture of terror. He was wearing a rather surprised look on his face, and Kate could not help laughing. The laughter sounded good in the still air. "It was only a butterfly, my friend. Surely you aren't afraid of that?" Natty Bumppo had the grace to look abashed, as if he understood her. Kate sobered almost at once. It was not as simple as that. There had been something . . .

There was a rustle in the dry needles behind her; the sharp snap of a broken twig. Kate tensed and turned, then immediately relaxed as she recognized Chip emerging from under the shadowed trees. "You scared me for a moment. I thought you were—"

"A butterfly?" he asked, cutting her off.

Fleetingly Kate wondered just what she would have

said, then dismissed the thought as Chip emerged into the clear sunlight, bringing with him a whiff of oils and turpentine to meld with the tang of wind-borne brine. "He's a city dog," she said as Natty Bumppo ran to greet Chip, blissfully oblivious to everything save his joy in seeing his master.

"He's a coward," Chip stated, then relented, reaching down to tug the dog's silky ears. Kate turned her back and walked to the cliff's edge, her joy in seeing Chip so unexpectedly blunted by the harshness of his attitude.

After a few moments Chip joined her. "He is, you know, and pretending otherwise will not change the fact."

"I felt something also." It was a flat statement.

"Did you think the butterfly was going to mug you?"

Kate ignored the caustic tone and responded as honestly as she could. "It had a compelling aura of . . . well, of menace." The minute the words were spoken she knew how implausible they were, yet she refused to retract them. Even when Chip stared at her, incredulity lifting his eyebrows into an almost straight line.

"Menace? A delicate little insect? Be serious."

Kate kept silent, stubbornly refusing to be drawn into an argument. She pulled her light cotton sweater more firmly about her shoulders and stared straight ahead. The sun was shining strong and clear, dancing in diamond points of light across the water. The view was magnificent, the sparkling air painting the scene like a glossy varnish. Faraway birds were circling the waves in their ceaseless hunt for food. Their thin cries were carried across the distance. Her eyes lifted toward the birds and once again they sang their sad lament. The children. Oooooh the dead children. Medea. She shuddered, horrified that she had thought of her again.

Chip, misinterpreting her action, put his arm around her shoulders, and gave her a gentle squeeze. "Let's forget it, huh?"

Kate nodded, took a deep breath and let her eyes drink in the clean purity of the open vista. Today the bay was calm, its waters a deep grayish green. The breeze that chilled the woods was ruffling the moderate swells flowing in from the ocean, capping them in long curls of frothy white lace. Boats, as always except on the stormiest days, dotted the waterways. Most of them were small pleasure craft, except for a ferry making its regular run to one of the larger islands over toward the northeast. The local fishing boats and lobstermen were a recognizable presence. Squinting into the glare, she caught a glimpse of a sleek sailing craft—a Friendship by her lines—disappearing around the southern end of a neighboring island.

She transferred her gaze from the panoramic view to her husband's face. He was staring out at the picture-postcard view. "Inspiring, isn't it?" she whispered, totally in awe of nature's magnificence. Chip flinched and dropped his arm, creating a space of only inches between them, yet which felt to Kate in that moment to be an inseparable gulf. She had said the wrong thing. Sensitive, prickly Chip; he was having trouble settling on a theme. A motif to give his work coherence. Not that he was not trying. He spent almost every waking hour working. He was early to leave and late to return. He bathed, ate and slept with her, but he was nothing more than a guest at the house. A roommate. Kate

57

sighed, silently admitting to feeling a bit lonely, more than a bit neglected.

It was not difficult for him to read her thoughts. "I'm not like other men," he said, never taking his eyes from the view. "You know that. You also knew what it would be like here, that it would be lonely." His hands clenched into fists. "It's not easy for me either. God, Kate, the burden, the responsibility . . . the imperative to do something unique."

Kate melted with this rare glimpse of his fears. He was right. He was not like other men. A life of commercial art, with its compromises, its anxieties, its frustrations was not for him. Neither was commercial art's triumphs, its big money. No, not for him. He burned, burned with a flame to create, to pioneer, that drove him more mercilessly than any commercial venture ever could. He had been honest about it right from the start. She had known what to expect. His art held him—mind, heart and soul.

She captured one of his hands and lightly kissed the paint-speckled knuckles. "You'll be fine," she said reassuringly, "and so will I."

Chip's hand uncurled and moved up to cup her chin. He turned his body so that it blocked her view of everything but him. She looked up into his familiar hazel eyes, saw the power and the passion burning down into her. He lowered his head and brushed his lips across her forehead, then claimed her lips in a hard, possessive kiss, while his hand roamed familiarly, intimately, down over her supple curves.

Kate responded to him willingly. She lifted her arms and twined them about his neck, bringing her body into close contact with his, allowing him freer access to the places he loved to caress. The first dizzying sensations of love were flushing her body when she felt him tense, then pull away. Her eyes flew open. Confused, she regarded Chip, who was standing with his feet spread apart, his head tilted upward, staring at something above them. She followed the direction of his gaze up to the yellow signal flag, a pennant made of strong oiled canvas, where it flew atop the flagpole.

"I forgot. The chief probably gets his jollies through his telescope. He most likely enjoyed our little show immensely." His tone was sour, tinged with the antagonism which he held for Puffin Landing's sheriff. Kate could not understand it, but she knew instinctively it was not a topic she wished to explore.

She struggled with disappointment at the rude interruption, not speaking until she was sure there would be no trace of it in her voice. Chip was sensitive enough, there was no need to give him another issue which could start an argument. "We *are* isolated, Chip. I'm grateful he keeps an eye on us. I feel . . . safer. It's our only line to other people," she said mildly.

The primitive communication system was simple, yet effective: yellow for status quo; yellow and white for send a boat; red flying alone for emergency, come as quickly as possible. As he had promised he would, Daniel Sheridan checked the island through the powerful telescope in his glass-enclosed office several times every day. Each time she had added a white pennant beneath the yellow, Norman Day had appeared within a reasonable time. She had no complaints, although the teenager was still refusing to set foot on the island. He was polite but adamant about that. On the mainland he carried her parcels, but at the island he left them on the dock, quickly steering the runabout away. Kate knew if she pushed the issue Chip would make good on his threat to fire the boy.

"Some people." Chip snorted. "A lazy kid who's good for nothing except to take my money, and a horny sheriff who ogles my wife daily."

"Chip!" Aghast, Kate stared at her husband. "You've got no cause to say that." Chip shrugged, but remained mute, a mulish expression marring his face. Kate accepted that she was not going to sway him from his misbegotten notion. She placed her hand on his arm, felt the involuntary jump of tense muscle. "How about coming to the house?" She let him read the deliberate invitation in her voice.

He shrugged her hand away. "No, I've wasted enough time already."

Kate stood and watched him disappear into the piney woods, leaving behind the faint aroma of paints and solvents. She thumped her hand against her side, gaining the setter's attention. "C'mon, Natty, let's go. We'll walk down to the beach and see what the tide's left us. How about that? A one-woof answer will do, sir."

Natty Bumppo responded with a wave of his tail. Kate took this for his assent and began the tricky descent to the beach. Deliberately she shut her mind, closing off the disturbing thought that Chip could have chosen his words more carefully. But then, that would have only served to mask his true feelings. Some things just did not bear thinking about

* * *

He was exultant. He could still do it. All it took was strength.

Power.

Patience.

He trembled, whether with the exhaustion of his efforts or with his desire to have everything now, at once, he did not know. But that was impossible. He knew that. He looked with scorn at the fragile yellow wings, feebly waving, barely moving the failing body above the ground. He had nothing but contempt for so frail a creature, although he did not scruple to use it. He was fading fast; he had not the strength yet to maintain even so small a form.

Power.

He could remember when nothing but strength pulsed through him. Nothing then had been too great, too arduous, too complicated for his skills.

Patience.

Time now had a meaning.

He rested in the grass, sheltered by the tall goldenrod, gathering his strength. He waited, and while he waited, he dreamed. She was part of the dream now; she was the dream reborn. His living dream. He ached again, as he had once long ago. He yearned to stroke firm, supple flesh, to set it to quivering, to feel it grow moist with the need to love.

Time flowed, taking him with it.

Kate prepared a simple lunch, then ate only half of it, carefully wrapping the remainder of her tuna sandwich in plastic and putting it in the refrigerator. She was feeling listless and more than a little disturbed. The thought of typing held no appeal, neither did the thought of another walk entice her. She might meet up with . . . with what? With the yellow butterfly? In retrospect her fear had been absurd. She must try to curb her imagination. She wished she could adjust to solitude as easily as Chip apparently had.

Having eliminated all other possibilities, she went upstairs to take a nap, suspecting that had been her goal all along. A half hour later, despite a dimmed room and the best of intentions, she was no nearer sleep than she had been when she first lay down. She abandoned the attempt and changed into shorts and a T-shirt before leaving the bedroom

Downstairs she poured a glass of lemonade and looked around for the open box of chocolate chip cookies, finally locating it behind the tea on the second shelf of the pantry. Taking the entire box with her she picked up her drink and the historical romance she was reading and took everything outside to the porch. She settled into a wooden rocker and tried to bury herself in the story.

She read for a half hour, gladly losing herself in the lusty adventures of the heroine, who had managed to get captured by a handsome pirate and was happily in the process of losing her battle to stay out of his bed. As she read she grew drowsy, lulled by her tiredness and by the sweet warmth of the spring air. The slats of the chair were beginning to press into her flesh. If she wanted to nap, she would have to move.

The bedroom was stuffy and too far away for eyes grown suddenly too tired to stay open. Kate left the shelter of the porch and stepped down onto the lawn, walking around the house until she reached the side lawn where there was a small clearing protected from the ocean's scouring winds by a stand of aromatic balsam firs. Within minutes she was curled on her side, asleep, her head pillowed on her arms. Slightly behind her Natty Bumppo settled himself in the long grass, his nose resting on his crossed paws, his eyes fixed firmly on his mistress.

Awareness returned to him slowly. He had been exhausted. He cursed his weakness, but he was stronger now than before. Rippling silently through the grass he searched the island until he found her. The one who was now as important to him as his dream. She was his dream. She was sleeping. Excitement built within him, until he shook uncontrollably with his wanting.

Power.

He must be strong.

She was open to him in her sleep. He reached out with long green fingers.

Patience. Soon he would share his dream.

CHAPTER FIVE

She was lost in a world consisting almost solely of sensation, surrounded by darkness, thick and velvety and full of promise. The very air caressing her skin was alive, perfumed by the sweet smell of wood smoke mingled with the pine scent of the forest and the moist richness of earth.

She was dreaming, but it was so real, so tactile that she could feel the fur pelts on which she was lying and the gentle breeze of aromatic air gliding sensuously across her flesh. She was in some sort of enclosure, the nature of the structure hidden by the dark. The blackness was saved from being absolute by a small open circle above her head, giving her a glimpse of a night-dark sky flecked with cold points of starlight.

As she lay in the near total darkness she felt her body begin to tingle, but whether it was with anticipation, awareness or arousal, she could not tell. Time passed in the way of dreams, seeming to rush by one minute and the next minute seeming to take forever. Kate waited in the cocooned darkness.

A change in the air, the slightest disturbance of the

very fabric of the night, and she was no longer alone. In silence a man drew near, the strong musky odor of his body filling her senses, filling her with a strange, yearning ache. He was an ebon shadow in a lightless world, blocking even the small sky view as he came to tower over her. He lay down, separated from her by no more than a puff of breath. The air flurried briefly, then settled about them, flowing around both bodies as if they were one. They remained like that for a moment or an eternity, she knew not which.

Kate turned her head and tried to see who lay beside her, but the darkness hid all detail. She was aware of a leashed power emanating from his body, a power so mighty, so strong, that she rapidly became afraid. If that power, that terrible, raw energy were to escape his control, were to touch her, she feared she would not survive. As if sensing her thought he reached out and placed the tips of his fingers on her arm, a touch so light, so gentle, so controlled, that she knew and understood his ability to leash the dreadful strength he commanded.

He did not withdraw his fingers, but left them resting, unmoving, on her arm. This contact, slight as it was, acted as a conduit. Kate felt herself engulfed by waves of longing, such acute longing, that her body began to throb to their rhythm. She grew icy cold and tears formed in her eyes as longing became loneliness, a loneliness so deep, so profound, that it sang with the sorrow of centuries.

Kate thought her heart would break. Just as she felt she could take no more his touch changed, subtly altering her feelings, gradually leading her away from despair. His fingers began to stroke her flesh, gently at first, then with more insistence, leaving a glowing trail as they moved up her arm to her neck, where they surely, knowingly explored the hollow at the base of her throat before moving up to carefully, lightly investigate every inch of her face. The blind touch, cloaked in the midnight dark, was the most erotic experience she had ever known. It was as if she were a flower, and he was learning the shape of her, petal by petal. The touch was openly sexual now, as his fingers trailed streaks of fire over her responsive body.

He withdrew his hand and Kate whimpered with frustration. In moments he was touching her again, his fingers stroking the soles of her feet, her ankles, moving up to her calves, past her knees to her inner thighs, where he lingered, stroking the sensitive flesh until she grew moist with longing. He pushed her dress above her hips and returned to the soft skin of her thighs, now trembling with arousal.

She wanted him, needed him more than she had ever needed anyone. He had unleashed a passion that only he could satisfy. With eager arms she reached up to clasp her dream lover, to draw him toward her, into her; to quench the fire he had stoked deep within her; to bring her the sweet peace of fulfillment.

The *putt putt putt* of a motor ripped through her consciousness, destroying and unraveling the meshed threads of the dream. Before she woke, still more than half-asleep, she felt a hint of rage within him, a blackness come from some unfathomable abyss, quickly flicker and as quickly die. As she returned to the real world she regretfully let go of him, felt him fade as her eyes opened and focused on the stately dip and sway of the balsam firs against the backdrop of a deep cerulean sky.

Vestiges of the dream still clung, but the details were fast receding, leaving her with a heavy dullness where before there had been nothing but fiery, bright promise. Bemused, Kate realized her body was moist and ready for love. She was lying on her back, a position she never slept in, and her legs were parted as if tautly open in anticipation of an eagerly sought lover. Looking down the length of her body she saw that the tall stalks of grass were bent over, touching her, some of them even pushed up past the bottom of her shorts.

The sound of the motor was growing louder. Kate sat up and closed her legs, pulling the long blades of grass away from the moistness between them. She felt vaguely alarmed, but ascribed this to her embarrassment at almost being caught in such a compromising position. Dull crimson flushed her face when moments later Henry Packer rounded the side of the house pushing a lawn mower before him. He stopped in consternation when he saw her and turned off the motor, returning the clearing to quiet.

"Why missus, I didn't think you were about. I called when I came, but there wan't an answer." No matter how many times she told him to, he never called her Kate. "Figured you was down t'the beach. Gettin' warm enough for it."

Kate arose and walked toward him, feeling unreal. A part of her wished to be back in the soft darkness, while another part of her, the part which had governed her being for almost all her twenty-eight years, was more than faintly ashamed by the vivid dream. Dreams were a manifestation of the unconscious. The interrupted lovemaking earlier in the day must have deeply disturbed her on some subconscious level.

Henry Packer was looking at her a bit oddly; this was not the time for self analysis. Since he was the only one from Puffin Landing who came to the island, she could not afford to alienate him. Forcing a smile, she ruefully admitted he had surprised her. "You caught me napping, Henry, and I didn't hear you arrive. But I'm very glad you're here. It gets a bit lonely." She bit her lip in consternation as the admission slipped out. She had not meant to say anything to anyone, much less to inadvertently criticize her husband to a virtual stranger.

Henry Packer nodded his head, his short, solid body planted firmly, with bowed legs apart. "Ayuh. Know just what y'mean. But a body gets used t'the feelin'." He peered beyond where she stood, Natty Bumppo close behind her. " 'Sides which, missus, you really ain't all alone," he said cryptically.

"What do you mean?" Kate felt her nervous edginess creeping back.

"Nothing. Th'dog there, is all. Got to get back t'work, missus. Only got one hour for th'island today."

"Henry, wait, don't turn that on again." Once he started the motor all hope of conversation would be lost. She just had to find out what he meant.

"No time. Sorry missus." The caretaker leaned over and swiftly urged the motor to life. The sudden roar was deafening, effectively preventing any further talk.

Kate stood and watched his stocky figure slowly guide the mower before him as he moved away. Another puzzle. That was just what she had needed today.

After dinner she followed Chip out to the porch and settled on the railing in front of him. He was staring up at the night sky, his eyes fixed unwaveringly on the dizzying sweep of the Milky Way as it swirled above the state of Maine. It seemed much closer here than it ever had in New York.

"Henry Packer was here today."

"Um."

"Chip. Are you listening?"

"Of course I am."

"No you're not. Please pay attention." He was still looking up. "What are you doing?"

He tilted his head, considering. "What I'm doing, Kate, is rearranging nature to fit the artist's eye. There, look up there. The lighter patch of blue. Pure ultramarine. A little to the left and several degrees upwards and it would give better balance to that bank of smoke-gray fog. See, there, it's rolling toward us." He lifted his hand, and with an imaginary brush made the change, stroking the air with several sure, sweeping movements. He brought his eyes down from the heavens and refocused them on Kate's face. "Was there something special about it?"

It was several moments before she realized they were back on the subject of Henry Packer. "No. Only . . ." She paused, a bit daunted in view of the guarded look which set Chip's features into stubborn lines. "Look, I know how it sounds, but there's something . . . something peculiar about this island. I'm not the only one who senses it. Henry Packer said some strange

69

things today. Alluded to . . . to *something*. I know Natty Bumppo feels it too.''

''I see.''

''No you don't. You're only saying that to calm me down.'' Willfully Kate slowed her speech. If she were hearing herself, even she would have doubts—serious doubts. Forcing calmness, she stared pointedly at Chip, daring him to dismiss her fears.

He did not disappoint her. ''It's urban withdrawal. Give it a few weeks. You'll stop seeing potential muggers behind each bush.'' He laughed, apparently pleased with himself.

Kate sat and smoldered, her anger directed at herself. She should have known better than to tell him. He refused to see things just past his nose, if they did not serve his purposes. They sat in silence, Kate's resentment building as Chip's features again took on that distant, otherworldly look. He had apparently dismissed the entire thing from his mind. She took his indifference as long as she could, finally using the dankness of encroaching fog as an excuse to go inside. There was a lot of fog on the island. Henry Packer said that it meant good weather, usually forming on windless, cloudless nights, but to her it meant distortion of familiar objects, turning them into alien, frightening shapes. *Anything* could be hiding in it.

Despite her afternoon nap she was exceedingly tired, weary, as if she had fought and lost an epic battle. There was no sense in waiting up for Chip. He could remain on the porch, lost in his own thoughts, for a long time. Being honest with herself, Kate admitted to not particularly wanting to be with him at the moment.

70

In their bedroom she changed quickly into a long-sleeved nightgown and turned down the bed. As an afterthought she opened the window a bare inch. Fifteen minutes later she was sound asleep. She did not hear Chip when he came up to bed an hour later. Nor did she see much later the stealthy invasion by tendrils of fog, slipping noiselessly over the sill and gliding into the room. Nor did she feel its dank clamminess as it hovered over her, descending to cover her sleeping form with a mantle of white.

The darkness was a friend. She lay on the plush fur pelts, waiting expectantly, her senses alive to the unseen world around her. All was quiet, the earth suspended under the camouflaging night. A rustle, a flutter of air, and she was no longer alone. Her pulses quickened, the soft rasp of her breathing accelerating with her heightened awareness. The musky odor which was uniquely his permeated the space. A soft wash of liquid desire flowed through her as she inhaled the scent. Tensely she awaited his touch, knowing disappointment when he bent and took her hand, understanding he wished her to arise and follow him.

Outside the earth was sleeping; nothing moved in the gloom. To the east the first faint trace of the coming day was apparent as a growing lightness against the horizon. They passed many structures, low circular buildings completely covered with woven mats of bark. They went through the village, traversing a large center space to reach the fertile fields beyond. These they crossed, the man now behind her, unseen, guiding her steps with the lightest of touches on her arm.

71

They entered a wood that bordered the fields, the ground underfoot changing to a springy carpet of leaves. They walked for some time, Kate frustrated by her need to see him, but prevented from doing so by the knowledge that he did not wish it. Light from the dawning day reached them through the overhead tangle of tree branches in full leaf. Still they walked.

Ahead was a clearing; the sound of running water. He stopped her on the edge, before she left the thick screen of trees. It was daytime now, pale sunlight filtering through leafy boughs down onto a stream that gurgled as it rushed over rocks greened by algae and moss. Birds chirped in the branches, their happy cries an echo of the life around them.

A young woman sat on a large flat rock plaiting her wet hair into one thick braid. She wore only a single garment, a skirt of animal skin wrapped about her waist, leaving part of her right thigh exposed. Her upper body was bare, the firm young breasts fully exposed to view.

The sound of a twig snapping to her left drew the girl's attention. She gave a small cry of joy as a tall man stepped out of the woods and stood in the shadow of the trees. With the grace of a young doe she leaped up and ran to him. The couple embraced, the man picking the girl up into his arms and swinging her about, so that his back turned toward Kate. He was tall and muscular, his skin smooth and bronzed by the sun. His torso was bare, his only covering pants which molded his well-formed legs. His hair gleamed blue-black as it fell straight to broad shoulders.

As Kate watched, the tall man gently lowered the

girl to the mossy ground, then quickly followed her down. They began to make love, each kiss, each stroke of his strong blunt-tipped fingers down her delicate, responsive flesh evoking a wave of longing from Kate. A burning jealousy built within her. She didn't want to watch. She wanted to be the one embraced, kissed, stroked to mindless passion. She tore her gaze from the broad back of the girl's lover, transferred it to the girl's face, which was dreamy with ecstasy. Kate stiffened and froze, feeling a cry rising from the very core of her being. The girl looked just like her—yet was subtly different. Why had she not noticed this before? Kate knew they were alike enough to be twins, yet were as different as two crystals. The girl was moaning now, twisting in the man's arms, begging him for fulfillment.

Kate wanted to run, to flee the scene that was a torment to her, but she was rooted to the spot, held by the will of the silent man behind her.

"Little Sparrow," the girl's lover whispered, his hand curved lovingly over her breast.

"Great Bear, my husband," she responded.

"Go," a voice whispered in Kate's ear. Suddenly it was she on the ground, she who was captured beneath the big man's body. She could feel his lips, teasing her earlobe, then the sharp pleasure-pain sensation as strong teeth nipped the tender flesh.

Kate's body writhed under his, her passion rising quickly, her pulses throbbing a wild beat. She yearned for him, her body ached with knowledge of his power. The desire to see his features, to learn his face, became overwhelming. She struggled to shift his weight

CHAPTER SIX

"Honey, why don't we have a picnic lunch today. What do you say? I could make fried chicken, deviled eggs, and if you'd like, I'll bake chocolate chip cookies. From scratch." Kate knew she was behaving badly. Baldly stated, she was trying to bribe Chip with his favorite foods, but she didn't care. She simply did not want to be alone. Not for another entire day. Not after yesterday. Not after her dreams. A blush stained her cheeks at the memory. So anxious was she not to be alone all day again that she was willing to disregard his insensitivity of the previous evening. She plunged ahead, although Chip was looking at her as if she had suddenly grown a second head. Or a third breast.

"We'll have wine. One of the good Italians. A Valpolicella. It won't take long. You won't lose much time. I'll come to the studio. There's a clearing behind it that will serve admirably." A clearing that is the perfect setting for love, her treacherous mind whispered.

"Kate." Flatly Chip interrupted her spate of words,

and then maddeningly, making her want to shake him, shoveled another spoonful of cornflakes into his mouth.

They were having breakfast in the kitchen, a large old-fashioned room with gay, red and white, checked curtains. Their brightness failed to cheer her this morning. There was also nothing of cheer about her husband. Kate had a feeling that things were not going well with him. They had been through these dry patches before. Chip would find his way. She, and now the trustees of the grant, had absolutely no doubt about that. She also had no doubt that she needed some help—or some attention.

"Well. What about it? The picnic?" She watched Chip's spoon as it returned to the bowl, ruthlessly pushing cereal out of the way as he hunted for raisins. Chip liked to finish even. Kate wanted to scream.

"No, Kate. No thank you," he repeated politely, as if his mother were present to remind him of his manners.

The flat rejection depressed her, although she had been expecting it. She geared up to try again, raising the ante this time. The second wave of Marines, storming the beachhead. "We'll have music. How about Vivaldi? *The Four Seasons* would be perfect. After . . ." she lowered her voice, vamping shamelessly, "after . . . dahling . . . you can have me. *Love in the Afternoon,* complete with music, wine and yours truly. How lucky can you get?"

"For God's sake, Kate."

A coldness was creeping into her. She was finished before she began. She watched stonily as Chip picked up his napkin and began to pleat it, a sure sign that he was fighting to keep his temper from flaring. Kate knew

76

he would lose the battle, that he really had very little interest in controlling himself. The artistic temperament with a vengeance. The only unknown in this equation was the time element: how long it would take him to vent his temper. He apparently was running on a tight schedule, for the expected outburst came almost immediately.

"Be reasonable," he began, a tip-off that what he was about to say would call for total surrender on her part. "You knew what to expect before we came here. You knew you would have to amuse yourself. I've got to work, you know. This is no vacation for me. Just how do you think I can concentrate if I've got to worry about my wife and her boredom?" He threw the napkin from him and stood up. "Look, I know you're nervous here all day alone. God, honey, don't you think I know that? You don't have to invent things to prove your point."

"Invent things? I'm not sure I understand you."

"You know."

"No, Chip, I don't know." The coldness within her was spreading, reaching out greedily, leaving a path of numbness in its wake.

"Come on, let's not play games. You've obviously let the remoteness get to you. Your imagination is working overtime. Has anything happened? Anything real, that is? I'm not talking about monster butterflies and old men who dribble nonsense." Henry Packer was neatly and ruthlessly disposed of.

"No." Her whispered answer was eloquent.

Chip spread his arms wide, a nonverbal "I rest my case."

She had no defenses against his logic. Only a feeling

of disquietude. That, and dreams. Dreams so real they frightened her.

"I'd like to write to your sister, ask them up for a visit. The kids would love it here."

The abrupt change of subject momentarily disconcerted Chip. Kate watched his face as he studied the question, examining it for the possible benefits, and detriments, to himself. She waited impatiently, all too aware just how important his decision was.

Chip looked thoughtful for another few moments. "If that's what you want, go ahead. I thought you'd like some time to yourself, especially after spending most of the year cooped up in a classroom with a bunch of savages."

As usual, Kate took the bait. "They're not savages. Some of them are rather sweet. They just need discipline and a firm hand to set them on the right road. It's very rewarding work, even if I'm only a substitute."

"If you say so."

"I do say so." Kate was grateful to be back on familiar ground.

"Look, hon, I don't want to fight with you, especially over this nonsense, and we both know that it will only lead to one if we continue. So, I think I'd better leave now before we say things we'll both regret." At the door he stopped and turned to look at her. "Inviting them isn't such a bad idea. Why don't you go into town today? Mail the letter. Do a little shopping. That ought to cheer you up," he suggested heartily. This ancient male palliative failing to elicit a response, he tried again, modulating his voice somewhat. "Fried chicken sounds wonderful. Why don't we have it tonight. I'll try to get back here a little earlier. We could make it an early night." He leered suggestively, his hazel eyes shining with earnestness. He picked up his lunch from the counter and left.

Kate thought dispassionately that that final gesture marred his overall performance, the entirety of which she had viewed with the detachment of a jaded audience. Chip's self-serving attitude never ceased to amaze her. He was quite adept at twisting things to suit his own ends. It was true she longed for a break in her solitary routine. Guilty on that point, your honor, with an explanation. It was not boredom that had driven her to seek her husband's favor. Boredom was something that she could handle. She was good at amusing herself, to use Chip's snide words. If only it were something as simple as that.

It was a matter of minutes to clear up the breakfast dishes. Her uneaten English muffin was hard and greasy, even the dog had no interest in it. She threw it in the garbage. Upstairs she gave the bedroom even less attention, making the bed and leaving before she could even contemplate dusting. The letter to Anita was written, addressed, sealed and stamped in under ten minutes. Then, purposefully, she went to the box where the signal pennants were kept. Taking the white one she called Natty Bumppo and set out.

The air was clear and crisp, sparkling and pure. Kate walked briskly, the setter cavorting at her heels. They entered the woods and as usual Kate increased their pace. It was hushed and quiet here, cathedral-like, although there was nothing of the soaring hopefulness that permeates sanctified places. She forced herself to slow down. There was nothing in the woods to harm her. One look at the dog was all that was needed to confirm this. He was trotting along, exhibiting none of the symptoms of fear Kate was coming to dread. Nevertheless, she was grateful when she left the close darkness and was once again on the cliff overlooking the small sandy beach.

She hoisted the white flag, secured the ropes and stepped back to make sure the signal was flying from the top of the pole. Maybe she would stay overnight in Puffin Landing. Chip could fend for himself. Just remembering his words made her angry again. Flinging in her face that he was not on vacation. She supposed that he thought all the housework, cooking and cleaning she did here was a vacation for her because it was not done in their own home. Some vacation.

The air was still, the bay calm and glassy looking. It was a perfect day for a boat ride. She really did not have it in her to be mean. Leaving Chip on the island overnight alone would be the act of a petty person, and that was something she had never been. She had no intention of starting now.

It was such a beautiful day that she did not want to hurry back to the house. Norman Day would come to the dock and ring the brass bell if she was not there waiting. There was time to enjoy the beach. She and Natty Bumppo made their leisurely way down the treacherous path. They made straight for the tide line where she dipped her fingers in the frothy white lace of a receding wave. The days were warming up, but the water was still frigid. Numbingly so. Her fingers were starting to tingle and lose feeling in the tips after only being submerged for a few moments.

"Come on Natty, let's go exploring," she called to

the setter, who eagerly came to her side. This activity was a delight to him. The small beach was ringed by clumps of rocks, and the two of them had discovered tidal pools in several niches on previous expeditions. Today there were some sea anemones, orange-pink tentacles waving sluggishly in the still waters, but none of the hermit crabs that the setter so loved to tease, putting his muzzle close and gently pushing until they scurried away with their distinctive movements. He searched for them, inserting his paw into the shallow water and stirring the massed clouds of green seaweed. In companionable silence the two of them visited several pools, but in none did they find any crabs.

Patience.

He watched the girl leave the island. The girl who was his memory reborn. She would return. The man was still here. Shut up in that little house. Like the ones before. He had no interest in him. Not now. Not until he needed him. Until . . .

Patience.

Power.

He needed power. He needed the power that had once been his. So long ago. So long that even the dust had no memory of it.

Power.

He was stronger now than he had been for a long time. He would be stronger still. Soon. He knew what he must do. Flowing on the air, he set out.

A light breeze carried him over the island. It swayed the branches of the tall firs, lifting them up and dropping them down like huge shrugging shoulders. It rippled through the long grasses, bending the heads of the wildflowers scattered in profusion everywhere. It brought him to the house, where the setter lay sleeping.

The dog dozed fitfully, ears twitching at the rattle of a window, the creak of the empty rocking chair, the soft fluttering of the pages of a book lying forgotten on a chair. He used the breeze to ruffle the silky auburn coat, blanketing the setter with the sweet breath of growing things.

Patience.

Not here. Not yet. But soon. Soon. Sheer force of will stayed him from rashness.

Power.

He caused a loose shutter to rap smartly against the wall. The dog came awake abruptly, snuffling softly in alarm. He sniffed the air, whined, then got up and paced to the steps, stopping there with head cocked to one side, ears perked upright. Soulful brown eyes looked toward the path, but there was no one there.

Power.

Abandoning the breeze, he took on form, becoming again a pale yellow butterfly. Fluttering on a beam of sunshine, he caught the setter's attention. Alighting onto a blade of grass, lazily folding and unfolding his wings, he dared the dog to remember, tantalizing him with each languid movement of the velvety, graceful body.

Patience.

Natty Bumppo approached.

Patience.

He must appear to be nothing but a fragile, teasing insect. Triumph surged through him as Natty Bumppo signaled his intent, tensed powerful canine muscles, sent the long, lean, beautiful body leaping through the air. Strength of purpose born of ancient cunning kept the delicate insect body immobile until the very last instant when he flew out from under the setter's shadow. The dog landed heavily, looked down, then whipped his head from side to side. Eager now that the battle was engaged, he rapidly fanned the yellow wings open and closed until Natty Bumppo saw him, leaped again. He took off, the setter in hot pursuit. The chase took them around the house, past the clearing, on into the woods. It grew dimmer, the sunshine fading as it streamed down through the dense, screening trees.

Patience.

He disappeared, right before the setter's eyes.

Natty Bumppo stopped, sides heaving with exertion, pink tongue lolling outside his mouth to cool his overheated body. He whimpered, began to pad about in aimless circles.

Patience.

From the midst of a clump of daisies, spectral white faces with yellow eyes, he produced the faintest of movements. Natty Bumppo dashed over, bent his redbrown head, pushed his nose into the flowers.

Now.

From his camouflage, masquerading as a daisy's eye, he spread the insect wings to their utmost, revealing himself. For an instant their eyes met. He saw awareness, knew when the setter's hunter's genes responded to the menace. Too late.

Power.

The contest was unequal. He discarded the butterfly for a bee. With savage purpose he rose from the flower and stung the defenseless dog over and over again on his sensitive nose until the membranes swelled and air could no longer enter. Eyes wild with pain, Natty Bumppo opened his mouth to breathe, gasping and gulping, whimpering as the venom's fire raced through his body. Jaws agape, the setter inhaled deeply.

Power.

Quickly he relinquished the bee, flowed into the flowers, forced the daisies into the dog's throat, down his windpipe, cutting off the remaining air passage. He felt the setter try to pull back, try to dislodge them, but strength pulsed anew and the flowers danced to his will. Natty Bumppo struggled, but weakened rapidly. Coldly, he thought they both welcomed the darkness which finally dimmed the dog's eyes. In the end death had come as a friend to Natty Bumppo.

CHAPTER SEVEN

Puffin Landing was no longer the quiet little town it had been in early June. While not yet bustling, it nevertheless hummed along with signs of burgeoning life. The all-purpose drugstore displayed out-of-town newspapers in outdoor racks, all uniformly bearing bold-type, bad-news headlines. Kate ignored them all without a qualm. An expensive jewelry store, that also stocked antiques and fine local crafts, was now open for tourist business. The town's only traffic light was on automatic, no longer subject to pedestrian whim. Pausing before entering the general store, Kate counted three cars stopped by the red light. A traffic jam. Chip would be amused.

The store was dark after the glare of the street. Kate loved the smell of it, bringing to mind as it did childhood summers in New York's Adirondack Mountains. There had been a store there, similar to this one but on a much smaller scale. Kate had never forgotten the special blending of odors: pine and balsam cushions;

lavender sachets and boxes of soapsuds; old, never-quite-dry wooden plank floors.

She shook off the memory and looked around. There were five customers, three browsers and two waiting at the back counter for Bess Perkins to attend them. Kate made directly for this group, anxious for her mail, and also to do a little discreet questioning of the post-mistress. There was very little in Puffin Landing that escaped her notice.

"Yes?"

Bess Perkins was addressing her in the tone she reserved for outsiders and, Kate suspected, alleged Democrats. She sighed inwardly, determined to remain pleasant. "Good day, Mrs. Perkins, I'd like my mail please."

"Name?"

"Kate Windsor. Mrs. Charles Windsor. We're out at Smoke Island this summer." Kate forced herself to be patient. Bess Perkins put her through the same routine every time. The woman was a civil servant with a vengeance. Kate wondered wryly if the federal government was aware of this gem in their employ.

"Ayuh." The postmistress accepted Kate's statement with a frosty nod. A thin woman, bordering on gauntness, with a weathered and worn face, she looked the very picture of a stern schoolteacher, Hollywood version. A tight bun, into which her thin gray hair was gathered, augmented the image. She took out a large key from beneath the counter, moving to unlock the metal grille that divided United States' property from Perkins property. Reaching into one of the cubicles, she withdrew a single envelope. The grille was carefully relocked and the key secured beneath the counter again before she released the letter to Kate, who stuffed it into her shoulder bag without a glance. "Anything else?" Mail puts no money in the cash register, her expression unmistakably said.

It was a slim opening, but Kate took it, conscious of an approaching shopper. "Uh, yes. That is, I—" Hastily she proffered her shopping list, a sop to the woman who would not even unbend enough to offer her a smile. For the first time in her life Kate knew the true meaning of the phrase "the only game in town." "If you could fill this, Norman, that's Norman Day, will pick it up for me in a couple of hours."

"I know who Norman Day is." The flat statement left Kate in no doubt about Norman's importance, as an insider, compared with her own, a mere summer person. The list changed hands.

"Uh, Mrs. Perkins, I was wondering . . ." Kate swallowed, unaccountably nervous. "That is, I just wondered if you knew anything about Smoke Island. The people who used to live there, that sort of thing."

Bess Perkins cut right to the heart of the matter. "Somethin' wrong out at th'island?" The beginning of interest kindled in her eyes.

"No, nothing is wrong. Whatever could be?" Kate was proud of the lie, of her ability to deliver it. Bess Perkins closed her face. Too late Kate perceived her error. There would be no information forthcoming today. Kate could recognize defeat, certainly when it was spelled out in neon lights, or written on a Down East face.

"Norman'll find this ready and waitin', missus."

The dismissal was obvious. Kate mumbled a "thank you" and left. It had been hopeless from the start, the notion of Bess Perkins being cooperative, if not friendly. Kate did not feel too disappointed.

Outside again she stood in the shade beneath the store's green and white striped awning, undecided on her next move. A rumble in her stomach was a reminder of her uneaten breakfast. There was a coffee shop along the street, more properly a cafe, as they called it here.

Cora Best's Cafe had limp yellow nylon curtains framing a flyspecked window, through which Kate could just make out several tables, two of them occupied. She decided on grilled cheese and coffee before entering; packaged bread and processed cheese washed down by hot coffee could not do much damage. Her hand on the doorknob she felt someone else's hand on her shoulder.

"I wouldn't, if I were you, but I'll deny I ever said it with never a flicker of conscience."

A smile lit Kate's face as she turned to face Daniel Sheridan. "Am I being arrested?"

"Let's just say I'm arresting an irrational act." He smiled down at Kate in return, the action spreading fine crinkles outward from his dark eyes bright with humor. "Cora's a good woman, but only tourists, summer folk and Walt Perkins, who is addicted to her coffee, frequent the place."

"Surely it can't be as bad as that." Kate was infinitely grateful for his warmth, his friendliness, after the formidable Bess Perkins.

"You're right, it's not." He moved his hand to her elbow, gently guiding her away from the cafe. "If you're hungry, Puffin Landing can do better for you than Cora's, especially now with the start of the season. If you wouldn't mind some company—?"

"I'd love it."

"Good. There's a lobster pound down at the wharf. I promise you won't be disappointed."

The day had grown warmer as the sun ascended a cloudless aquamarine sky. There were many people on the streets. Most of those they passed had a greeting for the sheriff. Kate received a few fallout nods, more than a few curious stares, but mainly she was ignored. She did not mind. She was enjoying herself: taking pleasure in the presence of other human beings; in the hum and thrum of noise; in the feel of pavement beneath her feet. She was a starving urban addict getting a small dose of what was familiar—comfortable. They exchanged few words, nevertheless established an easy relationship in the short time it took to walk from the center of town down to the dock area.

"Here we are. Why don't you wait out here. I'll get the food." He steered her toward a rustic picnic table near the railing on the deck overlooking the wharf where the fishing boats berthed.

"But—"

"Let me surprise you." He was gone before she could either agree or protest.

Kate relaxed and looked about her with interest. The restaurant was nothing more than an offshoot of a commercial lobstering concern. There were no frills, everything was plain and functional, although someone had taken the trouble to plant long boxes with masses of white and purple petunias. Only one table was unoccupied, and this was only a technicality, for a large sea gull sat on it, black eyes alertly watching the diners.

"Subtle, isn't he?" Daniel Sheridan shooed the bird and deposited a tray loaded with lobster rolls, potato chips, donuts and mugs of steaming coffee before her with all the panache of a waiter at a five-star establishment.

"You must be very hungry." Kate looked with dismay at all the food.

"You're expected to do your share. You look like you could use it." He sat down across from her and picked up one of the rolls. If he noticed Kate's startled reaction to his personal comment he did not let on.

Her first bite told Kate that she was more than hungry—she was almost ravenous. The food was delicious. Conversation while they ate was confined to Puffin Landing's emergence from its winter chrysalis. One of the most noticeable changes was the sheriff's dress—he had forsaken his work clothes for a neat khaki uniform, complete with gleaming star. Kate missed the Yankees cap.

Over coffee Daniel Sheridan abandoned his distant, polite air. "How are things, Kate? Everything going smoothly out there? Everyone's well, I take it, including my friend, the Pathfinder?"

He had opened the door for her, all she had to do was take a step inside.

His gaze sharpened when no answer was immediately forthcoming. "Okay, what's wrong?"

The sharp question, the change of tone, demanded a response. Deep down Kate knew that this was the real reason she had come into Puffin Landing today. Daniel Sheridan was a good listener, and she knew instinctively that he would take whatever she said seriously. She was not alone out there, had not been the only one who had sensed—something. Natty Bumppo. Loyal, sensitive Natty Bumppo. Animals had acute senses—and no imagination.

"We're all fine, Daniel. Truly. It's just that sometimes—well, with the loneliness . . . being so isolated . . ."

"Imagination working overtime, Kate?" It was not said sneeringly, nor was it said unkindly.

"No. No, it's not. Forget what I just said about the isolation. That has nothing to do with it. I know what I saw." This last was said stubbornly.

"Perhaps you'd better tell me just what it was you did see."

Kate needed no further urging. Calmly she recounted the incidents that had disturbed her, mentioning also the feelings of disquietude that assailed her wherever she went on the island. "I know how it sounds," she said defensively, "there's really nothing much here. Chip tells me that often enough. But Chip was there when that butterfly acted . . . strangely. That's the only word for it. He saw the way it behaved. Even though he won't admit it."

The sheriff was regarding her gravely. Kate had a sudden idea. "Is there someone else on the island? Could someone be living there? A hermit? Maybe living in the woods? I suppose you could live off the land, if you knew how." A new idea occurred to her. "Have you heard about someone missing . . . or escaped? A fugitive." Kate knew she was reaching into left field, but she was anxious to have her fears given a rational basis. An unseen person hiding on the island would not explain everything, but it would account for her feeling of being watched.

The sheriff did not laugh. "No, Kate. There's no one missing. Or escaped. There are no known fugitives in this area, and I would be notified if there were. There is no one else living on Smoke Island. Hasn't been since 1957. Not since Nate left and moved back here to the mainland."

"Nate. Old Nate? The same man who . . . who said all those horrible things to me?"

The sheriff looked surprised for a moment, then understanding replaced surprise. "Chip didn't tell you? No wonder, he probably didn't want to upset you."

"Sure." Kate felt betrayed. The feeling passed quickly. Annoyance with her husband—self-serving, impossible, talented Chip—rose within her. It was a familiar feeling. "Now that the big secret's out, don't you think you'd best tell me all of it?"

"It's no secret, Kate. There's nothing mysterious. Nate was the second recipient of the Voss Grant. Elwell Nathaniel Smith—Nate, for short. He went to the island one summer—and . . ."

"Yes?" Kate prompted.

"He failed."

"Oh no." Kate felt a deep sadness for the old man. Chip—vulnerable Chip—afraid of a similar fate. "What happened? No—not with his art, I know how that can happen. Only too well. Chip has friends—some, well, they just don't make it. They go into advertising, real estate—one's driving a taxicab nights to pay the rent. It's a common ending to most dreams in that field. But it's not what I meant." She gazed out over the gleaming, busy bay. "Out there. What happened to Nate out there?" She frowned as a thought occurred to her. "Do you think those strange notions

92

of his are rationalizations? Excuses to explain his failure.'' Daniel Sheridan looked momentarily blank. Kate
persisted, ''Remember? I told you about his warning.
You said it was stories. Legends.''

''Yes. I remember.'' He looked beyond Kate, waved
to someone. ''There's Nate now.'' Kate swiveled
about. Behind her Daniel Sheridan spoke, his voice
filled with understanding, and a hint of pain. Kate had
to strain to hear him, for the tone was pitched low.
''You're probably right. Life is sometimes very cruel.
So cruel, so hard, that explanations are needed, explanations that somehow absolve us from the harshness of
truth. I would guess that Nate simply had to have some
explanation—for himself—for his failure.''

It was all so reasonable, so plausible. An old man
needed his pride. ''So there's no truth in what he says?
The warning was symbolic?'' That still did not explain
the uncomfortable atmosphere on the island. Nor the
mirror that distorted her image. Nor the butterfly.

''Howdy, missus. Sheriff.'' Old Nate smiled a wide,
almost toothless smile.

Kate nodded, smiled. Daniel Sheridan waved casu-
ally toward his bench. ''Have a seat. How about some
lunch?''

''Thankee, no. Coffee'ud go down real easy.''

''Sure thing.''

To Kate's consternation, the tall sheriff left. She did
not feel comfortable alone with the old man. To her
chagrin, Old Nate sensed this.

''No cause to fuss, missus,'' he said quietly, then
raised his voice to catch Daniel Sheridan's attention.
''A piece of blueberry pie would sure make the coffee
a lot more interestin'.'' He smiled his almost-toothless

smile at Kate, who offered him a somewhat shaky smile in return. "Never meant you nothing but good, missus. Th'island's not for you."

"What do you mean?"

"Wan't no good for me and mine. I had a woman there. Wouldn't stay. Lost her. Lost ever'thing."

"I'm . . . I'm sorry."

Old Nate waved a gnarled hand in the air, either acknowledging Kate's sympathy, or dismissing it. "Long time gone. Happened afore. Feller 'bout twenty years afore me had his troubles. Course there was worse, long afore him. Th'island's no good."

"Blueberry pie a la mode." Daniel Sheridan re-seated himself next to Old Nate and watched him attack the sweet dessert.

"Mr. Smith was just telling me that Smoke Island has a history of 'er, problems."

The grizzled man looked up from the rapidly disappearing pie. "Nate'll do, missus. Or Old Nate. Whichever you're more comfortable usin'. An' you're right there. Th'island's no good."

"Why?" Daniel Sheridan asked peremptorily.

Old Nate placed his fork neatly beside the now empty plate and carefully wiped his hands and lips before answering. "Legends, sheriff. Stories. You should know. Your people figure in 'em often enough. Things'll get twisted in 'em, but most times there's a truth hidin' under all the tales."

The sheriff nodded his head slowly. "You're quite right. So much of history, the legacy of my people, is lost. Shrouded in mist, as if it never was." He sounded bitter, but his strong-featured face registered nothing but resignation. "Almost all we know about my direct ancestors, the Algonquins, comes to us as oral history. Nate has quite an ear for it. I've been trying to get him to write it down."

Kate looked at Old Nate. Elwell Nathaniel Smith. He favored her with another gaping smile. Disconcerted, she transferred her gaze back to the sheriff.

"Did you know, Kate, that a little over three centuries ago an entire people virtually disappeared?" he asked fiercely. "Gone from the face of the earth as if they had never existed. Scattered, assimilated, swallowed up—whatever. A few beads, some incredibly crafted tools—that's all that remains."

"What happened?" Kate asked softly, moved by the deep feeling he was allowing her to see.

"It's an old story. It's familiar in many guises. Progress, civilization—what have you. The result is always the same, although the names and the players change, of course. In this case two civilizations met and found they could not both live on the same land. The Indians gave it a good fight, they almost won, but almost was not good enough. It never is." The corners of his mouth quirked in a rueful smile. It disappeared with his next words. "Disease was the final blow. The Pilgrims did not know it at the time, but they carried the seeds of destruction within them across the sea. We were always doomed. Now we know so little about them, a people who had a culture equal to—but different from—those who superseded them. Most Americans today only think of the Indians of the southwest when they think of American Indians. If at all."

"I'm sorry."

"No, I'm the one who is sorry. I never meant to get into all that. Nothing lasts forever, as they say. Just look at me," he teased, "a mixture of bloods. All co-existing very nicely under the same roof, so to speak."

"You look all right to me," Kate allowed, responding to the lighter tone. "But what about the island? Specifically. What legends are attached to it?"

Daniel Sheridan looked thoughtful, then he shrugged. "It's strange, but now that you ask, I realize that I don't know. The villagers have always had a fear of the place. For as long as I've been here, which is a good many years." He transferred his attention to Old Nate, who had been growing perceptively nervous in the past couple of minutes. "Of course, no one's ever lived on the island, not since Nate. He left . . ."

"Look over yonder," Old Nate interjected. "Young Norman isn't lookin' too happy."

Kate turned and saw Norman Day slouching down the dock in their direction. "He won't set foot on the island," she blurted out.

"Smoke Island's reputation has had a salutary effect. The extended coverage, vandalism and malicious mischief insurance premiums are exceptionally low. The place is a good risk," Daniel Sheridan said with a straight face. "What the—?" Old Nate scrambled over the bench and hurried away, almost trampling the sheriff in his haste.

"What happened? Why did he run away like that?"

Daniel Sheridan shook his head negatively, but his eyes held a thoughtful stare. "Nate doesn't take to too many people. I wouldn't attach too much importance to it."

Kate accepted the explanation without comment, transferring her attention to the approaching boy. When the teen reached their table he stopped, thrust his hands deep into the pockets of his worn denims and shuffled his feet in place. "Miss Kate, ma'am, could we leave soon. My mom wants me home early tonight. Before dark."

Kate assured him that she would be leaving soon. Alone again with the sheriff, she offered him her slim hand. "Thanks for lunch, it was certainly much better than what I would have done for myself."

"My pleasure. You have an open invitation anytime you're on the mainland." To his surprise, he waited eagerly for her response.

Kate hesitated before favoring him with an open, engaging smile. "You're on," she said.

Daniel Sheridan waited until Kate had disappeared from view before he got up to leave. Before the day was much older, he intended to learn everything he could about Smoke Island. Puffin Landing was a small village, despite its swollen summer population. There were only so many places the old man could be, and Sheriff Daniel Sheridan knew every one of them.

CHAPTER EIGHT

Kate finished wrapping the pizza in foil and placed it on a cookie sheet. It was a surprise for Chip, who loved pizza. She had juggled the box on her knees all the way across the bay, trying to keep the sea water from soaking through the cardboard. She had thought of pizza just before she left, and not even Norman Day's scowl at the delay could deter her. Not after what Daniel Sheridan had told her about Old Nate, the last recipient of the Voss Grant. No way. The current recipient was going to get special treatment from now on.

She put the rest of the groceries away and then glanced at the clock. There was time for a relaxing bath before she could expect Chip back. The time reminded her that she had not seen Natty Bumppo since her return. He was never far away, was usually right on the porch, barking her a welcome as she walked up the path from the dock.

She went outside. "Natty. Here, boy. Come here," she called. There was no answer. Nothing. She walked a full circle around the house, calling for him as she went. A stiff evening breeze whipped her long hair about her face. "Nat . . . ty, Natty Bump . . . po," she cried, and the wind moaned a mock reply. She stopped, listening, and had the eerie sensation that the grass, the flowers, the very air itself was listening too. Still nothing.

She called one last time and then went back inside, leaving the door slightly ajar. She filled a glass with wine and went upstairs, starting the water running into the tub, adding a capful of scented soapsuds. While waiting for the huge old-fashioned bathtub to fill she remembered the letter. She went into the bedroom and fished it out of her bag. Ironically, it was from Anita, inviting herself and her family to the island over the Fourth of July holiday. Kate grinned. Impulsive Anita, so unlike her sober brother.

Wineglass in hand, she wandered back into the bathroom, now dewy with mist, redolent with the scent of lavender. Something was bothering her, teasing her mind just out of reach of her memory. She worried it for a bit, but whatever it was, it remained elusive. She undressed, now more relaxed, her mood mellow from the wine. How simple everything was once there were no more secrets. Chip had been wrong not to tell her about Nate. Daniel Sheridan had been wrong not to tell her about the legends. Nothing was as bad as the unknown.

The water level finally crept up to where she wanted it. She leaned over to turn off the spigots, using all her strength to make sure they were firmly closed and would not drip. The legends! That was what had been bothering her. Too bad Norman Day had interrupted her conversation with Daniel Sheridan.

She took one more sip of wine and then put the glass down on the floor. She had one long leg into the warm water when she heard a sound that froze her in place. It came again, a sound like a thud, followed by strange, unidentifiable scrabbling noises. Kate hastily withdrew her leg and reached for the towel, wrapping it like a sarong about her body. The peculiar sounds were getting closer.

Quickly Kate reviewed her options. There were only two: she could stay behind a locked door and pray that whatever it was would go away, or dissolve into thin air; or, she could go out and discover what it was. Cowering behind a closed door held no appeal. Before she could change her mind she slipped out into the hallway. It was dark, the ornamental stained-glass window over the stairs had not been fashioned to admit much light. That was too bad, for the noises were issuing from the part of the staircase just beyond her vision. She wanted to see what she was facing before it saw her.

Her eyes scanned the hallway, feverishly searching for some kind of weapon, for anything to make her hand feel less naked. Just then a new sound reached her ears. It took several moments for its significance to penetrate her consciousness, and when it did, when she identified it as nails clicking on polished wood, she gave a glad cry and rushed forward.

"Natty! There's a good boy. Come here. Come to Kate. Oh, my God, you're hurt!" The setter was lurching drunkenly, as if he no longer had control of his body. Kate ran down the steps and knelt beside the panting animal. She ran anxious hands over his body but could detect no wound. Relieved that her hands were not sticky with the setter's blood, she half-dragged, half-carried him up the remaining stairs. "Come, Natty, come in here where it's light. Let me see what's wrong." He seemed to be walking better now, although his gait was awkward. He looked as if he had forgotten how to make his legs work, and was taking it one paw at a time until the knack returned.

Kate led him into the steamy bathroom. She dropped to her knees onto the bath mat and went over every inch of his body. She could find nothing wrong. The dog was leaning heavily against her. She fondled one silky ear. "It's all right, boy, you're safe. There's nothing to worry about." She leaned over to pull him even closer. The towel she had so hastily fastened parted slightly. The dog pushed his head past the edges and licked her right breast with his slightly rough tongue. Kate felt a shock course through her, and for one dizzy moment was back in the velvety dark of her erotic dream. The towel slipped completely open and slid to the floor. Kate automatically reached for it in an instinctive desire to protect her modesty. She felt the setter at her breast again. "Oh, no," she moaned, while one part of her, something hitherto unknown, responded to the foreign caresses.

"Kate?"

She had not heard him come in the house, much less climb the stairs. She pushed the dog from her and stood up to face Chip, who was standing in the doorway, a puzzled expression on his face.

"I came home early . . . after . . . after this morning. You know—"

101

It took her several moments to remember. The morning could have taken place ten years ago, so much had happened since. The dog was pressing against her, heavy and warm on her bare legs. To her horror he turned his head up and ran his tongue slowly, deliberately, over the soft flesh of her thigh. She flushed and tried to push him farther away, but he stubbornly resisted her efforts.

"Here, that's enough of that. I'll take over now." Chip picked the setter up and deposited him in the hallway, closing the door on his nose when he tried to reenter the room. He turned to Kate. She looked rosy and very beautiful. "The dog has good taste," he remarked. The casual comment caused Kate to blush an even deeper hue. "Rubens. Definitely Rubens. Come here, little girl."

Kate saw the desire burning in Chip's hazel eyes. "Rubens, huh? Are you trying to tell me something, buster?"

Chip put on his innocent look. He moved toward her, yanking his clothes off.

"Call the love of your life fat, will you?" There was a catch in her voice as she watched him.

He was naked now. He reached out and drew her into his arms, held her close, so that she could feel the hardness of his arousal as he pressed himself urgently into the soft flesh of her belly. "Skin tone, my love, that was my reference," he murmured into her ear. Scooping her up into his arms he stepped into the tub, settling down into the warm, scented soapiness. Grasping her hips he slowly lowered her down onto his lap, impaling her. Slowly, exquisitely, they began to rock together, their movements sensuous, unhurried. Neither of them saw the door slowly open. Nor did they see a rusty muzzle push past the door's edge. Nor did they see a pair of flat, black eyes stare unblinkingly at them.

Locked in their own, private world, they made love.

CHAPTER NINE

JULY

Two weeks after they found Natty Bumppo's body and buried him under the shadow of a huge white spruce, Kate awoke from a vivid dream to find Daniel Sheridan standing over her. She had gone to sleep in the small clearing on the side of the house. It was close to the setter's grave.

"Kate. Kate?" Daniel Sheridan's voice pulled at her from outside the boundary of her dream.

She forced herself wider awake. The dream clung, confusing her. For several wild, thrilling moments she thought that he had come for her, the tall virile Indian who haunted her sleeping hours; had come to spread her legs and thrust himself deep within her willing flesh. She quivered, deep inside. It was an awful, burning hunger. It was only a dream.

Looking up into his concerned face she blushed with the wanton thought. He hunkered down beside her, concern clouding his dark eyes. "What's the problem? Why are you sleeping out here?" When she started struggling into a sitting position he quickly moved to help her, placing one strong hand behind her nape and gently exerting pressure until he could slip the other hand behind her shoulders and ease her up. "Why, Kate?"

"It's better here. The dream is better." Her voice was heavy with sleep. The sheriff frowned. Kate realized too late what she had said. She couldn't explain. The dreams were coming more often; they were as vivid as her waking hours; they frightened her. It was as if she were living two lives, one awake, the other asleep. She was fascinated, yet afraid. They had begun in the dark, the voluptuous dark, and were permeated with a frustrated longing so intense, so concentrated, that it was painful. Always, she wondered where they would end; if she would be able to bear it, when they did.

Daniel Sheridan knew it was none of his business, dreams were personal, but something nagged at him. "What do you dream?"

"Oh, different things," she said lightly, knowing the answer would not satisfy. "Sometimes I dream about an Indian village." That was safe enough, and it was true.

"Indians lived all around here, came to this area from inland during the summer to feast on seafood. Mounds of shellfish have been found up and down the coast."

"I know. It's sad that they're gone."

"Sometimes I imagine they've just left. Perhaps will return at any moment."

"It's easy to visualize them here." Sometimes when she woke from a dream she was surprised not to see the bustling Indian village.

They smiled at each other, perfectly in tune. "I must look a mess," she blurted out, suddenly aware of him as a man.

"You look beautiful."

Kate was startled; it was not said lightly. She gave a shaky little laugh. "Thank you for the white lie." He regarded her gravely. Alarmed, she tossed her head, the wild tumble of her hair falling forward. Impatiently she pushed it back. "Nothing's wrong, is there?"

"No, nothing. I brought you another guest. Wilma Thompson showed up on my doorstep this afternoon. Norman was not to be found, so I ran her out as soon as I could get away."

Kate gaped at him for a second and then laughed, the sound floating about the clearing. "Wilma? Here?"

"I hope I did the right thing. She said you wouldn't mind."

"Of course I don't mind. I'm delighted, in fact." She laughed again, only this time the notes sounded slightly off key. "For weeks I've longed for company, and now I've got a full house." Chip's sister Anita, her husband Gus and their two children had arrived two days previously. "No problem. The more the merrier, as the saying goes."

"That's good. Miss Thompson didn't seem to be too concerned."

This time her laugh was a sound of pure delight. "That's Wilma, all right. Where is she? Wait, let me guess. She made a beeline for the studio, if I know her."

The sheriff chuckled. "Right you are." He checked his watch. "I've got to go. I promised my deputy he could take his wife to dinner tonight."

"Deputy?"

"Part-time summer help. It's mostly traffic duty. Information. That sort of thing. Puffin Landing gets more tourists each year." He sounded proud.

Kate walked with him to the small dock and watched his boat go out of sight. It was too early to start dinner. She decided to go to the cove. Anita and Gus were there with the kids. Melinda and Paul loved the water. It was still too cold for Kate.

The woods were free of menace today. Kate did not need poor Natty Bumppo to know it. Poor, unlucky dog. He had died from bee venom, his system going into shock as a result of multiple bites, according to the report Kate had insisted on. She missed him terribly.

She was more familiar with the woods now. More at ease. The cove was not too far ahead when suddenly, shocking in its unexpectedness, sounds of screaming, not the usual sea gull screams, but pure, unadulterated human panic shattered the peaceful air. Dread spurring her on, she ran, bursting out of the woods above the cliff. From her vantage point she saw her brother-in-law Gus running into the surf. Anita was in the water frantically tugging at twelve-year-old Melinda. The child was emitting sharp, piercing yells. Paul, a thin, undersized eight-year-old, stood at the surf line, his arms hugging his shivering body.

Kate ran down the path heedless of the many dangers. She reached Paul and put her arm about him. "What's going on? Did Melly get a cramp?"

107

Paul shook his head no, mumbled something she couldn't hear.

'What?''

"Her foot's caught in some . . . something. It's, it's pull . . . pulling her down.''

Horrified, Kate saw Anita struggling to keep her daughter's head above the water. Gus reached them just as a big wave washed over them. Only two heads reappeared; ominously, the screaming stopped. At once Gus and Anita dove again.

"Melly's drowned,'' Paul said matter-of-factly, immediately bursting into tears.

Kate felt a cold hand squeeze her heart. She tightened her arm about the little boy. Sea gulls circled overhead, their sharp, piercing cries now the only voices to be heard. The children. Oooooh the dead children. Kate waited, almost not breathing, aware of her nephew's thin body pressing against her.

There was nothing to be seen now, nothing but the incessant roll of the waves as they rushed to fling themselves on the jagged rocks. The moments stretched out, each an eternity. A head broke the surface of the water. It was Anita, her sandy hair plastered tightly to her skull.

Paul started to whimper. Kate snatched a towel from the picnic blanket, noting without conscious thought the basket of food, the paperback novel with damp-curled pages riffling in the salt-laden breeze, the single wet green flipper, all mute indications of happier moments. She placed the towel about her nephew's thin shoulders and gently began to rub his back. She concentrated on the task.

Anita was no longer visible, having dived again beneath the gray-green water. Kate began to despair.

Three heads popped up, turned automatically toward land, like curious seals surveying unknown territory.

Paul ran into the water. Kate caught up with him before he could throw himself into the surf. She noticed abstractedly that he was wearing the mate to the green flipper. "Wait, Paul. They're coming in." He ignored her, intent on reaching his sister. Kate put her hand on his shoulder, physically restraining him.

"Melly! Melly!"

The little boy's taut body fought against her restraining hand. Kate released him as his father struggled out of the water, Melinda pressed tightly to his chest. She was crying. Anita and Gus were both trying to talk at once, while Paul kept plucking at his sister's hand, trying to get her attention.

Kate hunched her shoulders, drawing herself inward. Above, the gulls circled, their harsh cries blending in a raucous crescendo.

Kate's attention was snatched away from the birds by the high, piping voice of her nephew. "I thought you were dead, Melly. I thought you were dead."

Anita reached out and drew him into her embrace, making clucking mother noises to calm him. He struggled free of her arms, almost striking her in his frenzy to get to his sister again. "I thought you were dead," he sobbed, "I did."

Anita recaptured him, hugged him close. "She's safe, honey. Melly's safe," she crooned.

Paul stopped his spastic movements. He looked up

at his mother with large hazel eyes, his legacy from her Windsor blood. "Sa–afe?" he hiccuped.

"Safe." She nodded reassuringly. "It's all over now."

Kate looked at her brother-in-law. Augustus Barth showed every one of his forty-four years. There was a pinched look to his handsome face, his features somehow diminished in the aftermath of shock. He appeared shorter than his five feet ten inches, as if fear had compressed him.

"What happened?" Kate asked, trying to keep her voice even.

"Damned if I know. There was seaweed wrapped around her legs. It was the toughest plant I've ever seen. The tide was pulling her into the rocks. If . . . if she'd got caught in them, we . . . we never would've pulled her out." He shuddered.

"It's over. It was a freak accident. Let's not dwell on it," Anita said.

Kate looked hard at Anita, an older, female version of Chip, at least in looks, and wondered for perhaps the thousandth time why her husband had not inherited some of his sister's placidity.

"But—"

Anita shook her head sharply, interrupting Gus. "There are no 'buts.' Everyone'll be fine after a hot bath and something to eat. Tomorrow we'll all be back in the water." Unless we make a big fuss and scare them, her fierce look said.

There was nothing more to say. They gathered their paraphernalia and straggled up the path to the top of the cliff. Paul turned toward his sister, who had stopped crying and was staring out over the water with rounded eyes. "He wanted you," he whispered.

Rage filled him. He trembled, his glistening green length swaying aimlessly with the tide's ebb and flow. Useless.

Power.

Soon. Soon he would be strong.

Patience.

He forced himself to calm. So close. She had almost been his.

Patience.

He would rest. Husband his strength. He rode the waves, cresting each one with sinuous grace. He dreamed. When he woke his way was clear.

The boy was young. Afraid.

Patience.

CHAPTER TEN

Little Sparrow hummed happily, the pure notes of her joy floating on the air as she prepared journey cakes for Great Bear to take on the hunt. Over and over again she pounded the dry corn meal in the stone bowl. Finally satisfied, she moistened the meal, formed little balls that she dropped onto a red oak board, then swiftly moving her hand down the rows, flattened them slightly. She placed the board near the hearth and made sure there was enough wood to cook the cakes thoroughly on both sides.

She sat and waited, giving the oblong board an occasional shake, dreamily thinking of the night to come. Great Bear always took her, many times, before he left at the first hint of dawn. There would be little sleep tonight. Little Sparrow smiled in anticipation, feeling her body soften, grow liquid with only the thought of her husband deep within her.

His voice outside their wigwam roused her from the reverie. Hastily she stood up, smoothed her skirt until the material lay snugly across her hips. Great Bear would know with one look how she wanted him.

She started to go to him, but stopped just inside the entrance when she saw that it was Iye, the shaman, who held him in conversation. Hastily she stepped back, into the shadowed interior. She was afraid of the medicine man; he was powerful, more powerful than any man had ever been before, controlling the world of spirits as easily as she could pound corn into meal. Even the sachem, wise old Rain Cloud, was careful not to anger the powwaw lest he call down the lightning to punish him.

At last the shaman stalked off, walking past the wigwam. Little Sparrow retreated farther into the dark, but she knew he saw her. She suspected, with superstitious awe, that should he wish to, he could see through the walls of woven mats.

Great Bear stood still, watching Iye walk away. She concentrated very hard, letting her love flow outward, willing Great Bear to feel it. She measured him with admiring eyes, the width of his shoulders, the leanness of his waist, the long, powerful lines of his legs. They were so strong, so hard, so right, between her own.

"My husband," she whispered. It was enough. He heard her.

Just as Great Bear turned, Kate woke up. Damn, she thought, then quickly looked at the other side of the bed, afraid she had said it aloud, disturbed Chip. She was alone.

It was very early. A few opportunistic birds were chirping, the clear notes carrying far in the still air. Slipping out of bed, she reached immediately for her robe, belting it tightly against the chill. The window was open; cold air streamed inside. She closed it, wondered why Chip had left it open, then sighed as she realized the simple answer was that he had not noticed.

The hall was still night-murky; the staircase descended into gloom. Kate went down as silently as she could, trying to remember the places that creaked.

The kitchen light was on, a warm, welcoming beacon in the shadowy house.

"Chip?" The room was empty.

She walked into silence, inhaled the unmistakable aromas of coffee and cinnamon raisin toast. The toaster was faintly warm; dishes were piled in the sink, two of everything. Wilma. Chip would have left them on the table.

Kate went upstairs to wash and dress. A more suspicious wife would probably wonder, but she was married to a man with a one-track mind, set firmly on art to the exclusion of almost all else, long enough to know that her competition was not another woman. An affair took time and a degree of effort; Chip was stingy with both.

Ironically, it was Chip's sister who could not accept the circumstances. Hearing the younger woman moving about, Anita came sleepily down to the kitchen to share a cup of coffee before the demands of the day began. "If it were Gus and that green-eyed honey blonde I would be in that studio right now."

Kate smiled, amused by the adamant gleam in the hazel eyes. "We're talking about your brother. Remember?"

"We're talking about a man. Don't you forget it," Anita replied hotly.

"An artist. Wilma Thompson is his agent, and a

good one. They're a lot alike, you know. Two sides of the same coin. She lacks creative talent, but has the ability to recognize it in others. In her own way she's as ambitious as Chip, maybe more. Her own success depends on his. She's not interested in Chip as a man, and I'm sure that Chip has never looked at her as a woman.''

Anita grimaced, giving her features an impish twist, producing lines around her eyes and mouth.

''You can believe me or not, but that's the truth. It would be a lot simpler if it were the case; it's easier to fight another woman than an abstract like *Art.*''

''That bad, huh?''

''Not quite.'' Kate heard the note of bitterness in her own voice; was surprised at it.

''What can I do? Should I talk to Chip?'' Anita regarded her soberly, a true friend, despite her natural loyalty to her brother.

''No. Please. It's all right. It's just . . . sometimes . . . the loneliness. It's exaggerated here, on the island. I miss Natty so.'' This last was whispered. Kate still found it difficult to say the setter's name without her throat closing in pain.

''I know.'' Anita's voice was gentle, caring. ''You should have a baby.''

''Come on, Anita. I thought that solution was Victorian.''

''Edwardian, at least.'' She smiled. ''Think about it.''

The day turned out as beautiful as the one before it. Kate was mildly surprised when first Paul, then Melinda, demanded to go swimming. Anita calmly sent them upstairs to change into suits while she made piles

115

of sticky peanut butter and jelly sandwiches. "Their favorite lunch," she explained when Kate offered to vary the menu. "The taste buds do not develop until late in the second decade of life. By then the parents' wallets have expanded to accommodate more exotic preferences. One hopes."

Kate looked at the sandwiches, jelly already oozing through the bread. "This may not be a gourmet household, but I can do better for you and Gus." Anita made no protest.

There was still no sign of Chip and Wilma when they set out for the cove. Kate stayed behind, despite their protests, promising to join them later. She spent an hour typing, then picked up a science fiction paperback she bought in Puffin Landing and went outside to read. The front porch was in shade, perfect for her purpose. She settled into a comfortable rocker and quickly became engrossed in the story.

The sound of the brass bell clanging down at the dock preceded Henry Packer's appearance. Although the day was now quite warm, hot in the direct sun, he wore a cardigan buttoned over a shirt.

"How're you, missus?" He tipped his misshapen baseball cap in an old-fashioned gesture, taking the opportunity to wipe the sweat from his brow onto the sleeve of the sweater.

"Fine, Henry, and you?" The handyman allowed that all was well with him. Kate was better acquainted with him now, more understanding of his taciturnity, recognizing the innate shyness which barred fuller communication. "I didn't expect to see you this week, because of the holiday."

"Makes no diff'rence t'me. Mind if I do some work

round t'about here. Bushes look kinda scraggly. Need a firm hand t'keep 'em growin' right.''

"Of course not. Let me get out of your way."

"Ain't in the way, missus." He tipped the cap again and went off for the tools kept neatly stored in the utility shed.

He was still working two hours later when Anita returned. "Gus and the kids will be along shortly. They're waterlogged, all three of them. No problems," she answered Kate's unspoken question. Her voice changed. "I suppose my brother and that agent still haven't put in an appearance. Never mind," she said, not waiting for an answer, "I had a terrific idea. We're going to take you to dinner ashore tonight. Our treat."

"No."

"Yes."

"I meant 'no' to the treat. The idea sounds great."

"We'll argue later," Anita stated, meaning it. "Do you think he can take us?" She nodded in Henry Packer's direction.

Henry was obliging. Anita bathed and changed and when Gus returned sent him to the studio with firm instructions not to return alone. He saluted her saucily and left. "Smart ass," she said, then looked around guiltily for tender ears. "Mustn't ruin the mother image," she informed Kate in mock relief when her offspring were not found in the vicinity.

Gus proved himself an able persuader, returning with both Wilma and Chip. Kate found it curious that Chip was willing to leave his studio even for an afternoon. But then, he was full of enthusiasm again, likely buoyed by Wilma's supportive presence. Kate felt a twinge of jealousy, then quickly suppressed it.

Once in Puffin Landing they decided to go separate ways, since Chip adamantly refused to set foot in any local gallery, and the others were interested in seeing them.

"Where will we all meet?" Anita asked.

Chip looked amused. "Just try and get lost in Puffin Landing. We'll see you around."

It was a pleasant walk from the docks to the green in the center of the village. Chip looked startled at the transformation from spring somnolence to summer activity. They had to wait for traffic at each street; there was even a smell of exhaust fumes in the air.

Kate was happy to have Chip all to herself, for the first time in weeks, away from the island, away from his work. He was in a good mood. She took his arm, nuzzled her face against his shoulder. "I love your cologne. Eau de turp." He smiled the quirky smile she loved. "It's such a part of you."

They strolled about, window shopping, not caring to venture inside the crowded stores. Kate smiled at some of the townspeople she recognized, receiving chilly nods from a few in return.

"Popular, aren't you?"

"We're outsiders, Chip. You said it yourself when we first came here." She hesitated, then decided to say what was on her mind. "But it isn't only that. There's something else, something to do with the island. It isn't Norman alone who is afraid of it. Henry Packer comes during the day, but you just heard him say he couldn't take us back tonight, that we'd have to call the sheriff or hire someone 'willin' ' was the word he used, I believe." Chip frowned. Kate was afraid she had spoiled his agreeable mood. She braced herself for an explosion which never came.

"I guess there are some places like that," he said thoughtfully. "Maybe an accident happens, something unexpected. Rumors start, become myth. I suppose it's easier to do here than a lot of other places."

"Why here?"

"Use your head," he said with a return to his usual asperity. "This place is small, isolated. During the winter they all probably sit around gossiping. You know how it goes. Ever play 'rumor' as a kid?"

"We called it 'secret.' "

"Whatever. The principle's the same. It's a classic example of distortion. Say one thing, one simple thing, and it comes back garbled." He grinned down at her. "Mostly people hear what they want to hear."

Kate mulled over his explanation. It was reasonable, but still . . . There was something different about Smoke Island, an aura, a feeling, sometimes no more than the faintest of impressions, that the real world stopped beyond its boundaries. Little Alice must have felt much the same while wandering through Wonderland. On Smoke Island Kate was aware of her own senses, more acutely than at any other time in her life.

Then . . . there were the dreams. Surely the island's ambience influenced them. Here, in Puffin Landing, it might be easier to tell Chip about them. Before her fragile courage could flee she stopped, forcing him to stop also. "Let's sit over there," she indicated a slatted park bench. "I want to tell you something that's been happening to me . . . something eerie. Peculiar."

Chip looked surprised, then concerned, but said nothing, waiting for her to tell him what the problem was. They had the bench to themselves. "I . . . I've been having unusual dreams, strange dreams, always about the same place, the same people, and," she blushed, unable to control it, "they're very erotic."

Chip was silent for so long Kate thought he was not going to say anything, or worse, that his attention had strayed. He was staring fixedly at a family of tourists, posed for a self-conscious picture with a statue of one of Puffin Landing's founding fathers in the background. She sighed with relief when he asked a pertinent question.

"What place do you dream about?"

"I don't know where it is, only what it is. It . . . it's about Indians, and, uh, it takes place in and around their village." Chip made no comment; encouraged, she amplified the bare statement. "They are a woodlands people, not very advanced, but also not too primitive. They hunt, fish, farm for corn, which is the staple of their lives. I-I don't know too much about the men, the warriors—their weapons and all. The women have simple stone utensils for cooking, an open hearth, always inside the wigwams, which are stuffy and smelly. One . . . one of the women . . ."

"Yes? Finish it."

"She looks like me. Close enough to be my twin. I . . . I think she's the woman in the mirror. Remember? The first night. When Natty acted so odd." Chip's body stiffened. Kate automatically responded. "No, don't say anything about him. I . . . I couldn't bear it."

"I miss him too."

The simple statement almost finished her. But Chip

120

had not yet addressed himself to the problem of her dreams; the wait was not long.

"Have you thought about these dreams? Really thought about them? Look, I'm not Freud, but . . ."

She should have realized Chip would jump to the obvious explanation. She had toyed with it herself . . . until . . . until she realized that the dreams were serial; it was apparent she was dreaming a continuing story, although there were many missing chapters, or episodes.

"Think about it, Kate. You're an intelligent woman."

"I considered it, of course," she snapped, angered by the hint of condescension in his voice. "But I don't think Freud is the explanation. Nor do I think they are the product of reading local stories. This is so personal; so . . . *immediate.*"

"Well, what does she do, this woman who looks like you?"

Kate knew him well enough to know he would have dropped the subject and refused any further discussion if he had no interest. "Nothing out of the ordinary; nothing that the other women don't do."

"Has she a lover?" Kate slanted a startled look upward. Chip was staring at her intently. "You did say the dreams were erotic?"

"She has a husband whom she loves very much." She sounded prim, even to herself.

"I see. Who does he look like?"

He's tall, with broad shoulders, skin the color of burnished copper, hair a brilliant blue-black. His waist is trim, his legs long and muscular. His body is smooth, hard, exciting. His caresses are gentle as velvet, as exciting as fire. Little Sparrow

121

responds to him wildly, glorying in the feel of his hardness against her yielding flesh. She knew so much, yet so little; she had yet to see his face. Chip was waiting; there was only one answer. "I don't know."

"Kate." He tilted her chin up, looked directly into her eyes. "He is the focus of 'er, the erotic interest, I take it. Well, I can't help much with your dreams, but . . ." He paused, deepened his voice. "Perhaps if you had some *real* erotic interest, say tonight, it would help to banish this other fellow." He looked thoughtful. "It's been a long time for us."

Perhaps it would work, but somehow Kate doubted that making love with Chip would end the dreams. There was a reason she was dreaming about Little Sparrow and Great Bear. She was certain of it.

They resumed walking, detouring into the ice-cream parlor by common consent. They were leaving when Daniel Sheridan walked in. Chip stiffened, his instinctive reaction to him. If the sheriff noticed, he chose to ignore it. Kate greeted him warmly, genuinely happy to see him.

"I saw Henry not too long ago. He said you'll need a ride later. Any time after six o'clock is fine with me. I'm off duty then."

"I hate to impose," Kate began, only to be overridden by Chip.

"That'll be fine."

Kate was embarrassed; the sheriff looked amused. They exchanged a few more words, Chip not bothering to hide his desire to leave. Kate invited him to the clambake they were planning to celebrate the holiday. Daniel Sheridan hesitated, then capitulated when Kate persevered. "I'll have to get Ron, that's my deputy, to cover for me. It should work out if there are no major problems.''

''Fine.'' Kate was the product of a traditional upbringing. Now their numbers were even; Wilma would not be a fifth wheel.

Daniel Sheridan tipped his cap and went to order his ice cream.

Chip hustled Kate outside. ''Was that necessary?''

She understood him perfectly. ''I thought so. He's been a tremendous help to us.'' There was more she could say, but wisely she fell silent. It would be a no-win argument if ever it got started. She was grateful when Chip let it drop, but regretted the loss of the earlier, easier climate between them.

The afternoon slipped away. It was a relief to come across Gus standing outside a pricey gift shop. He grinned at them. ''Anita's in there doing what she does best. I'm feeling poorer already.''

''Why don't I believe you?'' Fond of her brother-in-law, Kate admired his relaxed attitude to life. A research chemist, patience was his greatest asset in the white-tiled laboratory where he spent his working days. At home his temperament was so agreeable that Anita once complained that she had to pick a fight every so often just to remember how it was done. ''Where are the kids?''

''Wilma took them back to the island. The kid that works for you left with them a half hour ago. It's good of Wilma to give us all this time alone.''

When Anita emerged from the boutique she was flushed with success. She handed some of the packages to Gus. ''Let's go. I'm starved,'' she announced.

The restaurant was noisy and crowded, crammed

123

with hungry, tired vacationers. The service was slow; the food marvelous. Chip and Gus argued good-naturedly over the check, but the fight was no contest since Gus had put in the fix with the maitre d'. It was late when they emerged into a cool, clear night. Anita made them laugh when she declared the bananas Foster with its gooey caramel sauce would haunt her hips forever.

They strolled to the public dock, where they were to meet the sheriff. Gus and Chip walked ahead and were almost to the end of the long dock when a shadow detached from the others and moved swiftly until it came up behind the two women. A hand reached out and touched Kate on the shoulder. She gave a frightened gasp and spun about.

Old Nate opened his mouth wide in one of his empty grins. "Didn't mean t'scare you none, missus."

"Well you did." Fright constricted her throat, making her voice raspy. She could feel Anita move closer to her, whether to protect or for protection, did not matter. It was good to have her so near.

"Sorry, missus. Missus," he said, nodding his grizzled head to Anita. "I waited for you. I saw the children."

Anita gasped. "What do you mean? What about the children?" Her raised voice reached the men.

"Take 'em away, missus. Take 'em away. Th' island's no place fer young'uns."

He started to back away into the shadows, but Chip grabbed his arm. He was livid. He shook the old man, none too gently. "Don't you ever annoy my wife or sister again." He shook him once more. "Is that clear?"

"That's enough, Chip."

"Stay out of it, Kate."

Old Nate mumbled something. Chip released his arm and the old man looked steadily at the younger one. "Take care of what's yours. Leave th'island."

"Just because you didn't make it," Chip began, but Old Nate ignored him.

"Go home, all of you," he said, and then walked away, back into the shadows.

Melinda woke up, not slowly the way she normally did, but with a snap. It was very dark. Very quiet. There were no car horns, like at home. Even the old house was still, not creaking the way it usually did. Settling its old bones, Daddy said. She didn't quite understand that, but it sounded funny.

"Mommy," she said, and then remembered that she was a big girl. Only babies cried for their mothers. But her mother was not there, was not even on the island. Instead of frightening her more, the thought made her strong. She was in charge, just like at home when her parents went out. She and the baby-sitter.

She lay in the narrow bed with the thing across the bottom her mother told her was called a footboard. She thought it was dumb. It made the bed harder to make. A door opened and closed, right under her room. The back door. She got out of bed and went to the window. Wilma was walking away, going in the direction of her Uncle Chip's studio. She relaxed. The baby-sitter never left them alone. Her parents must be back.

She crossed the room to the door, careful not to bump into anything with her bare feet. She hesitated, then grasped the pretty glass doorknob and quickly pulled the door open. The hall was dark, scary. Something moved, sounding slithery, coming from the direction of Paul's room. Melinda wanted to go back into her room, shut the door and climb back into the bed, right over the footboard, and pull the quilt over her head. She wanted to forget about being brave. Instead she stepped into the hall.

CHAPTER ELEVEN

Puffin Landing sparkled under the influence of a brisk wind that swept up through New England from the middle Atlantic states. The village green was decorated in patriotic hues, the red, white and blue scalloped bunting puffing out like a trumpeter's cheeks. The volunteer band would give its annual Fourth of July concert in the white wrought-iron gazebo when dusk fell.

Norman Day was beginning to sweat as he worked to put up the reviewing stand for the village's elite. His father and several of his buddies volunteered to do this every year, citing civic duty. This year he insisted Norman help.

Across the green, sitting on one of the benches, long legs sprawled in front of him, spine curved low to maximize slouch, was Norman's best friend Joe Moody. Norman worked steadily, keeping an eye on his father, looking for the chance to slip across to Joe. It came six minutes later when the elder Day went into Fisherman's Haven restaurant.

Norman wasted no time, joining Joe in an identical back-twisting posture before the door of the Fisherman's Haven swung shut.

"It's a bitch," Joe offered by way of greeting.

"It sure is." Norman knew the reference was to the early-morning labor.

"I was thinking," Joe said, the amenities over, "about tonight."

"What about it?" Norman assumed they would do what they always did, grab a few beers and go cruising around looking for girls out at the new mall ten miles north of Puffin Landing.

"It being a national holiday, and all," Joe continued as if Norman had never spoken, "we should do something different. Exciting."

Norman thought about this. He couldn't imagine what would be more exciting than what they did, he and Joe and sometimes Fred Shackford, sometimes Billy Sproul. The only thing that could possibly be more exciting than drinking a few brews and riding around looking for girls, was actually to get some girls into the car. So far this had been the impossible dream.

"What?" Across the green the door to the Fisherman's Haven opened, Norman's father emerged, surreptitiously checked his fly. Next he would look for him. "What?" he repeated, jostling Joe with his elbow to convey the need for speed.

Joe told him.

The color leeched out from beneath Norman's tan, leaving his face an interesting shade of putty.

CHAPTER TWELVE

Anita groaned dramatically and patted her stomach. "It's the fat farm for me after this week. I never ate so much."

"She'll never eat again," Gus whispered sotto voce to Kate, who was not the least amused, since her own stomach felt uncomfortably full.

The remains of the clambake were neatly encased in huge black plastic garbage bags: steamer clam shells, lobster shells, corn cobs, chicken bones, all stuffed out of sight, along with the paper dishes and plastic utensils.

"Aren't we going to roast marshmallows?" Paul asked, eliciting a chorus of groans from the adults.

"What about the watermelon?" Melinda inquired, referring to Daniel Sheridan's contribution to the clambake.

"Later," Anita said firmly. "I'm for a nap."

Chip picked up a red and white beach ball. "Who wants to play monkey in the middle?" He pointed to the water. "In there."

"I do," Paul yelled, beginning to struggle out of his sweatshirt.

"I do," Melinda yelled, "choose me, Uncle Chip. Choose me."

"Choose me," Wilma yelled, and stripped out of jeans and T-shirt to reveal a taut long-limbed body in a sleek red maillot.

Gus grabbed the ball from Chip and was in the water first. The others ran after him, whooping like demented sea gulls. Even the sheriff stripped down to a suit and joined them. Once in the water the four "men" ganged up against Wilma and Melinda.

"Wouldn't you know it? Not that I have much sympathy for *her*. It's Melly I care about."

"I know," Kate soothed, "but I honestly think she was telling the truth. I believe she doesn't know why she left them."

She did not want to upset Anita any further. Not after last night, when they found Paul and Melinda alone, huddled together in total darkness at the top of the stairs. Melinda's arms were so tightly clasped about her brother's thin frame that they had to forcefully separate them. "Don't," she had whispered, "please don't."

"Why not, darling?" Anita had asked.

"Don't. Please don't," had been the only reply.

"Don't," Anita said, an eerie echo of Kate's thoughts, "excuse that woman to me. Whatever her reason, I don't care. It was unforgivable to leave them alone like that. Unforgivable."

"It's over. I'm going to read, how about you?"

"I'm going to sleep. I didn't get much last night."

Kate's gaze wandered up to the top of the cliff, to

the dark woods crowding the edge. "Sometimes I think there's something here . . . something—Oh, nothing," she said lamely. There was a flash of yellow above her. A butterfly. She shivered, although the hot sun warmed the land. She made herself comfortable and picked up her book. Another mystery unsolved. Another secret of Smoke Island. It sounded like a Nancy Drew title. Would that it were only that, she thought, as her eyelids suddenly closed and she too fell asleep.

The earth was hot and still, the way it is before a storm. Little Sparrow waded into the stream, the water cool on her hot skin, to place another stone in the long funnel she and Great Bear were making. She looked across the water to her husband. His side of the giant V was almost done. She applied herself to the task, knowing that once the final rock was in place they could position the sieve made of sticks and then sit idly by, waiting for the fish to come down the narrowed rapids, into the trap.

"Many fish will come for you today, Woman of the Rapid Water." Little Sparrow trembled with joy. He used her secret name, given her at birth. It meant he was pleased with her.

"The fish will come for us, Storm Cloud," she answered, using his sacred name and pleasing him with the gift of it and her answer.

"Let us finish the trap. There are better things to do."

Little Sparrow felt her heart grow big with her love. She worked faster, anticipation of the long, lazy afternoon in her husband's arms generating little quivers of delight through her eager body. Impatient now with the promise of passion, she imprudently lifted a rock

131

too large to handle comfortably, for once in place it would almost close the funnel. They would be finished.

For the last time she waded into the water, the rock heavy in her hands. In her hurry she tripped, sending it flying before her. She cried out and fell, landing heavily on her hands and knees. Dazed, she remained motionless, the cold rushing water numbing her, masking any pain.

"Little Sparrow!" Great Bear came splashing into the stream, sending a great spray of water cascading over her. The drenching coldness returned her to full awareness. He knelt beside her, began to examine her body, his hands gently running down her arms, her legs, searching for injury. Her body flamed into awareness, all memory of the jolting fall pushed out by an all-consuming need.

"That is not where I hurt, my husband." Her voice was low, raspy, ripe with the urgency that was coiling in her middle.

Great Bear tensed, then released his breath in a long exhalation as understanding flooded him. He moved behind her, slid his arms around her middle, placed his hands flat against her abdomen, slowly moved them forward until they cupped her breasts, made pendulous by her position. He began to move his hands in gentle circles. "Is this the place?" he murmured directly into her ear.

Little Sparrow arched her back, pressing herself more firmly into his palms. "One of them, my husband," she responded, her voice husky, deepened by her need. He was kissing her ear, his tongue sweeping the delicate whorls, flicking tantalizingly inside, retreating to start all over again. She groaned, her passions spiraling upward, escalating into a demanding desire. His hand moved along her side, slid sensuously over her hip, down her thigh. She gasped when he pushed aside her covering.

"Is this one, my love?" he asked, chuckling low in his throat as she groaned. Her readiness inflamed his senses. He began to straighten up, his intention to lift her out of the water and carry her to a mossy bed by the side of the stream.

Little Sparrow sensed his intent, but so great was her need that she stayed him with a single word. "Now!" she shouted, and a jay in a branch above echoed her cry.

He needed no further urging. Stripping her of her doeskin skirt he flung it toward the bank; his breech clout followed moments later. He positioned himself between her thighs and grasped her hips, holding her still. She was panting, each rasp of her breath increasing his ardor. A fish blundered into the trap, flapped its body, sprayed them with a shower of icy droplets. They both ignored it. There was no more time.

Kate's eyes snapped open in shock as cold water dripped onto her neck. Noooooooooo, echoed through her mind; a wail of pure rage, of frustration beyond endurance. Her body was tight, throbbing; the hot blood painfully pulsing, demanding release. More water dripped on her, ran down to pool in the hollow of her collarbone. Chip squatted next to her, his sandy hair darkened by the ocean, and leaned his face over hers so that the sky view above her was completely blocked. "Close your legs," he hissed, and then withdrew.

Kate automatically obeyed, slamming them together

133

with such force that her knees ached from the blow. Slowly she became aware that the others were ringed about her, staring down, witness to the scene. She turned her head and saw Anita, embarrassment slowly replacing fright on her face.

"She's all right," Gus said. He signaled to Anita and they both walked away, followed closely by Wilma.

"Chip?" Still held by the dream, she was beginning to feel afraid, vulnerable.

"Not now." He stalked off, his face set in hard lines of disapproval.

She drew her legs up, curled her arms tightly around them, rested her forehead on her knees. She started to sob, her body rocking back and forth, the pent-up tension within gushing forth in wild release. She felt someone come to stand near, the presence nonintrusive, comforting. The sobbing eased, ended in an inelegant hiccup. A handkerchief was thrust into her hand. She took it and wiped her eyes, blew her nose, looked up into compassionate black eyes.

Daniel Sheridan knelt in front of her, shielding her from the others. He smiled, and it was such a normal smile, so uncritical, that she felt better immediately. "You had a dream," he said, "a very intense dream. That's all that happened." He got up and walked away, leaving her the privacy she needed to settle back into herself.

When she rejoined the party her hair was combed as neatly as the salt-laden breeze allowed, there was new color on her cheeks and lips and a heaviness around her heart. She accepted a slice of watermelon from Gus and began to pick out the glistening black seeds, avoiding eye contact with the others by paying attention to the task.

They replenished the fire and soon the flames crackled and popped as they consumed the wood. The age-old fascination with fire drew them; they arranged themselves in a rough circle around it. When she finished the watermelon Kate sat in the only space left, between Wilma and Gus. Paul and Melinda were peeling branches under the direction of the sheriff, readying them for marshmallow roasting.

"It's ready, isn't it?" Paul waved his branch, narrowly missing his sister's face.

Daniel Sheridan put his large hand over the boy's. "Remember what I told you. Safety at all times." He checked both branches, declared them satisfactory. Paul whooped, stuck four marshmallows on his stick and plunged it into the heart of the flames. Melinda wrinkled her nose, carefully chose one marshmallow and squealed in excitement when fire blackened the sugary whiteness.

"It's still a little early, but shouldn't we tell ghost stories?" Wilma asked. "This is the perfect setting."

"It sure is," Gus agreed, putting his arm around Anita, hugging her close.

Kate looked through the fire to where her husband sat, slightly behind his sister and niece. He was part of the circle, yet was not entirely of it; an estranged person by his own choice. Her eyes traveled from his face up to the cliffs, looming dark and mysterious over the small cove. When she lowered her gaze she found Chip staring at her.

"Aunt Kate, Daddy says you probably know lots of scary stories, from school and all."

135

Paul was looking at her with rounded, credulous hazel eyes. Usually she would do anything he asked, but she knew she couldn't honor this request. There was no way she could organize her thoughts, much less render a narrative with appropriate drama.

Daniel Sheridan saved her. "This is the perfect time and place to tell Paul and Melinda the legend of this island. After all, it's not everyone who is lucky enough to stay where there is a ghost." All eyes turned toward the sheriff.

"For real? A real ghost?" If anything, Paul's eyes were even rounder than before.

"So the story goes. I have it on good authority from a friend of mine. Old Nate. Nathaniel Elwell Smith."

Anita frowned, obviously trying to place the name. Wilma straightened and gazed thoughtfully at Chip, who was glaring sullenly at the sheriff. A knot on a branch exploded, sending sparks showering out. Anita gasped at the sudden noise and then giggled nervously. Daniel Sheridan leaned forward and poked it back into the heart of the fire with the tip of a green branch. He swept the circle with his dark eyes, letting his gaze rest for a moment on each of them in turn, ending with Chip. The peculiar tension between the two of them intensified, until it was almost visible, almost tactile, like static electricity from friction on a wool rug.

"Go ahead, Chief, you don't need my permission."

The sheriff gave Chip a long, level look and then smiled at the rude remark. He inclined his dark head in a mock bow. "As you wish." He began to speak, his voice pitched low so that they had to draw close, increasing the sense of intimacy created by the fire and the fading light as huge storm clouds rolled toward the mainland from the open sea.

"The legend of Smoke Island is a tale so old, so powerful, that many believe today that what happened here long ago is but yesterday, and what happened yesterday can happen again today." He paused, waiting for them to settle, letting his opening remark set the mood. No one spoke; they waited raptly for him to begin again.

He filled them in on the background, talking knowledgeably about the Algonquin Indians and their culture, setting the scene with vivid word-portraits. The Indian village, the portable wigwams arranged around a central green, the cultivated fields planted with corn, the communal activities, the sports of the adults, the games for all ages came alive for them. He sketched some of their religious beliefs, recreating for them a wonderful world guided by the invisible, for the Indians surrounded themselves with spirits big and small, good and evil.

"So the Indians needed someone to help them with these spirits, or gods, if you prefer to call them that. The person who did that had to be very strong, very powerful, for the spirits would crush anyone weak who dared to interfere in their world."

He looked at Paul, then at Melinda, who was still roasting marshmallows one at a time. "Do you know what a shaman is? What he does?" They shook their heads, Melinda not bothering to take her eyes from the sizzling marshmallow. "Okay. Another name for him is medicine man. His job was the intermediary between the tribe and the spirit world. Remember, the Indians believed that the spirits controlled everything,

137

nothing was too small, nothing was too big to escape their influence. They were in the rocks, the mountains, the clouds, the sea. They could send down lightning and terrible storms; they could withhold the rain, causing drought and famine. They were very powerful and everyone feared them. Everyone except the shaman. He could communicate with the spirits, sometimes control them."

"How?" Paul asked.

"Ah, a very good question."

Paul grinned, offered the sheriff a clump of melted, gooey marshmallow. Daniel Sheridan accepted it, then resumed the narrative. "The shaman was adept at magic; he could control the spirits through his drum and the rattle of his tortoise shell. He had supernatural powers and recounted fantastic dreams and visions as proof. He cured illnesses through the gods. His was a position of respect in the tribe. Even the sachem, the chief, honored him."

"What kind of magic?" Paul asked.

"Look at this." All of a sudden a knife, long and sharp and shiny, and very deadly looking, appeared in his hand. They all gasped. Wilma leaned as far away as she could without actually getting up. The sheriff ignored them all except for Paul, whose eyes were big and round and fixed intently on the wicked-looking blade. "If I stab the air, like this," he said, punching the knife upward, "and it comes back covered in blood, would that be magic?"

Paul's eyes got even rounder. "Oh yes. Can you do that?" he asked, never taking his eyes from the fire-bright blade.

The sheriff turned his hand and the knife was gone,

138

as fast as it had appeared. "No, I can't, I'm only part Indian, but the shaman could do that and more. But we're not even talking about an ordinary powwaw, for the one of the legend was the mightiest, the most powerful shaman of all time. He was not only revered but feared. The people knew of his exceptional abilities because he demonstrated them often, for his ego was as great as his ability and demanded constant adulation."

"That's praise. Flattery," Anita whispered to Paul.

"He was known by many names, one of which was Iye, meaning smoke in the Algonquin language, for he was able to change himself into any shape or form."

Iye. Kate stared at the sheriff, the name reverberating inside her skull. *Iye. Iye. Iye. Iyeiyeiyeiyeiyeiyeiyeiyeiye. Little Sparrow was afraid of Iye; superstitiously afraid. She concealed herself behind the woven mats, hiding from the shaman's view, lest his piercing coal-black eyes should fall on her, should look at her with the burning intensity which contained some unpriestly element that frightened her, deep down inside her soul.*

The sheriff continued, speaking to Melinda and Paul, but aware of the dazed look on Kate's face. "I-Y-E. It's pronounced *Eye-yuh*. It is believed the island is named for him."

"Why?" Kate's lips were stiff. *Why do I know his name, know his face? Is it his rage I feel, his frustration which haunts my dreams?*

"Ah, that's where it gets interesting. Even medicine men are prey to mortal urges, it seems, and Iye, strong and awesome and walker with gods, fell in love, madly, passionately in love with a warrior's wife. He wanted her, but—" He glanced at the children, cleared his throat. "He wanted her, but there was, 'er, no honorable way he could have her."

She was afraid of him. Little Sparrow hid in the dark, waiting for him to leave.

"It's a very old story, a man coveting another man's wife. Iye didn't care about anything save his craving for this woman. So great was his desire, his lust to possess her, that he resorted to trickery."

The words flowing across the circle, through the fire, brought bright images of long ago to life again. The story unfolded; the treachery was revealed.

"Calling upon his awesome powers, perverting his position as a religious healer, he took the shape of the woman's husband, came to her in that guise and took what was good between husband and wife and twisted it for his own dark pleasure."

Little Sparrow must have suffered so. "What about Gr— the woman's husband?" Kate asked, catching herself before she said his name.

The sheriff looked at her thoughtfully but made no comment about the slip. He took up the thread of the story, answering the question. "Unfortunately, the legend doesn't mention him. Only Iye, the Shapechanger, the mightiest shaman who ever lived. In the end it was his own vast ego which contained the seed of his destruction. He had the woman, possessed her at will. She was loving and giving, everything he desired. But—"

Kate closed her eyes. *Poor Little Sparrow.*

"One day he decided to show her how clever he was, or perhaps he was so vain that he couldn't stand using her husband's face and form. He changed into smoke and then into his own body. She was horrified and went to the elders, who confronted the shaman. Iye

140

mocked them, destroying their respect for him. In secret council they determined to punish him.

"But how do you punish someone stronger than you, stronger even than all the other medicine men combined?" The sheriff looked at the faces around him, saw that his audience was engrossed. "The answer came from a council of medicine men. Iye's peers. They passed sentence on him, but to carry it out they needed to be deceitful, for they knew the only way they could discipline him was with his own weapon—trickery.

"They proclaimed a contest for themselves only, so secret, so sacred, that it must take place away from all other eyes. They gathered on an island and encouraged Iye to show his powers. So boundless was his ego that he complied, dazzling them with a display that far exceeded anything they could imagine."

He looked all around, as if checking for eavesdroppers. Then he lowered his voice even more. "But, stealthily, one by one, the other shamans slipped away to their canoes. They paddled in a great circle about the island, raising their voices as one, chanting a spell, weaving magic around the island to keep Iye there, imprisoned, forever."

"Forever?" Melinda whispered.

The sheriff's tone was hushed. "Forever. They could not kill him, although taking another man's wife demanded it under their code of conduct, for they didn't have the power, even all together. But they could punish him. They could keep him away. Alone. All alone."

He paused, let the rapidly approaching night and the spitting fire silently speak of imponderables. After a time he went on, his voice easily sliding around the

141

flames. "Round and round the island they paddled, establishing the boundaries of his prison: the heavens above, the earth below and the sea, to the circumference of the circle made by their canoes. When it was done, when the circle was secure, they left. Not until it was too late did he realize he had been tricked. Iye was alone. Alone for eternity."

A bolt of lightning crackled the air and bounced off a rock near Anita. Thunder boomed directly overhead.

"Let's get the hell out of here," Chip yelled.

Kate automatically started to gather their possessions, and was picking up a picnic basket when another bolt of lightning sizzled nearby. A wind churned the water, howled through the trees on the cliff above, bending them into impossible bows.

Hail started to fall, huge chunks of frozen rain. It pounded down, pummeling Paul. Only Paul.

Melinda shrieked in fear. Kate dropped the basket, watched in horror as the hail began to burn with a blue flame as it struck the little boy. Lightning crackled around him, scorching the earth, filling the air with the reek of ozone.

Paul was screaming, they could see his mouth opening and closing, but the sound was lost in the rushing wind. Anita reached him first, tried to pull him into her arms. The stream of hail widened. It struck her face; blood streamed into her eyes, down her cheeks. Gus grabbed them both. Lightning sizzled around them, intensifying into a continuous flash of pure white light.

Kate started to run toward them. When she saw the sheriff struggling to pick up the blanket in the howling wind, she ran to help him. Together they raced toward the little group, wrestled the blanket up, trying to cover them, to smother the flames. The sheriff cursed. Kate could hear it clearly, as if there was no roaring wind. Hail drove against her, touched exposed skin. She was back in the dark, the velvety, voluptuous dark. A lover stroked her, tenderly built her passion.

"Kate. Kate!" Daniel Sheridan was holding her, his arm firmly around her waist. "It's over," he said, and when she looked around, she saw that it was true. "Are you hurt?"

She shook her head, stirred. Instantly he let her go. The storm had moved off, roiling just offshore. Rain began to fall, plain, cold, wet rain. "Iye's still here," she whispered, and looking up saw something flicker deep in Daniel Sheridan's dark eyes.

CHAPTER THIRTEEN

Power.

Up, up he swirled, using the heavily charged air, the boy's essence giving him strength, fleshing his will, enabling him to feel again. So close.

Patience.

He had acted too soon. It had seemed right. Fitting. After so long, so long that he had almost forgotten it himself, to hear the sound of his name on another's tongue.

Iyeeeeeeeeee. He screamed it aloud, used the voice of the wind.

Power.

So close. He would have had him, been stronger yet, but she had touched the boy, and he had felt her, really felt her, for the first time. He shuddered. His need was overpowering. So firm, so supple, the flesh that had been his, had been denied him for time immemorial.

Patience.

Up, up he whirled, exhilaration racing through him although frustration gnawed within. So close.

Power.

He was not yet strong enough. The boy alone would have been his, but they had been quick, surrounded him, made it impossible to separate the young, vulnerable essence. In unfulfillment he cried aloud, his voice the voice of the thunder, roaring over the island, sweeping over the sea.

In rage he screamed anew, his voice smiting the land, pounding it with his fury. He had seen him again. The other.

Up, up he spun, his anger, his rage, his frustration building within. In a frenzy he whipped the water until it writhed beneath him, huge gray waves capped by frothy white foam.

Patience.

A voice counseled within him, remnant of earlier, craftier days. He quieted, was about to drift, to dream, when something caught his eye. He raced toward it, a new vigor infusing him.

Power.

He sent a sizzling bolt earthward, piercing the racing clouds with deadly accuracy.

Patience.

Power.

It would come to him. They would come to him. All he had to do was wait. Time was now a friend.

The closer they got to Smoke Island, the less Norman Day liked it. This time it was not only the fear, the wormlike, gnawing finger of dread which lodged in his belly each time he approached it, but also the weather, that was deteriorating rapidly. He hunched his shoul-

145

ders, the gesture more from an inner chill than from the misting rain. "Looks worse ahead," he yelled over his shoulder, back to the other three boys. The wind grabbed the words, twisted and thinned them into a tinny-sounding shrillness.

"That so?"

Norman had no need to turn to know that it was Joe Moody who answered, but he did, slowing the boat, postponing for a short while their headlong rush toward the dark island. The sea was running high under a leaden sky. Behind them Puffin Landing—with its twinkling lights, its tourists and locals gathered on the village green for the holiday concert—was hidden behind a thick screen of opaque fog.

"Wan't no rain when we left." Fred Shackford leaned down, hunched broad shoulders against the wind, and managed to light a cigarette on the third try. The tip glowed red, eerily, in the deepening gloom.

"Sea's diff'rent from land," Joe said.

"Not this close to shore." Norman looked at Billy Sproul as he spoke, figuring he was the likeliest to chicken out first, to demand they turn around and go get a pizza. In the dim light Billy's most noticeable feature, large splotchy freckles covering most of his face, looked like army camouflage, the resemblance strengthened by the greenish tinge under a normally pale complexion. Norman judged the green was half seasickness, half fear.

Under the bravado they exhibited in front of each other, they all had their fears about Smoke Island. You couldn't escape it, not if you were born in or near Puffin Landing. Norman wasn't quite sure why that was, but it had always been that way. Even his father, who under the influence of more than a few Olands down at Salty's Tavern had been known to boast that he feared no one and nothing, had never set foot on it. Bad things happened to people who did. Norman was not anxious to break a family tradition.

"Whaddya think?"

Although he was looking directly at Norman, Billy addressed the question to Joe, their natural leader. Disappointed, Norman tightened his features, afraid of revealing his inner panic. He was always afraid of Smoke Island but tonight the terror was much worse. Something was different; he could feel it.

They all turned to look at Joe. Of average height, with neither the muscular, iron-pumping physique of Fred Shackford, nor the slight, unathletic form of Billy Sproul, he and Norman could have been brothers. There was nothing to distinguish him physically, but where Norman had a teenager's ability to blend into any crowd of his peers, Joe always stood out. It was something about his eyes, something sharp and knowing, gazing out of the clear pale blue irises, that set him apart.

Norman knew he wasn't going to like Joe's answer. Since it was his boat, and since he was the one most knowledgeable about the sea, he felt it his duty to acquaint them with his doubts about the weather. Deep inside he understood they already knew about his terror; it had a recognizable odor; he could smell it about himself, thick and sour and growing stronger with each swell that propelled them closer to the island. "Water's tricky, round about th'islands. Clouds're low to th'water, up ahead. Hard to see th'rocks."

Joe smiled, and Norman knew he was finished. He

started to accelerate even before his friend spoke, sure that there would be no going back until they had done what Joe had said they would do. Nothing would change his mind. He could hear Joe, his voice assured, saying the same words he had said that morning, a hundred years ago. "One beer, that's all. One beer and we're out. We'll leave the cans as proof, anybody doubt us."

"Yeah," Fred agreed.

There was silence from Billy.

Norman concentrated his entire energies on the boat and the sea. The waves were growing higher, deeper, with long sliding troughs between them. To Norman's fevered imagination they looked like old yellowed maps, where the oceans were undulating sea serpents, white froth topping each reptilian coil, while fire spewed forth from gaping toothy jaws. The rain was heavier too, hard and cold and driven by a wind that was picking up force with each passing second. He heard a moan behind him, turned in time to see Fred Shackford retch, bend over the side, his broad shoulders looking oddly headless in the dim gray light. Billy Sproul was greener than before, while Joe looked just the same as ever. *Damn him,* Norman thought, and returned his attention to the boat and the heaving sea.

From directly overhead came a loud crack of thunder, the booming echo of it rolling across the waves. A bolt of lightning sizzled out of the pewter sky, a jagged stepladder descending from a moisture-laden cloud to the pitching sea. Another sliced through the murk, closer yet, followed by another, then another still. It was a dazzling, deadly light show.

"Holy shit," Fred Shackford yelled, his voice a high, squeaky, unintended imitation of Donald Duck.

"What in hell?" Joe shouted, then screamed, so loudly, so piercingly, that it penetrated the booming thunder, the screeching banshee voice of the wind.

Norman glanced over his shoulder in time to see a bright finger of lightning swoop out of the raging sky, race in a direct path towards them. It sideswiped Fred's head, burning across the tip of his ear. Fred howled, jumped up, one huge hand going to cup the charred ear, the other clapped across his mouth. Another bolt descended, aimed at them, grazed the back of Fred's neck. His big body convulsed; vomit seeped out from between his fingers. His eyes were wide, disbelieving.

"Turn the fuckin' boat around. Let's get the hell outta here." Joe had lurched his way forward, had a painful grip on Norman's arm.

Behind them Billy Sproul was keening, the sound primitive, more frightening even than the churning frenzy around them.

"Lemme go," Norman screeched, finding it impossible to fight the sea with Joe constricting his movement. The boat was bucking beneath them, the wheel jerking, almost as if it were animate. Norman nearly lost his grip on it as he strove to keep them afloat. "The wheel," he screamed directly into Joe's ear, "help me." Joe looked dazed, the aware blue eyes glazed, staring. Norman kicked him on the shin, hard. "The wheel," he screamed again, and this time Joe obeyed. Together they fought to keep it steady, but it was too late, for it wrenched out of their grasp when the boat slammed down directly onto the water from the peak of a giant wave. The wheel began to spin wildly, the boat rolling helplessly without a guiding hand.

"Jeeesus," Joe yelled as another bolt of lightning aimed out of the sky. It speared Fred's shoulder, knocking him down. There was a hole in his windbreaker, the edges smoking, even with the pounding rain soaking into him.

Norman wanted to close his eyes, make it all go away. Instead he lunged for the wheel, rode it like a cowhand rides a bucking bronco, desperately trying to control it once more.

The lightning plunged down again, stronger, brighter than before. It penetrated Fred's body, entering through the same hole as before. The big, powerful muscles Fred worked on so diligently jerked spasmodically as the pure energy pumped into him.

A clap of thunder deafened them, but they watched in horror as Fred's lips opened, drew back exposing his teeth in a rictus of pure agony. The lightning pulsed, feeding on him, and then was gone.

Silence assaulted their ears, painful because of its suddenness, its unexpectedness. It was as unnatural as was the calming of the sea. The clouds lifted, although rain continued to fall. Dead ahead of them loomed Smoke Island.

"Is he dead?" Joe asked.

Fred lay limp, his head slapping from side to side against the hard wood of the deck with each roll of the boat.

"Go see." Norman grabbed the wheel, tried to start the engine. It coughed, died.

"He's unconscious. Breathin' poorly. You'd better get us goin', right fast."

Instead of jumping on Joe, beating his face to a bloody pulp—what he wanted to do to him for getting them into this mess—Norman concentrated on starting the flooded engine. Little wavelets slapped against the hull, the sound magnified in the unnatural stillness. Joe's fast, rasping breath was an irritant. Norman cursed steadily in a low voice, as if he were doing it in church. He wished Billy would shut up; his keening was thinner, weaker, more eerie.

Almost as soon as he thought it, his wish was granted. Billy shrieked one word, a long, drawn out *"Nooooooooooooooooooo."*

Norman whipped around so fast he knocked his elbow painfully against the wheel, the sound of it a sharp *crack*, the last sound he heard before it all started again. Thunder crashed above them, the clouds descended in great writhing masses of gray and black, the wind came screaming across the water, swelling the waves into huge, heaving gray-green mountains.

Norman whimpered in fright, for he too saw what Billy had seen. A long, pointed, brightly pulsing finger of pure energy was streaking down toward them. It arrowed through dark clouds, lighting them from within, an unholy picture of tortured beauty. It stopped, inches above Fred's flaccid body, then veered, drove itself deep into Billy Sproul.

Norman started to pray as he watched Billy lifted up, his hair spiked outward, his arms and legs jerking like a puppet. His head whipped about, then snapped violently forward. The lightning left. Billy's body collapsed, falling gracelessly to drape over the gunwale. Norman needed no one to tell him Billy was dead.

151

"Shit. It's comin' again!" Joe was screaming, trying to scrabble out of the boat.

Another bolt of lightning was zooming at them, this one bigger, brighter, more awesome than the others. Ozone filled the air. Norman started to pant. The lightning dove down, danced above his head. "Noooooo," he moaned, and remembered it was Billy's last word. It hovered above him, teasing him with dread until he thought that his heart would stop beating in total surrender. Then it passed him by, circled Joe, who was gibbering in terror, to plunge again into Billy Sproul, lifting his dead body up, forcing him to dance a final, cruel step, before tumbling him overboard. The last they saw of him was one pale hand following the rest of him beneath the waves.

CHAPTER FOURTEEN

Kate was more tired than she could ever remember. Wearily she pulled the brush through her hair, long habit making it impossible to skip the nightly chore although she ached for sleep, her body heavy and drained by the day's events.

It had been a strange day, made even stranger by the unexpectedness of the storm, its unnatural violence and the uncanniness of the hail. Paul was unhurt, frightened more than anything by something he couldn't understand. No one could understand anything so bizarre.

Rain rattled against the window. It was a foul night, although the storm had moved over the water. She could hear it in the distance, its intensity undimmed. Chip had stalked out to the studio shortly after they returned to the house, uncaring of everything, their guests included. Before he went he had looked at her coldly, the hazel eyes hard, probing . . . *condemning*. Your fault, they said, as if she could control her dreams.

There was nothing to be done about it now. She sighed, realizing she was happy not to have to placate him at this moment. Even with its problems, its strangeness, she had enjoyed the day, relishing the company.

The weather was worsening, the rain now sluicing against the window. Chip wasn't the only one out in the storm. Daniel Sheridan had insisted upon returning to Puffin Landing, despite her urging him to stay the night. Thankfully he had delayed long enough to help calm Paul and Melinda and to treat the cuts on Anita's face.

She put the brush down and climbed into bed. For a long time she looked at the other side of it, the neatly turned down cover, the plump, smooth pillow. They were growing apart, perilously distant. The danger was that they would drift, not communicating, and ultimately lose everything. How could they resolve their problems if Chip ran away? Was his art more important to him than their marriage? A wonderful bedtime thought. She turned out the light and despite her troubled thoughts, was asleep almost instantly.

Little Sparrow awoke to a twilight world. She lay without moving, her mind savoring the peace of the sheltered place. She looked up to the dark blue sky, seen as patches through the tips of the tall spruces. Her naked body felt full, sated; she was still moist from love. Against her back, fitted protectively around her curves, was the hard, warm body of her husband. She could feel him breathing deeply, evenly, in the serenity of his sleep.

Careful not to awaken him she slipped out of his

grasp, for even in slumber he possessed her, his arm wrapped securely around her waist. When he awoke he would be hungry. Quietly, not bothering with her skirt, since the night was soft and still warm, she went to the stream. The trap contained enough fish for a meal. She prepared them, working efficiently with the stone knife shaped like a leaf. When they were all gutted and cleaned she wrapped them in leaves and placed them on a flat rock where the cooling water could wash over them.

She stopped and listened, her ears trying to pick up sounds of human movement. There was nothing save the rustle of a night bird's wings as it stirred in its high perch, the distinct *click whir click whir click whir* of insects in the tall grasses and the lapping of the water against the rocky bank of the stream.

Little Sparrow waded out into the middle, where it was still deep enough to bathe. She sank down, luxuriating in the coolness, the sensuous feel of the water as it glided over her hot skin. She slid down farther, until by leaning back she was almost covered by the water rushing downstream from the trap. Only her face, the tips of her toes and her breasts were exposed to the air. Her long black hair flowed behind her, a rippling, silky ribbon that captured little phosphorescent bubbles from the foam. Like bright far-off stars they glittered in the ebon strands.

Lazily she half-floated, half-reclined, the water soothing, lulling her into tranquility. Minutes passed, Little Sparrow savoring the hushed serenity, until, without warning, her skin pebbled, just the way it did when the cold, icy winds of winter swept the land and penetrated even the warmest of mantles made from the skins of two bears. Someone was watching her. She sat up, splashing loudly in her abruptness. She looked toward the forest, but could see no one.

"Great Bear?" she called, but of course he did not answer, for it could not be he. Her body would not react this way if it were her beloved whose eyes beheld her.

Nothing moved, not even the leaves stirred, for there was no breeze to animate them. She was alone, but still she felt watched. Hastily she scooped fistfuls of rocky soil from the streambed, rubbing her body with it, then totally immersing herself to rinse the residue from her skin. Anxious to return to Great Bear, she collected the wrapped fish from the rock and hurried off. The short distance back to where they had made their bed seemed very far away, for the night was closing in, the forest coming alive with the rustlings of night-hunting mammals. Above, high in the concealing foliage, came the shriek of a raptor. Every step of the way back she felt alien eyes on her.

Great Bear had started a fire, its rosy glow welcomed her even before she left the concealment of the trees. He was kneeling before it, feeding sticks into the heart of the flames. Quietly she approached, wanting to surprise him, all alarm forgotten in the first sight of his familiar broad back with its rock-hard muscles clearly defined beneath the bronzed skin.

"Hello, Woman of the Rapid Water," he said before she had taken more than two steps into the clearing. His voice was husky, low, full of tenderness.

Little Sparrow's heart contracted, then expanded, freeing her blood to flush her body with the knowledge of his love. It was there in his voice, in the way he held his body, listening for her footfall, sensing her presence before she made herself known. She came close to the fire, knelt and placed the fish near to the stones that ringed it. She could feel Great Bear's eyes on her, inflaming her. "I have brought you food," she said, the gift of her love in her voice, not the words she spoke.

He turned and caught her in a tight embrace, crushing her face into his shoulder. "You are the food I need," he said, his voice a rough growl.

Little Sparrow reacted as she always did to the passion in him. Her own passion woke, spiraling into a core of need, tightening her belly, making her skin sensitive to the slightest of his caresses, the feel of his breath on her neck. She was aware of his arm, sliding down her back, past her hips, coming to rest behind her knees. He picked her up and walked to their aromatic bed of pine needles, where he gently placed her on her back, then quickly dropped down to lie beside her.

Kate stirred as she felt the mattress shift and dip under added weight. She rolled over, reached out. "Chip?" she murmured, her questing hand stopping when it touched flesh. Satisfied, she descended again into deep sleep.

Kate arched her back. Great Bear's tongue was teasing her skin. His lips skimmed across her chest, his tongue licking the valley between her breasts. Then he shifted his weight, moving down her body, using his lips and tongue to blaze a path of fire.

Kate writhed under Great Bear's clever tongue. Her body was aflame, the feelings real, immediate, for she was now a participant, not forced to watch in anguished frustration as he loved another. She wanted to give him pleasure as well, but his hands held her shoulders, pinning her down, allowing him unrestricted access to all her tender places. She felt the pointed end of his tongue enter her navel, groaned as it circled inside, sending a hot shaft of desire coursing through her. His lips trailed downward. Her breathing caught in her throat, stopped.

Kate wanted him, all of him. She lunged upward, broke his hold on her, and reaching down, grabbed his hair, tugging him to move up her body. She was almost sobbing with her need. He responded, reversing the path, awakening each tender part of her as he again traveled her quivering length. He moved to settle himself between her legs, and she surged up, impatient, and heard him chuckle.

A mewling cry escaped from deep in her throat. *At last,* she thought, as her hips rose to accommodate him. He rotated his hips, torturing her with the little circling movements, only allowing her part of himself. She wanted all of him, deep within her. Her hands roamed his body, pressing, urging, telling him of her desire. He was magnificent, the muscles beneath his heated skin sliding beneath her fingers like ropes of silken steel.

She was learning his body, yet she did not know his face. She whimpered, but still he resisted, holding back. In a frenzy, heedless of what might be the consequence, she twined her fingers in his hair, forcing his head up, and looked at his face.

As she recognized the face of Daniel Sheridan she screamed, then her passion overrode her mind as her hips took over and she rose to meet him. Her inhibitions gone, her desires escalated into a wildness which peaked with a great bursting of the tight nugget within her. She felt him shudder. He rocked her, helping her descend from the dizzying height. She fell asleep in his arms.

Screaming, high and harsh and unending, pulled Kate from her sleep. Reluctantly she opened her eyes, remembered the dream, blushed a deep crimson. Automatically she looked at Chip's side of the bed. It was empty, the covers thrown back, the pillow dented. She reached over, felt the sheets to see if they were still warm. They were damp. A briny smell teased her, reminiscent of the salt-laden breeze that blew off the ocean. Something green caught her eye. She reached out, touched it. It was wet. Slimy. She dropped it quickly, then bent over to examine it more closely. It was seaweed, wet sand caught in one limp fold.

The screaming stopped, so abruptly that the silence was more shocking than the noise had been. She got out of bed, surprised to find herself naked, and hurriedly pulled her clothes on. Downstairs she found a hysterical Melinda being rocked in her mother's arms. A pale-faced Wilma was holding Paul.

"What's wrong?" Kate looked wildly about, saw that both Chip and Gus were not there.

Anita looked at Kate over her daughter's head, the cuts from the hail looking raw, livid, on her pale face. "Melly found someone in the water. Down by the dock. Gus went to look." Her eyes were anguished, afraid.

Kate's thoughts flew upstairs, to the wet bed, the smell of sea water, seaweed, a glistening dark green, alien and disgusting on the pristine white sheets. "Oh, my God," she cried, and raced from the house.

She ran down to the dock, her feet pounding hard, hurtfully, against the packed dirt, using all the air she had to pump her legs as fast as they could go, so that she was unable to talk when she reached the granite steps. She leaned over and saw her brother-in-law bending over something. Her heart leapt into her throat, choking her, making it doubly impossible for speech.

Gus heard her harsh breathing. He looked up. An eternity passed. Then he moved aside. Kate stared down at the poor drowned face he had been shielding. It was stark white, except for great splotches of pale beige freckles. Long, thin strands of dark green seaweed were wound about the body, one snakelike piece draped grotesquely over an ear. As she looked down at the dead Billy Sproul for the first and last time, Kate felt herself sway, felt the world tilt. Behind her she heard the sound of racing feet. She turned, saw Chip running toward her, his face unshaven, wearing the same clothes he had been wearing the day before.

"Anita told me," he panted.

Kate stared, the blood draining from her face. "Did you come back to the house last night?" she croaked, her voice reluctant, rusty.

Chip gaped at her as if he had never seen her before. "Where's Gus?" He started to brush her aside, but she grabbed his arm, hung on until he answered. "No," he said.

160

Kate released him. The world tilted again. She felt a rushing in her veins, heard a roaring in her ears, and then saw nothing but gray spotted with dancing yellow and red lights as she collapsed in a heap at the top of the stairs.

the store.

CHAPTER FIFTEEN

Daniel Sheridan carefully mangled a paper clip, twisting the thin loops of metal into a tortured, unrecognizable shape. His dark eyes moved from Chip, who was belligerently airing his grievances, his hazel eyes more green than brown in his annoyance, to Kate, who sat with her dark head bowed. He silently willed her to look up and meet his gaze. The force of his desire amazed him, so strong and compelling was it. Ever since the day of the clambake, during the storm, when they had touched . . . He shook his head as if to clear it, the memory now, more than a week later, still disturbing.

"So what are you going to do about it?"

Chip's bellicose tone begged for a sharp retort. Daniel schooled himself to patience, unwilling to play the other's game. "I've already told you. Henry and I will share the responsibility. I can't get anyone else."

"I'm going to let the trustees know about this. I'm sure they'll be interested in hearing how you've botched things."

"I've already explained that none of the boys I've spoken to are willing to take over Norman's duties. Norman himself won't even speak to me about it. It's unfortunate, I'll grant you, but entirely understandable, especially after what happened. They, ah, ascribe some supernatural causes to the accident. In plain language, they're scared stiff."

Chip made a sound of disgust. Daniel Sheridan dropped the now useless clip onto his desk.

"That's not good enough. I want—"

"I don't care what you want." Daniel cut him off rudely, his tone short, careless of his hitherto carefully schooled temper. Kate lifted her head. Black eyes met black eyes. There was something new, vulnerable, in her gaze. He wanted to explore it. Instead he broke the contact, swung his head to look at her husband, where he stood leaning against the wall, his body taut, every tense muscle speaking of his anger.

"Look. I've got one dead boy, another away in a Portland hospital. The county coroner tells me lightning actually struck twice. That's his official report. I believe him. What else can I do?" he asked, raking a hand through his hair. "I believe him, but the people out there sure as hell don't."

"You're a superstitious, ingrown lot."

"Chip!"

"That's all right, Kate. He's not the first to suggest it." Daniel was regaining his humor. It was stupid to let Chip's complaints get to him. Just because he disliked the man . . . but that thought was dangerous. Ever since he met the Windsors the question of just why he felt such antipathy had bothered him. Sometimes, very late at night, when honesty was unavoidable, he answered the question. His eyes briefly touched Kate, then veered away again. He had no right.

She arose, her thin body turning stiffly toward her husband. "He's only trying to help us. You heard him. I'm . . . I'm grateful that he's willing to do it. We're so isolated. We *need* him."

Daniel wanted to take her in his arms, protect her, erase the note of pleading from her voice. Over and above that, he thought he would like to take Chip Windsor somewhere out into the woods, somewhere very private, very far from human intervention, and pound some sense into him. The man was insensitive and selfish in the extreme. He was abusing his wife. Not in the conventional sense of the word, but it was abuse, all the same.

Above her head the two men glared at each other. Chip pushed away from the wall and took Kate's arm, urging her toward the door. "I've wasted enough time on this. I shouldn't be annoyed with such petty things. That's where you're supposed to be earning your money, Sheridan. See that you do. I don't want to have to bother myself again with this." He didn't wait for a response, striding from the room without a backward glance.

Embarrassed, Kate turned to the sheriff. "He's really not so . . . so insensitive. It's just that he's under such pressure, such—"

He cut her short with a finger on her lips. Startled, her eyes flew up to his face, her mouth parted slightly. He quickly withdrew. "I'm sorry. I shouldn't have done that." His finger retained the feel of the full, soft lips. She nodded and then was gone, leaving him with a headache and also with something else, a knowledge

164

of something almost as old as man's tenure on Earth. He wanted another man's wife. The pain in his head was as nothing to the one in his gut. There was not anything honorable to be done. He welcomed the pain.

Kate found Chip standing outside, glaring at the single window with the legend "Sheriff's Town Office" stenciled in gold. She flushed, feeling guilty, wondering if he had seen the final, intimate gesture.

"It's about time. Let's get out of here. I don't know why I bothered. These locals are all the same. Incompetent, the lot of them." He started to walk rapidly away, back toward the waterfront.

He was still fuming when Kate caught up with him. "Now what are we going to do?" He checked his watch, frowned. "There's still an hour until we meet Packer. Damned inconvenient. Maybe he'll leave earlier."

To her surprise, Kate lost her own temper. "I don't know what *you're* going to do, but I've got some shopping that must be done. Even great artists eat, I've noticed. It would be nice if you gave me a hand." Chip looked astounded, making her even angrier. "We're supposed to be partners, remember? Where is it written that I get to do all the fun things, like shopping and cooking and cleaning? As for Henry, I wouldn't dream of rushing him. He's doing us a favor."

She marched off, leaving Chip standing there, watching her. As she walked to the store she told herself she did not mind that he let her go. Her life was so strange lately, so different, her perception of what

165

was real and what was not, so blurred, that a fight with her husband had no cosmic significance.

She did her shopping and suffered Bess Perkins, who was taciturn to the point of rudeness. When the items were bagged and paid for, the gaunt woman shoved them toward Kate, her plain features tinged with malevolence. "Ethel Sproul's buried her boy. Daisy Shackford don't know yet iffin she'll be buryin' hers."

Kate recoiled, horrified. What did that have to do with her? A picture of seaweed, dark green, slimy, *wrong* on snow-white sheets, rose before her. Bile churned in her stomach, threatened to reach her throat. The shopper behind her banged a large can on the counter. Kate tensed, picked up her packages and turned to depart.

"Have a good day," Bess Perkins said behind her.

Kate whirled around, knowing the California phrase to be a mockery at this time, in this place. The postmistress and several shoppers were staring flatly, accusingly at her.

It was a relief to get back to Smoke Island even though she was again alone, now that all their guests had left.

She thanked Henry Packer for the ride, doing her best to ignore both Chip's hasty progress up the ladder and the spot where poor Billy Sproul had washed ashore.

Henry disconcerted her by not moving away at once, as he usually did. He cleared his throat. Kate waited patiently, knowing that speech would come, given time. "You want me, you raise yonder pennant," he finally got out. "Understand, missus?"

"Yes. Yes I do. Thank you, Henry. Thank you very much."

He was in a hurry now. With economical, practiced movements he was away from the small dock and heading back toward the mainland before Kate had wiped the first tear from her cheek. He was a friend. His kindness had undone her, though, where Chip's insensitivity and the surly antagonism of the villagers had not.

Typically, Chip had left her with the groceries. Kate hefted the two bags and climbed the ladder. It was late afternoon, the path to the house was shady, cool. Kate walked slowly, savoring the feeling of being home. A sea breeze fluted through the trees, stirring the ponderous branches of the firs. As she passed, a low-lying bough swayed, grazing her bare arm with sharp needles. Kate smiled. It was a lover's caress.

CHAPTER SIXTEEN

Days slid by, one into another, the rhythm of their passing a lulling, soothing flow. Outwardly Kate was the same, careful to maintain her established routine. Neither she nor Chip ever alluded to her outburst, that day in Puffin Landing. She did her household duties uncomplainingly, never asking Chip for help he was unwilling to give. In the mornings she typed, her fingers growing more proficient each day, the pages piling up into an impressive stack.

In the afternoons she wandered around the island, carrying with her the awareness of herself, her body, in new, exciting ways. The tall grass caressed her legs, spoke eloquently to her of their shape, the long, strong length of them. A passing butterfly alit, briefly, on her arm, and she knew the delicacy of her skin, felt its resilience, its textured fineness. The dewy hidden center of a wildflower mirrored her own honeyed recesses. The soft warm breezes of July molded her frame, flowing over her in restless waves.

She walked until exhausted, and then lay down,

wherever she was, and napped, entering a new world, one where everyday existence was ruled by love. Since the dark night of the storm, the terrible night of discovery, she had never again been a direct participant in the dreams. Now she watched, bemused by the lovers, more than a little jealous of their passion, their unselfish love.

She knew now that Daniel Sheridan was not Great Bear, just as she was not Little Sparrow. So close were they, so alike in face and form, that sometimes she pretended, and doing so, felt guilty, for in her mind she had taken a lover and that act damned her in her soul.

On a hot, still afternoon she put on a bathing suit and went down to the small cove to swim. The walk through the woods was a heady delight. The mingled aromas, the tangy smell of the pines, the damp, dark smell of the earth, the lighter, tingling freshness of the flowers, that grew wild and abundant in the least expected places, enchanted her, making her wonder how she had ever felt dread in this place. She was at peace here now. Happy. Once she thought she caught a glimpse of a familiar, rust-colored body. "Natty!" she cried in joy. "Natty Bumppo." It was not him, it could not be, but for that moment she was content, watching the shadow dog cavort, play as he used to, in total, dedicated abandon.

The water was warm enough for even the most timorous soul. Kate swam, her body buoyant, floating on the glass-smooth waves when her arms tired. Above the sky was clear, the blue intense until it lightened, hazed with white where it skimmed the horizon.

When her eyes grew heavy she left the water, made

her bed on the sand. The dream when it came was vivid, as they all were now. Kate watched fascinated as Great Bear and Little Sparrow sat arguing over their evening meal of samp. The meal was the center of the argument. Kate was amused to hear Great Bear complain he was tired of the taste of fish, boiled with the pounded ripe corn to make the porridgelike concoction. Little Sparrow pouted, for she had worked hard to prepare the food.

"The moon shines bright over the water tonight."

"That will not alter the taste of fish," Little Sparrow replied tartly.

"Very true, my sharp-tongued wife." Playfully he reached out, tugged a long dark strand of her hair. "The moon will point the way to the rock where the great black birds with the orange throats live. Our great sachem, Rain Cloud, has not allowed a hunt there for the past two years. Now he gives his permission to hunt. The birds should be plentiful, enough for many days."

"A seabird hunt!" Little Sparrow's eyes sparkled.

It was not difficult for her husband to read her mind. "A woman's place is close to her fire," he said sternly, before she could beg to go along.

"Perhaps you will change your mind." Playfully she ran a finger lightly up and down his arm. "There is time before the moon lights your path." Artfully she began his seduction.

Kate smiled in her sleep, seeing the lovers entwine. Their bodies were like fine instruments, responding each to the other, eliciting the sweetest music from the joining of their beings. When the night winds cooled the earth they still lay together, side by side, their bodies relaxed in the aftermath of love.

"It is time for us to go. The moon paints the water for us. We shall be successful tonight."

"Yes, we shall be," Great Bear concurred, for they both had known from the start that the night's hunt would not be a solitary one.

Kate watched as they launched the birch canoe. It skimmed the water, propelled by the smooth muscles which rippled beneath Great Bear's bronzed skin as he sliced the paddle expertly through the waves. When they neared the island, lying dark and still in the sea, he cautioned Little Sparrow to silence. "The birds set out a guard. They rely on it to alert them. Once I kill this watchman, the rest will be easy. You shall have fowl in your pot, my love."

Little Sparrow admired his hunting skill as Great Bear quickly dispatched the sentinel, then moved through the sleeping cormorants, taking what he needed. When he had enough he gave a mighty shout. To Little Sparrow's delight, the air filled with birds, the rocky island abandoned in an instant as the survivors fled.

The trip back was slower, Great Bear paddling the canoe with sure, steady strokes. When they reached the shore he lifted Little Sparrow into his arms, revolved slowly in a circle, as if offering her to the moon. She wound her arms about his neck, lifted her lips for his kiss. He found a soft spot well back from the tide's intrusion. There, bathed in the soft light, they again made love.

Kate smiled and stretched, her body stiff from the

bed of sand. A shadow covered her. She looked up and smiled.

"You look pleased."

"I am." She raised her arms. He bent down, grasped her hands, and helped her to her feet. He brought her in close, melding the heat of their bodies, intensifying the awareness which pulsed between them, heightened with each measured beat of their hearts. He had not let go of her hands. Without knowing who moved first, their arms slid around each other, drawing them closer still. He lowered his head, hesitated. She raised hers, waiting breathlessly. Then there was no more space between them. His lips found hers, touched, then plundered deep, his tongue entering to find hers waiting to join him in a kiss so wild, so elemental, that when he finally withdrew he left her shaking, panting for breath.

He looked down into eyes as black as his own. "I'm sorry," he said, "I had no right." His voice was bleak, harsh with the remorse which scoured him from within.

It was then that Kate realized who he was, that this was real, not a dream of long ago. "Daniel," she said, and touched his lips with a finger, wonderingly, astonished that she felt no guilt.

He set her from him, but not so far to break the flow of heat between them. He studied her, the hunger in his gaze naked, unashamedly bared, the message plain for her to see. "This is wrong," he said, knowing that they had already declared themselves, spoken a silent, primitive message almost as old as time.

"I know," she replied, "but I don't care."

He groaned and reached for her. She came willingly, joyfully, into his arms. He molded her slim body tight against his long, hard length and could not control the moan which rose from deep within.

Kate lifted her face to his, let him see the desire flaming in her eyes. He bent his head and took her lips again, as one questing hand roamed her supple curves, stroking, caressing, pressing her, until her body quivered into arousal. His touch was fire, was velvet, was magic gliding over her skin. She moved closer to him, felt his desire rise against her, knew the ancient female satisfaction as she softened into liquid readiness.

A wind churned the water behind them, stirred the sand beneath their feet, where only moments before a gentle breeze had washed the air. He pulled his lips from hers and raised his hand to cup her chin. "Open your eyes," he commanded, and when she did, he reeled with the passion blazing forth. The wind strengthened into a roar, snatching her long dark hair, whipping it stingingly across his face. He captured it with one hand, the other still held her chin. "Not now, love," he said, "it's going to storm," and although he shouted, it sounded but a whisper in the screaming wind.

Disappointment flooded her, making her weak. She read the strength within him and knew she also must be strong. Belatedly she became aware of the tossing waves, the scourging wind. This was not the place. "He doesn't wish it," she said.

Daniel stiffened, felt his blood chill at the look on her face, the tone of her voice. He picked up her towel, draped it over her shoulders, then led her up the path and into the woods, where the voice of the wind was muted and they could talk. "Who doesn't wish it?"

He bent close to her, studied her features with anxious eyes.

Kate shrugged, waved a hand, vaguely encompassing the space about them, the entire island beyond. "The powwaw. Iye, the shaman. The Shapechanger, you called him."

"Kate." Gently, he shook her, his brow furrowed, his eyes filled with concern. "It's only a story. A legend. Nothing more."

"No, Daniel, you're wrong. Iye lives; he's still here."

The sheriff had no doubt she believed it. It was there in her face, a conviction, a certainty, that what she said was true. His reaction was a strange mixture, a blend of emotions which warred within him: anger at himself, for telling her about the legend; rage against Chip, whose selfishness had left her lonely, vulnerable; sadness; pity; but above all, love, a shining presence within him, a need to protect, to cherish, to *possess*.

Kate saw it all, for he made no move to hide it. She felt a rush of warmth, an answering emotion which responded to the deep well of feeling emanating from him.

The light began to fade; the woods closed in. Kate started to feel afraid, the way she had in the beginning, when she and Natty Bumppo raced through them, the setter sensitive to something she could not see. Natty Bumppo! A buried memory, strange, almost obscene, surfaced. She remembered the setter's tongue licking her breast, traveling up her thigh, evoking unnatural, erotic desires.

The atmosphere was becoming thick, gray clouds had chased the sun. Lightning danced in the pewter mist, casting the sheriff's chiseled features into sharp relief. Kate was reminded instantly of the night of the big storm, and the fear within her burgeoned into panic. Great Bear possessed her that night, was hard and real inside her, and the next morning Billy Sproul lay dead, washed ashore, wrapped in seaweed, slimy and green, so alien on him; disgusting in her bed, damp and smelling of brine where that night a body had lain.

She plucked at Daniel's sleeve, stark horror churning inside her. "You must go, it's not safe for you here. He'll kill you," she sobbed.

"He's not real. Don't be afraid." Again he damned her oblivious, self-absorbed husband, who cared so little that he left his wife alone, prey to dark imaginings.

Kate forced herself to calm, hearing herself, knowing how peculiar, how unbelievable she sounded. For his sake, she must convince him. "Listen to me. I'm not imagining it. It . . . it started with . . . with Natty Bumppo's death." Tears welled in her eyes when she said his name.

He reached out, carefully wiped the moisture from each cheek. "He was allergic to bee venom. You know that."

"What about the boys? They died because they came to this island. He doesn't want anyone else here. Please. You've got to believe me!"

Daniel took her in his arms, stroked her hair back from her face. "Fred Shackford is alive. He came home from the hospital this week."

"Oh, I'm glad." She placed her hands flat against his chest, felt the heat of the big muscles under her palms. "The other boy died, though. I . . . I saw him, that morning. At first I . . . I thought it was Chip. He

175

. . . he wasn't in bed when I got up. He . . . he hadn't been to bed, he said. But . . . but, the bed was . . . uh, damp. There was . . . was seaweed, in it.'' She turned stricken eyes up to him. *''Someone* was in it.''

''Kate.'' Lightly he brushed her cold lips with his own warm ones. He began to slide his hands up and down her back, trying to bring warmth to her cold flesh, but he could see that the cold was not of her body, but of her mind. ''Billy Sproul was killed by lightning. It was an accident, nothing more. Those damn fool kids had no business being out on the water during an electrical storm. They should have known better, but the problem was that they had been drinking to bolster their courage. The only thing they succeeded in doing was in dimming their wits, what little of them they have.''

''They must have been close. The . . . the body came here. The . . . the seaweed—''

Daniel put his hands on her shoulders and shook her, forcing her to pay strict attention to his words. ''Stop it! Stop this nonsense! The body didn't 'come' here, it washed ashore. Those idiot boys were coming here, it's true, to drink beer and then to boast to their buddies that they'd done so. It was supposed to be a macho demonstration. They picked the wrong night.''

Ruthlessly he suppressed Norman Day's hysterical report of rogue lightning that came again and again, aiming purposefully, deliberately, like a guided missile. *''Then it came again, the last time, after Billy was dead. You could tell he was dead, his head hangin' down, all floppy, his body lyin' like a pile of wet wash. It came and it buzzed me and then Joe and then it spiked itself into Billy again. It lifted him*

176

up and made him jerk around, like he was dancin'. It jerked him over the side, into the water. It did. It did. I swear it."

He shook his head to clear it. He could get little out of Joe Moody, and even less from Fred Shackford.

"Daniel—"

"No, Kate, listen first. What you think—it's impossible." She shuddered and he pressed his lips to her forehead, silently cursed again at the torment she had put herself through. "There's an explanation, a rational explanation, love. There always is."

"What?"

"That's better." He smiled down at her. "It was a wild night, remember? Things had happened to you during the day, and then the storm came unexpectedly, violently. You were upset. Now you tell me your husband abandoned you, left you with a houseful of people, all of you tired, a little bit shocked. You weren't yourself. Perhaps you left the window open a bit when you went to sleep. That would account for the dampness of the bed. The wind that night was awful."

"The seaweed—"

"Was brought into the room on your clothes. Or Chip's. He came back to the house with us, I remember. He could have gone upstairs to your room for something before he left."

He was right. There *was* an explanation: a rational, *normal* explanation of something unreasonable, that no sane person would believe. Kate knew she would have to tell him everything. It was the only way. She shifted in his arms. He had to bend to hear her, so low was her voice. "I dream, Daniel. Strange, exotic dreams. He's the one who sends them. I know he does. There's no one else."

The wind had found its way into the woods. Above them a branch snapped, came crashing down. He could feel her heartbeat accelerate. "Come, the storm's getting closer. We can't stay here." He took her arm and urged her to move. They hurried across the island, Daniel never taking his hand from her arm. When they reached the house he picked up a package from the porch.

"What's that?"

"Milk, eggs, bread, coffee, a few other essentials. Oh, and your mail." He reached into his back pocket, handed her several envelopes. "You haven't been to Puffin Landing in quite a while. I got worried. That's why I came over today. I thought you might need these things."

"Thank you," she said, and they both understood that it was for more than the groceries. Thunder rolled overhead. "Go, Daniel. Leave now, while you can."

He ignored her plea. "I could do with a cup of coffee, and so could you." He walked toward the back of the house, into the kitchen. "Sit. I know where everything is." Before too long he placed two mugs on the table and took the chair next to hers. She was staring straight ahead, her eyes fixed on the windows with their red-and-white-checked curtains. "Tell me about the dreams. Everything," he ordered, and then listened, his face impassive, nonjudgmental, letting her spill the whole, fantastic tale without interruption.

Kate unburdened herself, leaving nothing out; nothing but the final revelation, the one thing she had not even told Chip.

Daniel knew she was withholding something. It was there in her eyes. Shrewdly, he guessed what it was.

178

"You haven't said who Great Bear resembles." Gently he prompted her, but she lowered her head and refused to answer. He felt something inside him tighten into a hard, painful knot. "Who is it?"

"Don't ask. Please."

She was looking at him anxiously again, panic creeping back into her eyes. "Okay, I won't. Take it easy." When he saw her relax he rapped out a question, startling her into an answer. "When did you know who he is?"

"It was the night of the storm, the night of the Fourth of July, that . . . I saw his . . . his face for the first time. That . . . that was the night I felt him, he was real . . . it was me, not Little Sparrow in the dream. Then, the next morning . . . You know," she whispered.

"It was an accident. Billy Sproul died accidentally. Many people are killed by lightning each year. Too many."

"Accidents happen here. That's why you must go. Please."

"Come with me."

She lifted startled eyes to him, shook her head. "I can't."

The knot in his gut tightened, making breathing difficult. He had to get her away. The atmosphere on the island was poisoning her. "Chip doesn't deserve your loyalty. Ultimately he's the one responsible for everything that's happened here. His neglect is criminal." He brushed the backs of his knuckles across her cheek. "Come with me, Kate." His heart was in his eyes.

A loud crash of thunder rattled the windows. She knew he thought she imagined everything. Her fear

179

escalated, became terror. She could not bear it if he suffered because of her.

"No."

Daniel saw the fear blossom like a deadly flower. "All right. I'll leave. But you must promise me that you'll come in, get away from here. We'll talk. Don't be afraid." *Don't be afraid of me,* was the unspoken thought.

"I promise."

Reluctantly he got up, drew her up with him. She raised herself onto her toes, lightly pressing her lips against his in answer to the silent plea. He nodded gravely and left. Kate watched from the window, following him with tear-blurred eyes across the porch, down the steps and along the dirt-packed path until he was out of sight. She was not surprised when the threatening weather cleared soon after.

CHAPTER SEVENTEEN

AUGUST

"When are you going to Puffin Landing?"

"What?" Kate stirred her coffee, forgetting she no longer took sugar or milk.

Chip grabbed her hand, removed the spoon. "What's the matter with you?" he asked, then, typically, began to speak again, not waiting for an answer. "I'm low on canvas. I want you to call Wilma, tell her to bring it up with her."

"Wilma's coming here?"

Chip grimaced, exasperation flaring his nostrils. "I told you, Kate. It was in the letter she wrote. If you want to know the details, ask her when you call."

Kate shrugged, ignoring the querulous tone, unwilling to fight with him. She was happy to hear the agent was returning. Wilma was good for him; Kate knew she was not. "I'll go in the morning, if the weather allows."

"It's a nice night, it doesn't look like rain."

Kate spoke without thinking. "I saw a line of ants late today."

Chip pushed his chair from the table so fast it rocked back perilously on two legs. "I suppose that's more of the wit and wisdom of Henry Packer," he sneered. "Honestly, I don't understand how you can listen to that character, much less repeat the superstitious drivel he tells you."

"If I didn't listen to Henry," Kate exploded, "I probably wouldn't hear the sound of another human voice for days on end. You, it seems, only communicate with me when something displeases you, or if you want or need something. Henry may not be a mental giant, but he's a kind, caring, sensitive human being."

"Meaning I'm not."

Kate picked up her mug, went to the sink. "I don't want to fight."

"Neither do I." Chip placed his mug next to hers, stood by her side while she rinsed them. "This is not easy for me, this whole thing. I thought winning the grant would give me confidence. I thought that using the same studio Lothar Voss did, sitting at his easel, having the same light, the same air, the same atmosphere, would inspire me, help me to fulfill whatever it is that I have. I *do* have 'it,' " he declared fiercely, "however long it may take to come out."

"I never doubted it, or you." Kate turned her attention to the dishes, aware that two months ago she would have put her arms around him, held him close, assured him of her love, her trust, her belief in him. That was impossible now. The reality of it saddened

182

her. Chip wandered away. She heard the front door open, the squeak of the screen door as he went outside.

Tomorrow. Perhaps she would see Daniel; perhaps she would gain the courage to do so. She scrupulously had kept her promise, leaving the island several times since the day he had come to her in the cove. She had kept her promise, but that was all. She assiduously avoided anything personal with him. Timid, shy, exhilarated, fearful: she was all those things when he was near. She was not ready; perhaps would never be. He was patient, courteous, contained. She sensed the tight rein he kept himself under, sensed the passion radiating from him, appreciated the effort he made to give her time, space.

It was still early when she finished in the kitchen, nevertheless she went up to bed. The sooner she was asleep, the sooner she would dream.

He saw her smile, felt her sigh, turned with her in the deepening dusk. He was the air she breathed, the scent of dark-loving flowers that perfumed the night, the whispers in her mind.

He was stronger now, more powerful, but the strength he had gained made him yearn for more, made him ache with what was not; was not yet; was yet to be.

Patience.

Kate awoke to a gray day. Vindication for Henry Packer. She considered postponing the trip, then decided to go, whether for Chip, or for herself, she didn't know.

She bathed and dressed, then crossed the island to hoist the white pennant beneath the yellow, all before breakfast, before she could change her mind. She had her coffee alone, for Chip had left long before she was up. Within the hour the bell sounded down at the dock.

"Hello, Kate."

She looked down at Daniel Sheridan. She had expected Henry Packer. Daniel held his hand out and automatically she put her hand in his. "It's my day off." His spirits soared when he felt the leap of her pulse.

"Oh," she said, dragging her eyes from his face, finally noticing that he was out of uniform, wearing a pair of tan slacks and a blue knit shirt.

"I thought we could spend the day together. There's someplace special I'd like to show you."

Kate agreed eagerly, feeling a little shy, like a girl on a first date. "Am I dressed okay?"

He grinned, exaggeratedly examining her slim figure in white pants topped with a bright turquoise shirt. "You look terrific." When they reached his private dock he pointed to a small, silver car. "It's about an hour from here, do you mind?"

Smiling, she shook her head, happy just to be with him. They were silent for much of the ride, experiencing enough pleasure in each other's company without the need for talk. He took back roads, showing her places many summer visitors completely miss. They passed farms and orchards and small towns, some incorporated in the middle of the eighteenth century. On one quiet stretch, a doe dashed across the road.

"Oh, look at that!" Kate exclaimed. "She's lovely."

Daniel looked across at her. "Yes she is," he agreed. Kate blushed and he laughed, reached over and squeezed her hand.

Not long after he pulled up to a small toll box and bought two tickets. "Here we are. Pemaquid Point. One of the most beautiful spots on earth, I think." He parked the car and they got out to explore. A view of elemental beauty lay before them. The sky above went on forever, while below long bony fingers of rock extended into the sea, that crashed relentlessly against them, sending up flying sheets of spray. A prototypical lighthouse guarded the stark vista. Sea gulls circled above, gray on gray. Farther out several large dark herons fished the pelagic waters along with the ubiquitous lobster boats.

They visited a small museum dedicated to the fishermen of Maine. When they emerged Daniel pointed to another building. "That's a gallery for local artists. Do you want to see it?"

"No," she said firmly, "I'd rather not." He nodded in understanding, then frowned when she grabbed his arm. "I forgot! Chip wants me to call Wilma. That's why I wanted to go to town today."

"There are telephones all over. Even in Maine," he teased.

"You couldn't prove it by me," she retorted, an impish smile on her lips.

"Right. I forgot. Do you want to find a telephone now? There should be one in the restaurant back there." He waved toward the parking lot.

A telephone meant Wilma, and Wilma meant Chip. Kate made a selfish decision. "I'd rather go down

185

there.'' She pointed toward the granite rocks, that looked as if they had been combed by a giant hand, down into the sea.

They made their careful way down them, Daniel helping Kate over the steep places. In every tidal pool she searched for crabs, remembering Natty Bumppo's joy in the strange creatures. They found a shelflike rock and sat crowded close together. The wind played around them, capriciously ruffling Daniel's dark hair and blowing Kate's long strands around her face. He reached up and tucked a flyaway strand behind one ear. She trembled slightly when he touched her.

''Are you cold?''

''No. I'm happy.''

''Good.'' He smiled, and its warmth was like a protective shield. ''Now that I've got you alone, it's time to talk of important things, like pineapples and puffins, popplestones and pinnipeds.''

''Of course.''

''Of course,'' he agreed solemnly. ''Which one first?'' She laughed and shook her head. ''Then I'll start with pineapples, the symbol of hospitality. Our Maine sea captains were a hardy lot, voyaging far, for months on end. Many went south and returned with rich cargoes that they sold along the Eastern coast. When they reached home port they stuck a pineapple on their gateposts, a visual message that the master was home, all were welcome to visit.''

''What a lovely custom.''

''I agree.'' He picked up a small rock and skimmed it out into space. ''Popplestones, now, are a different story. The glaciers that carved the shore also polished rocks until they were round and smooth. Some of the

186

islands were littered with these giant marbles. Captains helped themselves to them, using them as ballast for their ships. They were free for the taking until some entrepreneur thought to sell them to the big Eastern cities to pave their streets.''

"Yankee ingenuity."

"With a vengeance."

She smiled. "What's next?"

"Puffins." He answered her smile and turned slightly, the movement bringing his legs into contact with hers. She didn't draw away. "Puffins are making a comeback from certain extinction because a dedicated group of people, ordinary citizens, cherish the clownlike bird and give their own time and money to ensure their survival." He fell silent, shifted, put his arm around her, drew her close.

Kate settled into his warmth. "Okay," she said. "That's pineapples, popplestones and puffins. Who, or what, is a pinniped."

"City girl," he scoffed, "and you a teacher, too." He got up, pulling her up after him. "Come, I'm starving. Let's get something to eat. If you're lucky, you'll see one. If not," he shrugged, "at least you'll be full."

He took her to New Harbor, a quiet, picturesque little town not far away. They ate steamers and lobsters, huge mounds of golden onion rings they washed down with beer, sitting on a high deck overlooking a busy dock where lobster boats pulled in every ten minutes or so to unload their catch. The air was brisk, invigorating, chilly where it blew in off the ocean. Kate never noticed its bite, so completely content was she for the first time in many weeks.

Daniel perceived the healthy red in her cheeks, the bright sparkle in her eyes, and was happy. Over her laughing protests he went to get dessert, returning with a tray laden with homebaked raspberry pie topped with creamy vanilla ice cream and steaming mugs of coffee.

"I can't possibly," she said.

"Try."

He watched in amusement as she dispatched the dessert with gusto. He looked beyond her, out into the sheltered harbor, where boats were tethered to sea anchors in orderly rows. "Look, a pinniped."

Kate hastily swallowed a mouthful of pie and sighted down his pointing finger. It took her a while, but finally she identified the creature. "It's a seal!" she exclaimed delightedly. The people at the next table heard her and rushed to the railing to look, jostling Daniel in their haste. He winked at Kate, who laughed for the sheer joy of it.

On the way back to Puffin Landing it began to rain, a steady downpour, slanting out of the sullen gray sky. Reality crashed around her, her mood turned heavy, weighing her spirits down. Daniel started to bypass the village, steering them toward his house. Kate stopped him with a hand on his arm. "I've got some things to buy, and I must make that call to Wilma."

He followed her into the store, staying with her, staring down Bess Perkins, who served her with pointed unsociability. He picked up the two packages, urged her from the store. "You'll make the call from my place."

Kate looked back, saw the postmistress purse her lips disapprovingly. "I'd better not."

188

Daniel understood her hesitation. "People like that don't concern me."

"But, you live here. Work here."

"They don't own me." Firmly he steered her back to the car. "Chip is right. They are an ingrown, superstitious lot. They'll probably never accept me completely, although I was born not far from here. I'm different."

Kate looked at his chiseled profile, the proud tilt of his head. "I'm glad," she said, eliciting a quick smile from him, "but I really shouldn't go to your house. There must be a telephone around here. I've got to get back. I've been away too long."

"Don't be afraid."

The simple statement was magic. It brought a new awareness, almost like a third entity, into the car. He smiled at her and she felt her body begin to tingle. She made no protest when he drove through town without stopping.

The rain became a drenching downpour. When they reached his house a few minutes later he pulled up as close as he could get, still they both got soaked in the few steps to the glass-enclosed porch. The office was chilly and dim, the only light coming from a lamp on the desk. He waved her to the telephone while he went to check the clipboard for messages. "Nothing important," he said and disappeared into the part of the house Kate had never seen.

She made the call to Wilma, then moved to the window, peered through the telescope. There was nothing to see, only gray rain, driving down relentlessly in gusting sheets.

"I wouldn't take you out in this."

Kate saw his reflection in the glass. "I know." Shyness overcame her as he neared.

He touched her shoulder, gently turned her around. "You'd better dry off. Come with me." He led her back into the house, stopping at the threshold of a bedroom. He gestured inside. "There's a bathroom through that door. I've put out fresh towels."

She found herself alone, the door quietly closing behind her. She released her breath, which, unknowingly, she had been holding. Curiously she examined the room. It was neat and Spartan: a dresser, a straight chair, a bed with splashes of bright color in blue and yellow throw pillows on the blue quilted comforter, a framed Van Gogh poster of a field of huge sunflowers from the New York Metropolitan Museum of Art on one wall. The room was lived in; she knew it was his bedroom.

The bathroom was small and clean. She hesitated, then stripped and showered, letting the hot water warm her chilled skin. She found a terrycloth robe hanging on a hook behind the door and knew he had placed it there for her. It was large and almost wrapped around her twice, but it was dry and although she wanted to put her own clothes on, they were too wet. She wrapped a towel into a turban around her wet hair and went in search of him.

He was in the kitchen, putting the finishing touches to a tray that held steaming mugs of tea, a plate of cookies and a bottle of rum. "Let's go into the den. I've got a fire going." He grinned at her outfit. "Where did you leave your clothes? I'll put them in the dryer."

"I'm impressed. You're so, 'er, together." She

pointed to the cookies, remembered the question she had asked Chip, so long ago. "Were you married?"

He threw back his head and laughed, the sound rolling around them, diffusing the air of the tension she had brought with her into the room. "No, I was never married. My mother trained me," he teased. "Now, madam, if there are no more questions, march."

Kate obeyed, preceding him down the hall into the den. She took a seat on the sofa. He set the tray on a low driftwood table, then left to see to her clothes. She looked about with interest, noting that this room showed signs of untidiness. Piles of books were on everything, even the floor. A newspaper lay discarded on a chair. It was a thoroughly masculine mess. It pleased her.

"I'm sorry about the disorder. I didn't know I'd have a guest."

He was standing in the doorway. Kate wondered how long he had been there, then realized he was telling her that he had not planned to bring her here.

From across the room Daniel saw the minute easing of her shoulders, the infinitesimal signs that she was relaxing. He came and sat down next to her. "Tea and rum," he said, pouring generous dollops into each mug, "has been known to cure just about anything." He handed a mug to her. "Drink."

"Mmmn. Good." The heady liquid spread a glow within her. She relaxed even more. She was very conscious of him next to her, the heat from his body was as warming as was the crackling fire that bathed the room in rosy light. She sipped the drink, not protesting when he topped it off with another tot of rum. She leaned back, watching the fire. She felt safe, protected.

Outside the storm strengthened; it grew dark. Inside the fire was the only light. It kept the shadows at bay, enclosing the two of them in a sheltered, glowing tent. Kate stared into its heart, mesmerized by the flowing dance of flames. She felt him take the empty mug from her hand, heard him place it on the tray. He tugged the towel from her head, released her long dark hair to curl in waves down over her shoulders.

"Kate."

Her name throbbed in the air between them. She turned into his arms as naturally as if she had done it thousands of times. He buried his face in her hair, inhaled its sweet fragrance. She turned her face toward him, gently rubbed her cheek against the top of his head. His lips found the fragile curve of her neck, settled in the hollow at its base, felt her pulse begin to race. He lifted his head and sought her lips. His kiss was slow, seeking. Her lips softened, opened under his. He deepened the kiss, letting her feel his passion as his tongue swept inside.

Kate responded to the hunger within him with a need of her own. She welcomed the ravishment of her lips, the possession of his tongue, accepted it and matched it with a fierceness born of her newly awakened desire.

When he finally pulled away they were both panting. He smiled down at her. She watched him with bright eyes as he lifted one large hand to tug at the belt around her waist. Her eyes never left his face as he succeeded in untying it, then inserted his hand inside to gently part the robe, easing it open until she was bared to his view.

His eyes found hers. He locked gazes with her, dark eyes shining into dark eyes, before he bent his ebon head and gazed at her. "You're beautiful," he breathed. Her creamy skin gleamed a pearly pink in the firelight. The flickering flames caused shadows to move across her.

Kate looked down and saw what he saw, and watched as his hand moved up, cupped her breast, cradling it in the palm of his hand. He leaned forward and a jolt of pure ecstasy made her arch her body upward as his lips closed over her. She brought her arms up to the back of his head, pressed him closer to her leaping heart. He raised his head and found her lips again. His hands stroked her, delicately traced her curves, moved slowly down her body, eliciting tremors from deep within her. She began to quiver, her body sensitive to his lightest touch.

Kate gloried in the slow, arousing exploration. His touch was flame, was ice, was a wonderful gift she embraced with both body and soul. She felt him touch her hip, gently move the robe aside. His hand brushed across her belly, then stroked downward.

"No! I . . . I can't." It was an anguished cry. Her hands gripped his arm, tugging at him, frantically trying to pull him away.

After one startled moment he realized what was happening. "Easy. Easy, love. Let go. Let go. That's right. That's the way." He crooned to her, verbally petting her, encouraging her to relax, to put her trust in him. When her grip loosened he covered her with the robe and then took her into his arms, holding her close, letting her settle, waiting until he could control his rampaging desire.

The fire hissed and crackled. Kate stirred, turned anguished eyes up to him. "I'm sorry."

He stroked the hair back from her fevered face. "I won't hurt you."

"I know."

He continued to stroke her hair, the rhythm of it soothing to both of them. She closed her eyes. He kissed the fragile lids with exquisite tenderness. "How long has it been since you've had a man, a real man, not a dream lover?" he asked.

Her eyes flew open. She turned her head away from his searching gaze.

He had his answer. Rage churned within him. He had to call upon all his strength to control it, to hide it from the woman he held in his embrace. Its intensity would frighten her; it frightened him. He cupped her chin, gently forced her to look at him. Her eyes held pain; black wounds filled with sorrow. He was glad Chip Windsor was out of reach. He wanted to punish him, make him accountable for the bruises he had put on his wife's soul.

He controlled himself, smiled down at Kate. "It's all right, love. I understand. You're not ready. It's all right." He began to stroke her hair again. Her eyes filled with tears. "Hush, love, it's all right," he murmured as she began to sob. He held her, rocking her in his arms, stroking her hair, murmuring endearments in her ear until exhausted, she fell asleep.

CHAPTER EIGHTEEN

Kate awoke with the pale gray light of dawn. She stared at the unfamiliar ceiling. Disoriented, she lowered her gaze, encountered a splash of yellow flowers, recognized the Van Gogh poster. Simultaneously she realized she was not alone and memory flooded her, bringing hot blood to crimson her cheeks.

"Good morning."

She turned toward the voice. Daniel was sitting in the straight chair close to the bed. His damp hair curled about the collar of his uniform. His dark eyes were regarding her gravely. He looked remote, official, very much the sheriff. She tried to slide completely under the comforter, realized she was naked, and blushed an even deeper shade of red.

He reached over and touched her hot cheek with cool fingers. "Did you sleep well?"

Amazingly, she had. She nodded, insufferably shy under the steady gaze. Involuntarily she glanced to the other side of the bed. It was undisturbed. When she looked back at him there was amusement crinkling the corners of his eyes.

"You slept alone, Kate. All night."

"How long have you been sitting there?"

He saw no need to tell her he had watched over her through the still hours, sitting in the dark, thinking, trying to understand, dreaming with his eyes wide open. "Long enough to know that you're as beautiful in first light as you are in firelight."

She levered up on her elbows, forgetting her modesty as the comforter slipped beneath her shoulders. She owed him an apology; an explanation, at the very least. "Daniel, I'm sor—"

He stopped her with a finger on her lips. "No. I told you last night. Everything's all right." He got up and bent over her, his dark eyes filled with tenderness. He kissed her lightly on each eye, the tip of her nose and then moved down to place a feather kiss on her slightly parted lips. Solemnly he pulled the comforter up to her chin and left.

Kate stared at the closed door for long moments, then transferred her gaze to the window. The light was stronger now, but it was still gray outside, with no hint of brightening sun. It had stopped raining.

She had to return to the island. The thought stirred the emotions she had buried the night before. Even as panic flooded her she sensed that something was missing, some feeling was absent, but she could not place it. She worried the thought as she showered and dressed, finding her clothes hung on a hanger on the hook behind the bathroom door. In the middle of brushing her teeth with the new toothbrush he had thoughtfully provided, it came to her. What was missing from the jumbled thoughts and emotions which worried her brain.

Guilt.

She felt no guilt.

In the misty bathroom fragrant with the scent of soap she bowed her head and cried, silently, letting the big, hurtful tears fall streaming down her cheeks. She cried for herself, for Chip, for both of them.

Daniel looked at her sharply when she joined him in the kitchen, but said nothing about her pale face, the puffiness under her reddened eyes. He handed her a mug of coffee, asked how she liked her eggs.

"Nothing, please. I . . . I must get back."

He nodded curtly. What was unspoken danced between them, choking off conversation, creating an awkwardness neither of them wanted.

He handed her a sweater when they left the house. The tide was coming in, running waves slapping rhythmically against the pilings of the pier. She helped him cast off, uncoiling the lines from the cleats and jumping down into the bobbing boat with the help of his strong, steadying arm. Once out in the bay he pushed the throttle forward. The boat accelerated, the roar of the engine making conversation impossible.

Kate watched him from her seat in the stern. The rushing wind ruffled his hair, molded the clothes against his broad, solid frame. She pulled the sweater more snugly about her shoulders, conscious of his spicy scent clinging to the wool. Her thoughts were still chaotic; she had no idea what she would do, would say, when she saw Chip.

When they reached the island he shut the engine off and made the boat fast. He leaned down from the dock above her and offered his hand. His face was unreadable, the eyes which had danced with amusement, melted with tenderness, were now hard and darkly inscrutable. She slipped out of the sweater and let him help her up. At the foot of the stairs she turned to him, put her hand on his sleeve, then quickly removed it, as if even that innocent gesture was somehow suspect.

A sad smile twisted his lips. Pain flickered deep in the dark eyes. "There's no one to judge us, Kate. What is between us is not wrong."

"I know," she whispered, and was rewarded by a genuine smile which erased the sad lines, chased away the hint of pain.

"If you know that then come back with me. Now. There's no need to stay here, none at all. You and Chip are finished." She shrank away from him, from the frank words. As much as he ached to take her in his arms he knew that it would be unfair. She must come to him whole. He wanted her mind as well as her body.

The confusion and panic in her eyes opened a wound within him, but he knew he was right and that these things must be said. "Ah, Kate love, it's not easy. I know it's not, but everything I said is true. You know it. You and Chip will never go back to what you had before."

"I can't leave. Not now."

"Why? Why not? He's not treating you very well. He's neither husband nor lover. He's left you alone, neglected you, the bastard, for the whole summer while he selfishly pursues his own interests. Surely there was room for compromise. His time here is not limited. He could have shown some flexibility."

"I . . . I owe him this time. I . . . I can't leave."

He frowned. Something did not sound right. He reached out and took her into his arms, holding her loosely, careful not to alarm her with his overpowering need. "We belong together. Let me love you. Come with me now, Kate, my love."

Tears welled in her eyes. Tenderly he wiped the moisture away, using the balls of his thumbs gently to blot the sensitive skin. Her eyes held his for long moments, then raised to the view above his head. He felt her body tremble. A cold finger of dread touched his spine as he comprehended the true enemy.

"It's those damn dreams, isn't it?" She went very still in his arms. He gripped her shoulders, shook her gently. "Listen, love, I understand. I really do. You needed them, the dreams. They helped you, made you feel good when you were lonely, perhaps afraid." She tried to look away but he captured her chin with one large hand and forced her to look at him while he spoke. "They're not real. They come from here." He pressed his lips to her forehead. "Think about it," he coaxed. "Think about what you've told me about them. They're happy the two of them, one who looks like you and one who looks like me."

"I never said he looked like you."

"You didn't have to, love." He sighed. "Come away with me. I promise you won't have to be asleep to be happy."

He read the answer in her eyes. His broad shoulders slumped. He knew no way to fight phantoms. "Come," he said brusquely, "I'll take you to the house."

"There's no need for you to go with me. I'm all

right. I can go alone." Panic licked at her. It would be bad enough, much worse with the complication of a showdown.

He gave her a long, level look. "I know, but I'm coming anyway."

"No! Think how it will look. To . . . to Chip. If we walk in together, like . . . like—"

"Like lovers?"

"Yes! We . . . we're not . . . not lovers."

"Aren't we, Kate love?" Her eyes blazed at him. He touched her hair. "Aren't we?"

She pulled away, but not fast enough. Without a word being spoken, he had his answer. He had seduced her mind. The rest would come. She was his.

"Soon, love," he said, just as if he could read her mind.

Desperation exploded in her. This was a dangerous man. He was prepared to fight for her. It could not happen. "He doesn't like you. He . . . he never has."

"The feeling has been mutual, I assure you."

Little laugh lines crinkled his eyes, but Kate was too agitated to notice. "Don't provoke him. Please. Not now."

Daniel sobered at once. "I have no intention of picking a fight with your husband. Trust me, Kate, I know what I'm doing. I need the assurance that you'll come to no harm because of me. Have you ever come back home with a man after a night spent away from your marital bed before?" She looked at him wide-eyed. "No? Then you don't know how he'll react."

They both knew the argument was ended. The short walk to the house was made in silence. Even the island around them was quiet, unnaturally still in the early morning fog. Kate shivered, moved closer to him.

At the house she turned, her eyes pleading, but he reached around her, opened the door and motioned for her to precede him. The hallway was dim. She reached for the light switch, changed her mind. "Daniel—"

Once again he stonewalled her protest. "I'll wait in the kitchen. Don't argue. I'm not leaving you here until I'm damn sure there isn't going to be any trouble."

Kate gave in to the inevitable. Upstairs it was dark, hushed. The bedroom was empty; the bed neatly made. She frowned, went to the bathroom, knocked on the door. "Chip?" There was no answer. The room was empty.

All the rooms were empty. She checked every one.

Daniel met her at the bottom of the stairs. "I heard you moving around. What's wrong?"

"He's not here. I don't think he slept here last night." She went to the kitchen, checked the sink, looked in the refrigerator. Everything was exactly the way she had left it, not quite twenty-four hours ago. She looked at Daniel out of panic-stricken eyes. "Maybe he's had an accident." She crossed her arms over her chest, and rubbed her upper arms with short, jerky motions.

"I'll make a search. Wait here."

He had the back door open and was on his way out when she spoke. "It'll be faster if we both do it."

He stopped and turned, letting the door bang into his back. "I don't want to have to look for you too."

Kate won the silent battle. It was still chilly outside, even more so under the tall firs that crowded close to the back of the house. Ground fog swirled around their feet, since the sun had not broken through the cloud cover to burn it away. "The island feels different. Hostile," she said.

Daniel threw her a sharp look. He wanted to hustle her back to the boat and take her away, far away, forever. Instead, he pointed to the path on their right. "Take that one. I'm going straight across the island. We'll meet at the studio."

She started in the indicated direction only to have him signal her to stop. He pointed straight ahead. Chip was walking toward them, his head down, his gait uneven. She started toward him but Daniel put out his arm, stopping her without speaking a word. Silently he urged her to move behind him.

Chip wavered toward them, still oblivious to their presence. Kate watched him from slightly behind Daniel's shielding frame. She was puzzled and more than a bit apprehensive. She wondered if he was drunk. He stopped and lifted his head. He was disheveled, his clothing stained and wrinkled, his chin stubbled with beard.

His manner changed the instant he saw the sheriff; arrogance and dislike both straightened his spine. He advanced, his gait now perfectly normal. "What are you doing here, Chief?" he snarled.

Daniel answered him calmly, his voice mild. "I've brought Kate back. I wouldn't take the boat out in the storm last night."

Chip ignored him, looked at Kate, who had stepped out into the open. He went to her eagerly. "Did you get Wilma? Is she sending the canvas?"

"No, she's not. She's bringing it with her. She

should be here in a couple of days." The smell of turpentine was so strong she took a step back.

"Good. Good." He walked past her, toward the house. "I'm tired. I didn't get any sleep last night." At the door he turned and glared at Daniel Sheridan. The two men silently measured each other. The air between them crackled with unspoken, unpleasant thoughts.

The sheriff deliberately turned his back on him, the gesture silently eloquent. "Good-bye, Kate," he said.

Kate heard the door slam closed as she saw Daniel disappear around the corner of the house. Alone, she wrapped her arms closely about her body in a purely defensive gesture. She knew nothing would ever be the same again.

He was angry, but the anger was mostly fear. He had lost her; he would lose her; she would never be his. It must not be. He had waited, dreamed, existed for her.

Patience.

CHAPTER NINETEEN

Chip slept for five hours, sprawled across the top of the bed in his dirty, smelly clothes. Kate checked him once, opened the window to let the air circulate, although there was no breeze. The day continued dull and gray, with an occasional light misting rain.

When he came downstairs she was in the kitchen, moodily staring into a cup of cold coffee. He had showered and shaved, but red streaked the whites of his eyes. She looked at him dispassionately; she had all morning to think.

"I'm ravenous."

A nervous giggle threatened to escape. She had spent the lonely time envisioning this scene, playing it in her mind a hundred different ways. Accusation, recrimination: those were expected. Not this.

"Breakfast or lunch?"

He stared at her.

Impatiently she repeated the question.

"I don't know. Whatever," he said unhelpfully. "I didn't have dinner last night."

"Do you want dinner?" She hated the edge in her voice, feared this would turn to farce.

"What's the matter with you?" He pulled out a chair, seated himself, treated her to a baleful stare.

Anger flared in her breast, hot and hurtful, choking her with burning pain. She wanted to scream an answer at him, provoke him, force some sort of interaction between them. She wanted anything but this distant, uncaring nothingness.

Last night I almost took a lover. I did take one with my heart, if not with my body.

She sighed, a great tearing sound that wrenched from her core. Instead of answering, she ignored the question, unwilling to be put on the defensive. "How about eggs?"

"Fine. Make it fast. I've got to get back to the studio."

You should be jealous. You should demand to know where I spent the night.

Kate automatically put the meal together, the anger leaving as suddenly as it had come. In its place was a hollow feeling, a great gray emptiness.

When he finished eating he rose to leave. They had not spoken while he ate. At the door he hesitated, then pulled it open.

Kate spoke to his back. "Will you return for dinner?"

He closed the screen door, turned to look at her. The mesh blurred his features. He shrugged. "I don't know."

A marriage should not die this way.

* * *

Two days passed and then a third. They existed in separate worlds, separate times. Chip kept to the studio, unconscious of night and day. At first Kate tried to keep the semblance of a routine, but soon abandoned it.

It was freedom such as she had never known. She cooked and kept the house, but there was no one to care what she did or when she did it. She spent the third lonely evening and part of the night typing. Cramping fingers forced her to stop, so she went to bed, falling asleep to dream of Little Sparrow, alone in the woods, gathering milkweed flowers and wild leeks to flavor her stews. The Indian girl kept glancing around, her big, dark liquid eyes darting to each plant that swayed, each branch that waved.

Where is Great Bear? Kate wondered, and knew that she and Little Sparrow shared the thought.

She awoke to find Chip sprawled beside her, fully dressed, lying on top of the covers. In the dim light he looked unreal. The bed was suddenly not big enough for both of them. She eased out from under the covers, long years of caring making her fearful of disturbing him, knowing how desperately he needed his rest.

The wooden floor was chill beneath her feet. She walked to the window, restless, troubled, the dream an overlay on the everyday world. She looked outside, letting the deep blue velvet of the night sky soothe her tight-strung nerves. A movement caught her eye. A shadow among shadows; someone watching the house. She inhaled sharply, trapping the breath in the back of her throat, then let it out slowly, in a thin stream, producing a faint whistle. The shadow slipped out from under the trees. A tall, broad man, moving with the

206

dark grace of a panther. Great Bear, she thought, forgetting she was awake, wanting to tell Little Sparrow not to worry, he was safe.

He approached the house, stopped, raised his face, surveying the dark windows one by one. Kate gave a soft, mewling cry. She jumped up and hurried through the night-dark house, her heart thumping loudly in her chest. She burst outside, a spectral figure in her white nightgown, her hair tumbling wildly down her back. "Daniel," she called, but there was no reply. She traced his path, searched the edge of the silent, sleep-hushed woods, softly calling his name. The wind replied, answering with a cosmic sigh. She was alone.

In the morning Chip was gone, the only evidence of his tenancy a pile of soiled laundry, a sodden towel, and dirty dishes left on the kitchen table. Kate went to the cove for a swim, then returned to have a solitary lunch.

In the middle of the afternoon the clamor of the brass bell disturbed the peaceful quiet. She sped down the path, heard the sound of voices before she reached the stairs. She slowed, composed herself, succeeded in placing a welcoming smile on her face by the time Wilma Thompson appeared.

Kate reached her just as Henry Packer came into view carrying a suitcase and a large, bulky package. Disappointment flooded her. "Hi, Wilma. Henry." She cleared her throat, her voice was rusty, unused. "Here, let me give you a hand."

Henry gave her a curt nod and started up the path. Wilma kissed the air next to her cheek. "No thanks. How's Chip? I can't wait to see what he's done. He said he's trying something new, using colors in a different way."

Kate was startled. "You've spoken to him?"

"No such luck. He wrote a few letters." Shrewd green eyes studied her. "He's had quite a summer, hasn't he?"

Kate swallowed her answer.

At the house Wilma remained on the path, looking up at Kate, halfway up the steps, and at Henry, who was waiting on the porch. "I hope you don't mind, sweetie. I want to get right to the studio." She held out the packages to Kate, who automatically reached for them.

"Of course not," Kate heard herself mumble, and knew that she spoke the truth. Wilma was not her friend.

"Oh, this one's for you." A red-lacquered nail tapped a thin parcel wrapped in pale lavender tissue paper.

Kate stared at the disappearing figure until Henry broke into her thoughts. "Where d'you want this?" He kicked the suitcase with the point of his toe.

"Oh, Henry, I'm sorry. It's all right. Leave it inside. I'll take it up later."

"No, missus. Can't. I promised I'd see to it. Just point the way." He disappeared into the house. Kate hurried after him and showed him Wilma's room. He thumped the suitcase down just inside the door, took off his cap and rubbed his sleeve across his forehead, in the gesture she had come to know so well. "Ayuh. Sheriff was right. Said that one would hare off as soon's she got here."

208

"I . . . I see." Her heart swelled with feeling. So he also remembered that day. It seemed so long ago.

"Well, got t'go, missus." He walked out, leaving her to catch up.

"You're not staying?"

"Can't. Not t'day." He was out the door before she reached the bottom of the staircase.

Alone again, she thought, suddenly bereft. He had sent Henry, rather than come himself. *Your own fault. You sent him away.* "Stop it!" she commanded the whispers in her mind. Her eye fell on Wilma's packages, jumbled in an untidy heap where she had dumped them on the hall table. The delicate lavender one looked incongruous amidst the sturdier brown-paper-wrapped parcels. The thin tissue paper ripped easily, revealing delicate robin's egg blue linen place mats. A proper house gift. Kate laughed aloud, the laughter teetering precariously on the thin edge of hysteria. Now all she needed was a proper house.

Wilma returned to the house alone. After dinner they took their coffee out to the porch. The darkness settled around them, concealing details, blurring expressions.

Wilma's long nails tapped a tattoo on her mug. "He's headed in the right direction, but he needs to concentrate his efforts more. I should have come back sooner. He needs a critical eye."

"Um."

Wilma shifted restlessly, causing the wicker rocker to creak. "Look, Chip needs help. He's close, very close, but he can't do it alone. He needs support more than anything else. I intend to give it to him, in any way he needs it, in any way I can."

Kate bristled, but let the challenge, if challenge it was, go unanswered. She was not about to fight over Chip, especially where his work was concerned. She stared at the pale disk which was Wilma's face, abruptly aware that she was happy not to be able to see her expression. "I hope you do," she said quietly, then excused herself and went upstairs to her bedroom.

Wearily she undressed, not bothering with the lights, then went to sit in a chair before the window, staring out at the night with dry, burning eyes.

In the next few days Wilma's presence on the island went virtually unremarked by Kate. She was an extra dish and mug in the sink, a damp bathing suit on the line at the side of the house.

On her way to the cove one afternoon Kate met Chip in the woods at the point where the path forked. He looked haggard, but there was an aura of barely suppressed excitement surrounding him; the familiar hazel eyes held an expression they had lacked for weeks. "It's happening. It's finally happening, finally coming right. It's pushing me from inside. It's like no other feeling I've ever had." His spare body was trembling. "This will change everything, revolutionize the way people think of art."

"I'm glad. I knew you would find it." Then, before she could stop them, hot words tumbled past her lips. "I hope it's worth it. We've both paid a high price for it."

Chip gave a short bark of laughter. "You don't understand."

"You're right. I don't." She left him standing star ing after her.

They were all together for dinner that night. Wilma raised her glass of wine. "A toast. To Pablo Picasso, Lothar Voss and Charles Windsor. The three giants of twentieth century art."

Kate sipped her wine, feeling alienated from the celebration.

Chip left them to go back to the studio shortly after.

Wilma leaned toward Kate, her green eyes glittering brightly. "I told you I'd do it. I gave him what he needed." If she had feathers she would have preened them.

Kate carried Wilma's grin of satisfaction in her mind for hours, long after they said good night. She fell asleep to dream of Little Sparrow, fashioning pots from long thin strips of clay wound round and round, using a hole in the ground as a mold, constantly looking over her shoulder as she worked. Even with her vigilance she was taken unawares, the soft footfalls of Great Bear went undetected as he came up behind her, put a proprietary arm around her waist. He took her in his arms and made love to her, there in the open field, in the light of day. The smell of wildflowers wove about them. The deeper scents of damp, clay and the body musks produced by their efforts as they strained together, invaded their senses. Great Bear stiffened and groaned, then went limp above her.

Little Sparrow's body was still tense, unfulfilled. She opened dark liquid eyes filled with puzzlement and a hint of pain and stared into the sharply chiseled features hovering so close above her. "I have need of you, my husband," she gasped. He seemed puzzled. She captured his hand and guided it down between them. With his strong fingers he stroked her, bringing her quickly to a shuddering release.

Kate awoke with a pounding heart. It was dark, still, the house around her felt empty. Vaguely disturbed, she got up and went to the window, looked out at the silent island. Great Bear was a considerate lover, it was unlike him to take his pleasure first.

Daniel Sheridan would be a thoughtful, perceptive lover. She shivered with the memory of his long, sensitive fingers on her heated flesh. It was always with her, an echo on her mind. She suspected he was staying away to give her time, time to think, to know her heart. She wanted him, but knew she would never go to him. He would have to come to her.

The house, the old walls, the shades of the people from the past all suddenly pressed in on her, making her feel claustrophobic. She went outside, the unlit world strange but not unfriendly. Her steps took her all over, to every place but one. She had no desire to see the studio, to see Chip, to see Wilma with him. The cove beckoned her, the dark water warmly welcoming. She swam and then let the air dry her body, falling asleep with aromatic pine needles for her pillow, her coverlet an infinite blanket of milky stars.

The next afternoon Wilma came back from the studio carrying several rolled canvases. Kate was in the kitchen, wrapping the sandwiches she and Henry had left over from lunch. Wilma looked flushed, her eyes were bright and shining. "I'm going to send these to New York," she announced, tenderly placing her burden on the kitchen table. The strong smell of oil paint invaded the room. "Henry said he'd give me a lift."

She went upstairs to get her handbag, leaving Kate alone with the first issue of Chip's creativity. Tentatively, almost afraid, she prodded the edge of the nearest canvas, coaxing it to unroll. Bright, pure sweeps of color blazed out, dazzling her eyes. Quickly she opened the canvas all the way, drinking in the revealed picture thirstily, unaware that she was doing so until Wilma's voice penetrated her concentration.

"Magnificent, isn't it?" Her voice was gleeful, gloating.

"It's breathtaking." She rerolled the canvas, reached for the next one. They were all different, yet they were the same, the same sure strokes, the same brilliance of concept, the same purity of color.

She surrendered them to the agent, who carefully wrapped each one in oil skin, then inserted them into hard cardboard mailing tubes. Henry came to the back door, announced that he was ready to leave.

Wilma gathered the tubes reverently, cradling them against her body as one would a precious infant. Kate felt a stab of jealousy; intense, penetrating, thoroughly unnerving. Anita's voice, telling her to have a baby, whispered ghostly in her ear. A baby had been born. Sired by Chip, its surrogate mother was Wilma Thompson.

Kate surfaced from the bitter thought to find herself alone. All at once she knew what she wanted to do. She ran down the path to the dock. Henry was helping Wilma wrap the tubes in a blanket, to keep them safe from spray, she assumed.

"Henry, wait," she called. "I want to see you for a moment." She went down the slippery granite steps faster than she should, afraid that if she slowed, even for a second, she would change her mind and turn around.

"Careful, missus," Henry shouted, seeing her precipitous descent. Wilma glanced up briefly but quickly returned her attention to the paintings. Henry met Kate at the foot of the stairs.

"Will you take a message for me?" She was breathless, her heart high in her throat.

"Ayuh."

"Please tell Da—,uh, the sheriff that I'd like to see him."

"Ayuh." He nodded and started back toward the boat.

For once Kate was grateful for his phlegmatic nature, although for just an instant, as he turned from her, she thought she detected a smile of satisfaction on his weathered face.

Alone on the dock she watched the boat dwindle in size as it sped toward the shore. She knew she had made the right decision. She was no longer able to hide on the island.

CHAPTER TWENTY

He watched the sun go down from high atop a tree, spread out in the leaves, absorbing the heat, the pure radiant energy, knowing he needed it for what was to come.

Power.

He pulsed with life, with new strength. It flowed through him, exciting, vital. It promised an end to waiting.

It promised him his dream.

He trembled with his need, with the ache that never stopped, his constant companion down through the uncounted years.

Power.

No longer would he wait, drifting, dreaming the days away. He was spirit, he was air, but now he was also the others. Small, insignificant, they had been enough to start. He swirled lazily, became the color of rust, a beloved dog. She had smiled the day he let her see him.

Patience.

He swirled again and grew, took on human form,

became a boy with pale face splotched with brown. It was not enough. He needed more. Soon. Now.

Power.

With darkness as his cloak he walked the wood, choosing his time, his place. He felt her near him, roaming the night like a restless soul. She prowled, the dreams he sent her clouding her mind, readying her, making her his. At last.

"Iyeeeeee," he whispered in her ear, using the soft night breeze to caress the delicate flesh. So sweet. So good. When she swam he flowed under her, over her, enveloping her in the wet warmth of his wanting.

Patience.

No more.

Power.

He took on form, used his borrowed shape. More, he needed more.

She would be his, again, before the sun set one more time.

From her comfortable chair out of the way in a corner, Wilma stretched like a cat and let her practiced eye sweep over the large, untidy studio. To the uninitiated it would seem that chaos reigned. The stacks of canvases against the walls, the sheets of paper with charcoal sketches pinned everywhere, the long table with its litter of paint tubes, brushes, palette knives, sticks of charcoal, cans of turpentine and linseed oil and rags—old rags, new rags, paint-crusted rags, filthy rags—all told her that a working artist was in residence.

She transferred her gaze to the artist. It was late in

the day and the room was filled with blue shadows. She had to strain to see him clearly. He was working like a man possessed, his body taut, his brow furrowed in concentration above hazel eyes which were narrowed to slits as he stared at one section of the canvas. She smiled with satisfaction at the sight. It had taken her the better part of a week to assure him that he was pursuing the right course.

She crossed the room, careful to avoid the piles of canvas, knowing that quietness did not count. Chip listened to an inner voice when he worked. Anything from the external world was simply filtered out, as if it did not exist. Kate used to laughingly complain about it, calling it Chip's artistic survival instinct. Kate was no longer complaining. Nor was she laughing. A fleeting frown marred Wilma's smooth brow. Chip acted as if his wife was not present, almost as if she had ceased to exist. Perhaps for him she had.

Wilma shrugged and dismissed the thought as nonproductive. She did not care what happened this summer as long as Chip produced. She was not alone in anticipating a huge success, a reputation established. Her eyes gleamed. While Chip was cloistered on the island she had been busy, planting hints, building enthusiasm, fanning the spark that ignited when he won the Voss Grant. She had done all the things expected from a better-than-good agent. She was ready; the world was ready; all they needed was for Charles Windsor to be ready.

"How about taking a break?" Her voice sounded unnaturally loud in her own ears, but Chip never even indicated he heard a sound. Wilma waited until he lowered the brush from the canvas, reluctant to risk startling him into an uncontrolled movement, then tapped him on the shoulder. He grunted, so she poked harder and repeated the question.

"Um?"

She reached around him and removed a brush from between his lips. "I'm going for a swim. It's still as hot as blazes. Why don't you come with me? You've been at it steadily for hours. You'll collapse if you don't get some rest."

In answer he swept his paint-speckled hand in the air over the upper right quadrant of the canvas. "What do you think about this? I'm trying to bring out the secondary theme, carrying it up and through, using the primary color, its direct complement and then, using pure titanium white, here and here," he pointed with the wooden end of the brush, "to highlight the direction the eye should travel."

Wilma stepped back a pace and squinted at the picture. "Interesting." She moved to view it from another angle. "Very interesting. I see what you're doing." Her voice hinted at the excitement always just beneath the surface when she looked at his work.

He turned back to the canvas and she remembered why she had interrupted him. "Chip, wait. It's getting late, and trite as it sounds, tomorrow's another day. There's enough time for a swim." He was staring at her uncomprehendingly. "Okay, forget it." She noted with amusement that he already had. "You'll have enough daylight for another hour before you have to go to the artificial lights. Try not to stay all night." She reached around him and inserted the paintbrush back between his teeth.

She enjoyed the walk back to the house, breathing

the fresh air and working the kinks out of her back and legs. This was not the way she had envisioned spending her vacation, but she was not sorry that she had come. She would do anything to get Chip to paint the way she knew he could.

At the house she called out to Kate, but there was no reply. After changing into a bathing suit she grabbed a towel from the linen closet and hurried down the path to the cove, half expecting to meet Kate coming the other way. She reached the cliff top without seeing her.

Wilma descended the steep path cautiously. She dropped her towel and kicked off her shoes. There was a rustling disturbance to her left in the trees that crowded the edge of the cove. "Kate?" There was no reply. She squinted and shaded her eyes with her hand. Something moved in the shadows; some animal.

She watched, not moving, for one crazy second thinking she saw the setter, the one with the impossible name, Natty Bumppo, slip from one shadow to another. "Natty?" she called, and then shook her head. "Wilma, my girl, you've been cooped up too long. The dog is dead and what you're looking at is probably a fox." Whatever it was, the sound of her voice must have scared it away, for it disappeared, almost fading from view.

Wilma smoothly shrugged her tanned shoulders and ran into the water. She didn't want to think about foxes or other predatory creatures with sharp, pointed teeth. All she wanted to do was relax. She swam with sure, strong strokes out past the line of the breakers, then turned and floated on her back.

The sky was beginning to darken into dusk. High cirrus clouds, flicking mares' tails, skittered across the delft blue. Wilma floated and dreamed, the dream of success she had entertained for a very long time. The gentle swells lulled her.

It was very peaceful. Content, Wilma rode the undulating sea until without warning a rogue wave peaked behind her, submerging her. She went down, swallowed some water and came up choking. She treaded water until the coughing spasms passed. It was time to head back in. When her feet kicked the shell-strewn bottom she stood up, feeling the undertow suck at her legs. She flicked her hair back out of her eyes and started to walk toward the small beach, the tide's rush pushing her from behind.

The figure of a boy stood at the water line, silent, staring, his fixed gaze never once wavering from her. Wilma stopped, her heart thumping painfully against her ribs. "Who . . . who are you? What do you want?"

He started to raise an arm, then he seemed to flicker and disappear, as if the gesture had erased him.

Wilma took a step backward. "Where are you?" Her voice was high, tight, panic-edged. She whipped her body around, searching the incoming waves. There was nothing.

A buzz near her ear distracted her. "Damn." She flicked at the sound with her hand. The buzzing persisted. She stepped to the side. The sound followed her. Afraid to leave the water until she was sure she was alone, she took another step sideways. The buzzing got louder.

Wilma turned to identify the insect. A bee hovered in the air, close to her right ear. "Get away," she yelled, and vigorously waved her hand. The bee darted forward and landed on the soft skin of her underarm.

Wilma felt the sting of its bite before she could brush it off. Fire raced through her veins. The bee landed again, on the back of her neck. Another sharp sting, another jet of venom went shooting through her. She splashed herself with water, maddened by the pain, in a frenzy to escape, but fearful of the boy.

The bee stung again and then again. Sobbing, Wilma turned and ran, back into the water, diving into a breaking wave, trying to keep submerged for as long as possible. When her head broke the surface she was quite a distance from the shore. She treaded water, her eyes searching the beach and the woods ringing it, trying to detect the slightest hint of movement. Her arms ached, her body on fire with shooting pain. Just a little while longer, she promised herself, just a little while, and then it will be safe to get out.

The air was cooling, but the water felt warm. Nothing moved on the land. No insect flew near by. Wilma waited until she thought she might pass out with the agony which seared her, threatening to cramp her arms and legs. All was quiet, safe. She glided into a side-stroke, using long sweeping movements to propel her through the water with the least discomfort.

Despite her striving she found herself drifting toward the rocks. She straightened in the water, reoriented herself to the shore and set out again. She had settled into a rhythm of sorts when she felt something brush her leg. She kicked out, losing her stride. Something under the water slid around her ankle, moved up her leg. She reached down to free herself. A hand closed over hers. "Oh God! Help me! Help me! Heeeeelp!" she screamed as Billy Sproul's head rose out of the green water only inches from her own.

In pain, exhausted, she faced him, for she knew there was no escape. "What do you want?"

He stretched his lips into a huge, gaping, *hungry* grin. Flat, black eyes bored into her. Her heart thudded heavily in her chest. She knew what he wanted, knew also she wouldn't give it to him easily.

"Come and get me, you bastard," she yelled, and swung at him with all her might. Her balled fist passed through him. She whimpered, but even this sound choked off, dying abruptly as the figure of Billy Sproul decomposed into thick, oily, slimy smoke that floated on the water. She stared, glassy-eyed, unable to move, as the viscous material stirred, reformed and once again took on the teenager's shape. He reached out and embraced her, pressing his lips to hers. Wilma never knew when he metamorphosed again, became a bee, and stung her on the lips.

She was dead before she slid beneath the waves. Seaweed wound around her ankle, tugged her toward the rocks. There, green eyes open wide, Wilma Thompson floated just beneath the surface, her body bobbing with the tide.

CHAPTER TWENTY-ONE

Daniel found Kate standing on a cliff overlooking the foaming, restless sea. A large orange moon, resembling a huge dimpled pumpkin, hugged the horizon, spreading a rippling apricot beam over the night-dark water.

Although she never heard his approach, she knew by the change in the air that he was near. From behind her he slid his arms about her waist, pulling her in tightly against his big, solid body.

She expelled her breath with a long drawn out sigh. "I thought you might not come." She moved back into his warmth, accommodating her soft curves to the hardness of muscle in chest and thigh.

"I've always been here, love," he said tenderly. He trembled when he felt her move. The pain of wanting her seemed eternal. "I've walked the woods with you, watched you while you swam and guarded you while you slept. You were not alone."

It was no surprise, for she had always known it, with her heart if not with her mind. He was the man shadow under her window, the snap of a twig in the woods.

She turned within the circle of his arms. In the dim lantern light of the low moon she studied him, but only the hard angle of his jaw, the high, wide cheekbones beneath dark, hooded eyes were discernible.

"But why—?"

He pulled her closer, settling her against his hips. "You were not ready." He answered the unspoken question that hovered between them. "I didn't want to push you, force you by my need into making a decision. I've waited so long, too long to risk losing everything."

"I want you," she said.

She both heard and felt his sharply indrawn breath. His body stilled, as if listening, and then he nodded and took her hand, leading her away from the cliff, from the open, unprotected place. He stopped in a small clearing ringed with tall aromatic firs. Cupping his hands beneath her chin, he tilted her face upward to study her features in the dim saffron light. "Are you sure, my love? Your eyes speak to me of desire, but I want more, much more from you."

She shifted her weight backward, but he would not let her go. His fingers moved into her hair, splaying out to cradle her head. The gaze which raked her features inexorably demanded she yield all to him.

"Please, I need you so," she whispered.

He took a ragged breath and expelled it in a sigh which ruffled her hair. "Ah, love, the need is mutual." Lowering his head he brushed her lips with his, a chaste, butterfly-light affirmation of their pledge. He withdrew his hands from her hair and stepped back a pace, so that they were joined solely by the fragrant night air that wove about their bodies. She trembled ever so slightly. "You need have no fear. I could never harm you. Not in this, tonight, or in anything that is to come. This I promise you. You are mine. I've waited a long time for you."

"Yes, I know," she breathed, and then they both understood that the time for words was past.

Kate stood still as he began to open the buttons on her shirt, slowly, one by one, starting at the top and working his way downward. When the last one was free he gently tugged the shirt from her pants, sliding it off her shoulders and down her unresisting arms. His fingers moved between her breasts to the clasp of her bra, deftly unhooked it, then peeled the wispy garment away. In another few moments her pants joined the little pile of clothing and she stood before him only in gossamer sheer bikini panties. He hooked his thumbs beneath the elastic and rolled them down her body so she could step out of them. When he straightened she was standing before him clothed only in the soft apricot wash of the low-riding moon.

His eyes drank in her beauty, the classic loveliness, the long, straight limbs and soft curves, the hollows, those mysterious places where shadows dwelt. He raised one hand and explored her face, using the back of his knuckles to limn her features gently. She stood breathlessly waiting as his hand began traveling down the long, slender column of her neck, pausing to rest in the tender, sensitive hollow at the base of her throat.

Kate felt her pulse leap under the feather touch, and then his hand was moving again, along her shoulder, down to her side, where the swell of her breast began. He traced the curve inward, then continued the downward line, lightly brushing the sensitive skin of her belly before dropping his arm to his side.

They remained motionless for several heartbeats, and then Kate reached up and unbuttoned his shirt. Separating the two sides, she pushed the fabric away from his broad chest. The big muscles tightened beneath her fingertips. Wordlessly she explored him, then leaned forward and pressed her lips to his taut skin, her tongue daintily licking him, tasting the warm, smooth flesh.

"Ah, love," he moaned, and shrugged all the way out of the shirt. She reached for the buckle of his belt, but he captured her hand, pulled it away. "Wait," he commanded, and bent down to spread his shirt over the carpet of needles, redolent with the fragrant scent of pine. He straightened and scooped her up into his arms, then knelt and reverently placed her on the sweet-scented bed.

Kate lay quietly watching as he quickly shed the rest of his clothes, finally standing tall and unashamedly proud in his nakedness. To her bewitched eyes he looked solid and beautiful, like the age-old trees that ringed the clearing. He dropped down beside her and took her in his arms, his lips capturing hers in a kiss which drove all thought from her brain. He kissed her long and hard, drinking deep of the sweet honey of her mouth.

She lost all sense of time and place with the feel of his lips on hers, the sweep of his tongue in her mouth creating a tantalizing expectancy when he started to slide it in and out, a foretaste of what was to come. She moaned when he pulled away, separating their bodies slightly. She reached for him, tried to draw him closer, but he denied her the intimate contact she sought.

"Slowly, my love," he cautioned, "or you'll soon have me at the point where I can no longer control my need for you." He picked up one of her hands and ran his tongue from her wrist to the tip of her middle finger. She shivered with the sensation it produced. He transferred his concern to the rest of her body, which was quivering with a smoldering awareness.

Kate felt fire race through her veins as his lips explored her, slow inch by slow inch, arousing her to a state of desperate need. Her body started to move, to roll urgently from side to side, under the sensuous attack. He left no place untouched, his hands stroking the curves and hollows, his lips and tongue tasting, licking, nibbling the sensitized skin. As his tongue entered her navel she moaned and grabbed his shoulders, urging him away, prodding him to lie back, to let her have her turn.

She let her hands and tongue roam at will, glorying in the taste and touch and smell of him. A smile of triumph curved her lips as he groaned, a sound torn from his being, deep and harsh and filled with need. She examined his broad torso, tracing each rib from the middle outward. She let one hand drift downward, only to have him stop her with a steel-fingered grip around her wrist.

"Please, I need you," she whispered.

"Not yet," he replied and quickly reversed their positions, once again taking the dominant one. She sobbed her disappointment in a choked cry. "Hush, my love. Soon. Very soon."

Through the agony of arousal, painful in its intensity, she felt him shift his body and move to crouch at her feet. He drew his tongue along the length of each sole from heel to toe. She thrashed from side to side, almost kicking him in her agitation. He grasped her ankles and held her still, then leaned forward and began to slide his hands up her legs, opening them ever wider as he journeyed slowly up her body, using tongue and teeth and fingers to blaze a path of fire.

She bucked and began to move her hips, blatantly inviting him to join her in the ancient rhythm. His hands moved up her thighs, and she stilled the wild gyrations of her hips.

"Yes. Yes. Now," she gasped, the words torn from the elemental force that now ruled her.

"Look at me!" he demanded. Her eyes snapped open in shock. He was kneeling between her legs, his body bent forward so that he could look into her eyes, could read her soul. He was shaking, trying to control his own raging desire. "Do you want me?"

"Yes, oh yes." She arched her back, trying to bring him closer to her, but yet he withheld himself, moving back fractionally until he was just out of reach. "Come to me. Now!"

"Who am I? Say my name." Her passion-hazed brain was slow to understand the demand. "Look at me, Kate. Yes, love, that's right, look into my eyes. Say my name, love, just say my name."

"D . . . D . . . Daniel?" She was abruptly aware of everything around her, of the night sounds of the woods, the rustling in the undergrowth, the deep blue dome of the sky beyond the face above her. Suddenly she knew what he wanted, and why he must have it before he made her his own. "You're Daniel. Daniel Sheridan," she stated positively.

"That's right, my love, my own Kate," he breathed, and leaned forward to take her in his arms. Her hands slid around his back, urging him down to her. Her legs came up to wrap around his hips.

Kate sighed in blissful satisfaction as she adjusted to the wonderful pressure inside her. She lifted her hips, hinting of her impatience to move, to begin the love dance.

"Impatient girl," he whispered in her ear, but he gave her what she wanted, what they both craved.

She traveled his length, the dizzying passion within her swirling to an unbearable height. She sensed his terrible battle for control, to give her release first. Then she ceased to think as the knot in her belly tightened and then burst, sending waves of pure sensation, clothed in marvelous kaleidoscopic colors of gold and purple and red, shooting through her body. He held himself unmoving above her until her wild thrashing calmed, needing only to thrust into her one more time to gain his own shuddering release.

He rolled over and took her with him, holding her close in his embrace until they were lying on their sides facing each other. Gently he stroked the damp hair back from her face, then placed a soft kiss on her passion-swollen lips. "Are you all right?"

"Mmmmn. More than that." The smile which lit her face radiated pure contentment.

He traced her lips with the tip of a finger. "You look like a cat who's about to purr."

She turned her head and kissed the roving finger. The dark eyes so close to hers were filled with love and understanding and joy. Her heart swelled painfully with emotion. "Daniel?"

"Yes, love."

"I . . . I think I'm falling asleep." She heard and felt the deep chuckle which rumbled through his chest, felt it in her breast and belly and thighs, all the places which touched his hard body. "Not fair. It's not fair," she mumbled as she drifted off, knowing complete peace for the first time in a very long while.

She stirred awake sometime later still clasped in his arms. It took but a moment for her to orient herself. "Hello," she whispered huskily, smiling up into a warm, loving gaze. He answered with a kiss on her lips. When at last he raised his head she stretched luxuriously within the confines of his arms. "I could get used to waking up this way."

"Why don't you? It would be my pleasure. No, don't pull away, love." Although he spoke in a light tone they both knew there was nothing frivolous about his words. He tightened his embrace. His voice deepened, became charged with emotion. "We both knew that this would change things."

Kate stubbornly shook her head, although her heart ached to tell him what he wanted to hear. "Nothing's changed. Not really. I still owe Chip his chance. I won't do anything to jeopardize that. It . . . it wouldn't be right."

Sadness filled his dark eyes. "Nothing's changed? Can you say that with honesty?" He traced the line of her lips with the knuckle of his finger. "Everything's changed for me, and I'm not afraid to admit it. I love you, Kate, my love. I loved you before tonight, but now that we've been together I know that I can never let you go. You're mine, just as I am yours. Come away with me. Live with me. Love me. I need you so." His big frame shook with the raw emotion. He groaned when he saw tears spilling from her eyes. "Ah, love, I didn't mean to make you cry."

"I'm not crying." She sniffled and gave him a very watery smile. She placed her hand flat on his chest, felt the strong beat of his heart beneath the warm, smooth skin. "I love you too." When she saw the hope leap into his eyes she shook her head. "No, don't say any more. I won't leave him until I'm sure his career won't suffer because of something I do. If he fails because of my selfishness, my need for you, I would never forgive myself . . . or you."

The last words were whispered so low that he had to strain to hear them. He kissed her tenderly on the tip of her nose. "My dear, sweet, loyal, stubborn Kate. What am I going to do with you?"

"Wait? Will you wait for me?"

This was said with such wistful hopefulness that he laughed, a short, almost gruff bark more nearly resembling a sound of pain than a sound of mirth. "Do I have a choice?" It was a rueful question to which he already knew the answer. "I guess I should have expected this. You wouldn't be you, the Kate I love, if you behaved differently. Yes, my beautiful, enticing, stubborn little witch, I will wait for you, but only . . . only if you now pledge yourself to me. Here, beneath the sky, with the stars and the moon for witnesses, promise that you will come to me when your heart is free. Promise it, Kate," he said fiercely, "for I find I need a token to carry in my heart."

"I promise."

No sooner had the words left her lips than a great wind arose, agitating the trees around them, swaying them inward, bowing them toward the earth, their branches dipping menacingly low. Kate shrank against him, fear trembling her body. "It's him. Iye."

Daniel could not hear her in the sudden, deafening din, but he read her lips and understood what caused her terror. He pressed her closer and threw back his head, roaring defiance into the night. "This woman is mine! I yield her to no one!" He bent his head and took her lips in a savage kiss, his passion rising strongly, a primitive response to the awesome play of nature. He transferred his lips to her ear, speaking directly into it to make sure she heard and understood him. "You're safe with me, love. Nothing will harm you. Nothing."

Kate moved her head so she could look at his face. She saw concern and tenderness and patience and passion and love. She put her arms around his neck and drew his head down, opening her lips under his in a kiss so filled with desire that she felt a tremor run through his big body. She pressed her body close, sliding her leg over his, slowly moving it up until it rested over his hip, telling him with her opened body of her need, the passion spiraling deep within her. She pushed against his chest, urging him onto his back. He rolled over and held her hips. Her long dark hair streamed out over his legs. Her eyes met and held his. He helped her to move, his hands cupping her buttocks as she set a pace as frantic as the furor around them. Their eyes never strayed from each other as they made love, heedless of the furious wind that was turning the island into a frightening, alien place.

Chip jumped awake at the sound of a branch crashing against the side of the studio. Sleep-fogged and heavy-limbed, he staggered to the door, reeling back in surprise when the wind pulled it out of his grasp. The scene before him was straight out of a nightmare: nature gone wild. It was a terrifying fantasy of huge, venerable trees twisted and bent over by a mighty force. It was a powerful vision such as a master like Albrecht Durer would dream. It was a picture of hell, of a world gone mad.

In awe, Chip rushed out into the night. The door slammed shut behind him. It was then that he became aware of the noise, the roaring, screeching, mad voice of the wind as it tore through the trees, playing the leaves and the sharp needles of the firs in a demented symphony of sound. The moon, risen high in the sky and shining brightly, bathed the spectacle in eerie white-gold light.

Chip added his own voice to the din, screaming in a primitive reaction to the insanity around him as his spare body was propelled forward by the force of the wind. Through the contorted, tortured trees he ran, pushed hard by an unseen hand. Through the wooded places he went, passing the edge of the secluded spot where his wife lay with her lover. He did not see them, for although his eyes were open he was blinded by terror and also by a vision, for in the maelstrom had come a revelation, a picture he would create of such raw, elemental power that it brought tears to his unseeing eyes. He ran until his tired body dropped and then he slept, surrendering consciousness for a world of tortured dreams.

The wind raced on, scouring the island with its fury. It whipped the water, building waves of monstrous proportion to come rushing, foaming in to the beach, to greedily suck up the sand.

Beneath the heaving, churning sea the body of Wilma Thompson was wrenched from the imprisoning rocks. Pushed and pulled by the current, it rose steadily upward through the aerated green-black water. It surfaced and rolled over, the fixed green eyes staring sightlessly at the moon. Slowly it rose perpendicular, turning until it faced the shore, riding the fierce waves as easily as a gull, before sliding again beneath the sea.

CHAPTER TWENTY-TWO

With the first hint of light Kate sent Daniel away. She went back to the cliff where he had come to her, starting back to the house only when she saw his boat round the island and head back to Puffin Landing. Everywhere was evidence of the fierce wind that had so frightened her the night before. Fallen branches clogged the path, trees that had looked to be immutable were uprooted, some lying like fallen giants on the ground, others supported by their neighbors, like drunken revelers on their way home. She saw some pathetic little heaps of feathers, broken bodies that had yesterday soared in the bright sky.

The house was silent, empty; Chip had spent another night away. She had just finished dressing after a quick shower and was combing the tangles out of her wet hair when she heard the screen door to the kitchen open and slam closed. Not wanting a scene in their bedroom, not after last night, she hurried down the stairs, almost running along the short hallway to the back of the house. He was standing in the middle of the kitchen, his face gaunt, unshaven; his bloodshot eyes focused on something unseen, inside himself.

"Chip? What's the matter?" She took in the rest of his appearance, the torn shirt and pants, the dirt smeared on them. "What happened to you? Did you fall? Answer me," she demanded, raising her voice when he failed to reply.

"What? Oh, Kate." He appeared to see her for the first time. "I'm hungry," he complained, like a child who must have its physical needs satisfied in the instant it discovers them.

Kate scrambled eggs and made toast, her actions so practiced she need give them little thought. While he ate he talked, managing to do both with no trouble, the words spilling out as fast as he pushed the food in.

Kate listened, understanding he had finally found the focus of his work. His enthusiasm was back, his eyes sparkling as he described the picture he would paint. "I'll start today. I've got wood for the frame and enough canvas to stretch it right away." He looked about the kitchen as if it were a strange room. "Do you have a pencil and some paper. I want to make some sketches now, while it's fresh in my mind. Oh, and more coffee." He held out his cup.

It was almost the old, arrogant Chip. "No. No more caffeine. Go upstairs and get some sleep. You look like the walking wounded. Everything'll still be in your mind when you get up." To her surprise, he listened, pushed back the chair and headed for the stairs.

Kate swiftly cleaned up, then poured a mug of coffee and took it out to the porch. She settled in the rocker, too tired and too full of the night just past to do more than sit and rock. Her life had changed in only a few

236

hours. Be honest, she chided herself, knowing that the few hours she had spent in Daniel's arms were the culmination of many days and weeks and months of change. The seeds of the marriage's dissolution had been sown long before they came to Smoke Island.

"The marriage is through, your staying here with Chip is nothing more than a charade," Daniel had said early that morning. "Leave him now, today."

It would be so easy. She would place her hand in his big, capable one and walk away. Get in the boat and never look back. Never dream of Little Sparrow and Great Bear again, for she knew the dreams were special to the island. She shook her head, the heaviness in her heart written plainly on her face. "I can't," was finally all she said.

"You are the only one who can decide who and what you want. I only hope you choose the living, not some dream which will fade like the morning mist." From the jerk of her body he could see that the remark had hit home. "I'd rather see you stay with Chip, than lose yourself in make-believe." There was pain in the dark eyes, a touch of bitterness in the deep voice. "I won't be back, Kate. You'll have to come to me."

"Oh Daniel," she whispered, and fell asleep with tears in her eyes.

It was dark in the wigwam, with only a small fire for light. At first it appeared to be empty, with the eating bowls stacked ready to one side of the cooking pot, and the sleeping platform along one wall unoccupied, but after her eyes became accustomed to the gloom she saw Little Sparrow, pressed close against the farthest wall, sitting as still as one of the decorated storage baskets that held her household necessities. She huddled, her arms wrapped around her body in a defensive pose.

It was hot, so hot that perspiration slicked Little Sparrow's dusky skin. She began to rock back and forth, her eyes wide open, staring at nothing, a high, thin, eerie melody issuing from her slightly parted lips. On the other side of the woven-mat wall one of Great Bear's dogs howled, the sound frightful, otherworldly. Little Sparrow shivered, but did not stop the measured movements of her taut body, nor the doleful muted wail which whistled past her teeth.

A feeling of dread settled in Kate's stomach. She wanted to shake Little Sparrow, make her tell her what was wrong; at any cost get her to stop the fearful, mindless tune. The heat was oppressive. Sweat rolled down Little Sparrow's temples, soaking her hair, turning the once bright, shining mane into limp, lackluster strands which clung damply to her bare back. The fire flared as someone pulled back the mat that covered the wigwam's opening. Little Sparrow abruptly fell silent, her lithe young body straining forward, concentrating her entire being on the person who stepped inside.

Kate whirled about, the sudden movement jarring her awake. Her eyes snapped open to a bright, dazzling world. Her clothes were sticking to her, her mouth felt fuzzy and her head ached. She went inside and ran the water until it was cold, splashing it on her neck and face, gulping down two aspirins with her second glass of water. It was past noon but she was not hungry. All she could think about was getting relief for her overheated body. The invigorating Maine water would cool her down.

Chip was still asleep, lying on his back diagonally

across the bed, loud snores issuing from his wide-open mouth. She knew they were alone in the house. Wondering what had happened to Wilma and if she had slept in the studio, Kate shrugged. She had long ago stopped caring about what Wilma did with her time on the island. Turning away from her husband's sleeping form, Kate grabbed the first suit her hand touched and went into the bathroom to change.

After a slow walk through the woods Kate arrived at the cliff and started down the tortuous path. She paused partway down and shaded her eyes, searching the area below. A rumpled towel and a pair of shoes were on the beach. Kate's lips curved in a smile. Wilma. The agent was no dummy. This was the best place to be on a scorching day.

Kate spread her towel near Wilma's and kicked off her shoes. The sand was hot. She lost no time running to the tide line and plunging directly into the foamy, breaking waves. Five minutes later she was cool enough to come out. Wilma was still not in sight. She cupped her hands around her mouth and yelled her name, but the only answer was from a circling gull. Puzzled, she turned in a complete circle, finally catching sight of a wet, honey-blond head bobbing about in the water near the rocks. She waved energetically, finally receiving a return wave from Wilma. Satisfied, Kate lay down and closed her eyes.

The sun was overhead, just beginning its slow descent to the western horizon. Kate saw red beneath her closed eyelids; red and gold and little dancing sparks of blue and green. She was looking into the fire, searching its molten heart for the courage to find out what was wrong, why she lived with dread in her heart, when seemingly nothing had changed. Perhaps it was the worry over Great Bear, two days late in returning from the hunt. But he was home now, his big body filling their wigwam, dwarfing everything within to insignificance. The deer he had brought home would provide meat for a long time; its hide would clothe them. Already she planned to fashion leg tubes for him to wear when winter chilled the earth. He would be protected from brambles and the dry brush that could so easily pierce the skin, and when he wore them for the ceremonials everyone would be envious, for his leggings would have the longest fringe, be decorated with the most intricate designs.

"It is hot. Let us go to the stream to cool our bodies."

Little Sparrow hesitated for a second, then followed Great Bear out of the wigwam into the night, thinking he was tired, and that was the difference she sensed in him. They undressed in silence and went splashing into the stream. The water felt good. Little Sparrow lay down and let it rush over her, throwing her head back to make sure her hair got wet. She floated peacefully, her world righting itself as her body cooled. After a time she left the water, lying down on her spread-out skirt.

Kate felt Great Bear's hands go around her. A wild, dizzying emotion swept through her at the touch. He lifted her torso, and she arched her back, pushing herself more firmly against him only to feel him pull back. Her skin pebbled immediately in the cooler night air. He squeezed the soft flesh of her breast. The rough treatment hurt the sensitive flesh. When she complained he laughed. "Pain is pleasure. I shall teach you."

Something was different; frighteningly alien. She felt Great Bear turn her body until she was lying on her stomach. She tried to pivot around, but he held her firmly in place. "Please, no," she cried with Little Sparrow's voice, yet it was her own trepidation which accelerated her heart until it was banging against her ribs. Her body stiffened in defense, her legs clamping together almost painfully in an instinctive effort to protect herself from an unwanted invasion.

She heard a low laugh and felt his knee between her legs, forcing them inexorably wider. As he moved to kneel between her thighs she started to whimper, afraid. He touched her, his hands rough and brutal. Through the pain and the shock she could feel his breath, hot on her neck, could hear him panting close to her ear. The long, blunt-tipped fingers began to move. "No, no, no," Kate and Little Sparrow cried with one voice.

"Pain becomes pleasure. You will see."

"Why do you seek to hurt me?" Little Sparrow asked in a puzzled voice, while the part of her that was Kate knew the answer. It was punishment for the night of love with Daniel. Fear entered her world of dreams. She managed to get her hands beneath her and pushed up, surprising him for the few seconds it took to roll over. The action forced him to withdraw.

She glared up at him, her breasts heaving from the exertion of fighting his superior strength.

"Ah, Little Sparrow, my love, I would never hurt you."

Kate grew icy cold. The choice of words, the tone, the inflection were all Daniel's, although it was Great Bear who spoke. He mocked her, but she knew not why. Using a feather touch, he began to stroke her skin, expertly, knowingly employing all his accumulated knowledge of her body to gradually, skillfully build her passion. When her breath became ragged he again touched her, this time finding her ready and open to him. "Does this give you pleasure, my love?"

"Yes, oh yes," Kate gasped, a helpless prisoner of her body's desires. She forgot everything but the demand of pulsing flesh. He captured the sensitive skin of her breast between his lips and bit down with strong teeth. Her eyes flew open.

"Pleasure is pain, my love, there is no difference."

"Noooooooo," Kate and Little Sparrow screamed together as the face of Great Bear wavered and turned to smoke, then solidified again into a grinning devil-mask.

"Iye," Little Sparrow whimpered, horrified, as the shaman leered down at her. She stiffened as the smirking face shifted again into thick gray smoke, became once more the face of Great Bear.

His fingers never stopped, moving faster and faster, heightening the tension which coiled in her belly. "You see, love, it matters not which face I wear. Your body responds to me, to this," he said and lifted her breast, shaping it with his palm. He licked it with the tip of his tongue, then brought it to his mouth.

Kate was both fascinated and repelled. Her traitorous body responded to the alien caresses while her mind tried to deny what she had seen. She looked down and wondered what face was pressed to her breast. Her hands clutched the head of midnight hair, her fingers curling in the coarse strands. She forced his head up. It was Great Bear's familiar face which raised to hers. Or was it? There were subtle, unmistakable differences. His face began to ripple, to change. He was Great Bear; he was Iye; he was both, a grotesque mélange.

Kate reached down and pulled his hand away from her, using a strength born of repugnance, just as Little Sparrow fainted dead away.

Kate woke up with a start. Wilma was bending over her.

CHAPTER TWENTY-THREE

"I was dreaming," Kate blurted, and jerked up into a sitting position. "It . . . it was a very . . . uh . . ." Her voice trailed away. Wilma was staring at her. Kate followed the direction of her gaze and looked down at herself. She gasped when she saw her bathing suit bunched around her midriff, leaving her breasts completely exposed to view. She started to turn her torso away, instinctively seeking to protect her modesty while she wrestled the slick material back into place, when an icy cold hand cupped her right breast.

Kate stared stupidly down at it for several moments, too stunned even for thought.

"You have very beautiful breasts," Wilma said.

Her voice unfroze Kate. She knocked Wilma's hand away. Her female hand. No woman had ever touched her in that way. She gagged as bile rose in her throat. She fumbled with the suit, her hands made clumsy by shock and revulsion.

"No, no, don't cover them. They're so glorious, so firm. Let me see them. Let me touch them."

"Stop it, Wilma, I'm not interested," she said flatly. A low laugh was the only response.

Kate's skin puckered into goose bumps. Flight was the only option, since it was obvious something had happened to Wilma; something had unhinged her. She would fix her suit later. Slowly she drew her legs up. The important thing now was to put distance between them.

Quickly she put thought to action and pushed herself up. Wilma moved so fast that Kate hardly had time to register the fact before she felt herself propelled backward. In the next instant she was lying flat on her back with Wilma straddling her lower body, pinning her to the ground. She leaned forward and grasped Kate's hands, holding them with surprising strength while her mouth sought and found Kate's breast.

Oh, God, no, Kate screamed inside her head, too horrified to produce sound. Wilma turned her attention to the other breast, using lips and tongue and teeth on the sensitive tissue.

Dimly she heard Wilma, almost crooning as she moved her head from breast to breast. "So soft, so good. Ah, yes, yes. Yeeeessss." It was unbearable. The world started to fade as Kate allowed reality to recede from her consciousness. In a semi-swooning state she felt a knee being forced between her legs. A new wave of revulsion swept her, causing sickness to churn in her stomach. "Let me love you. Open to me, let me in." Wilma was all over her, taking advantage of Kate's condition to roam her body at will. She wormed a hand between them and moved it downward, all the while still employing her knee to force Kate's legs to open.

Kate gave up the luxury of fainting. Wilma was not

245

going to have her, any part of her, not while there was a breath left in her. She willed herself to lie still while she gathered her strength, hoping to dupe Wilma into thinking her still in a semi-swooning state. It worked much better than she could have hoped, for Wilma began to murmur into her ear, responding with coaxing, cajoling words to the easing of the tense rigidity.

"Sweet. Oh, so sweet. Open to me. Let me feel you. Let me in. Sweet, oh so sweet, so sweet, so sweeeet," she crooned, dipping her tongue into Kate's ear. "Let me love you. Feel this, you like it, it gives you such pleasure," she said, and moved her hand between Kate's thighs.

At the very moment the alien female hand touched her Kate jerked her body to the side and kicked out hard, slamming her foot into Wilma's left side. With every ounce of strength at her command, she shoved her away. Rolling out from under her, she managed to get to her hands and knees. Wilma caught her ankle and tugged.

"Think; think what you're doing," Kate cried, as she unbalanced and fell flat on her stomach. The wind was knocked out of her as she landed hard. Wilma was on her instantly, sitting on her legs, one hand on the small of her back, pinning her immobile, pressing her into the ground. The coarse sand, interspersed with bits of broken shell, bit cruelly into Kate's exposed breasts.

"Let me up, you're hurting me."

A low, cruel-sounding laugh answered the plea. "Pleasure is pain, my love, there is no difference."

Kate stiffened as her blood turned to ice. They were the exact words in the dream. "What did you say?"

246

she whispered, fighting the nausea threatening to swamp her.

"Ah, love, so you remember," Wilma purred silkily. "I expect it's the position. So demeaning, so unsatisfactory, but it has its uses."

"Who are you?"

"I expect you already know, my love."

Kate's lips moved, formed a name. Using what remaining strength she had, she levered up on her hands, raising the upper part of her body. She threw back her head and screamed, hurled the name from her body as if the explosive force of the sound could exorcise it from her brain. "Iye," she yelled, startling a flock of small birds into agitated flight.

"Iyeeeeeeeee," Wilma responded. The sound reverberated in the air, a primitive declaration of being, an affirmation of power.

"What do you want?" Kate's voice was flat, unemotional.

"I only want to love you."

This was a waking nightmare; she could only look to herself for salvation. Wilma, impossible to think of her as anything else, must be stopped. Her cold hands were moving again, inching up toward her breasts. Kate shuddered and did the only thing she could, collapsing suddenly, taking Wilma by surprise. In the half a second grace period she gained by the maneuver, she pushed down hard against the sand and rolled over, bucking her body wildly, using her arms and her legs and her fists and her feet, striking out blindly, not caring what she hit as long as she hit something, until she forced Wilma off her body.

She was panting from the exertion, panting and sobbing both, for she found she could not control her mind's loathing of the female body she was trying to escape. It was clammy and cold and every time she touched it, or it touched her, her soul shriveled a little bit. She pushed herself upright and faced Wilma, who looked as strong and as fresh as if they hadn't just been in a tremendous struggle. Kate started to back away, looking for an opportunity to get past her.

"Do you remember the dream? The last time we loved?" the Wilma thing asked. "Surely you must, for you were left unfulfilled. Let me help you now. Let me touch you, your hair, your lips, your breasts. Oh, how I love your breasts, how beautiful they look in firelight, all dusky and glowing. So round. So firm."

Keep her talking, Kate thought, and said the first thing that popped into her head. "I'm Kate, not Little Sparrow. You don't want me, Wilma. Let me go." She started to edge around her, carefully avoiding looking at the path, her route to freedom.

"Not want you?" Wilma laughed. "I've thought about nothing else, dreamed about nothing else, through the long lonely years. I won't hurt you. I only want to love you." She held out her arms. "Come to me. I will love you like never before. I've always been your lover. Every time you slept I came to you. Now I have lips and a tongue, hands and fingers. All for you. For you, my love. You'll not be sorry. I can make you writhe with pleasure, make you call out for more." She took a step. Then another. "I need you. I ache for you. I've longed for you forever, my love. Come to me. Come to me now."

She lunged for Kate.

Kate turned and fled, heedless of the direction. She

had left it too late, had stood listening, mesmerized, like a helpless rabbit caught in a car's high beams. "No, oh no, oh no," she sobbed, as cold foamy water swirled about her ankles. She had run the wrong way. Wilma was right behind her.

Kate threw herself into the water, diving straight into the heart of a breaking wave. A hand grabbed her ankle, drew her down. Kate kicked, kicked hard, but could not dislodge it. She twisted around and groped blindly beneath her, found Wilma's head and clutched a fistful of hair. She gave a sharp yank and then another, kicking at her head with her free foot. All at once Wilma let go and Kate shot upward. She burst above the surface gasping for breath. Wilma shot out of the water not three feet away.

She was smiling.

The tide pushed another wave toward them. Kate turned and struck out through the surf, cresting the wave, riding it as it angled in toward shore. Wilma saw her intention and moved to cut her off, finally trapping Kate between herself and the rocks.

Kate was exhausted, unable to take another step. She watched Wilma stalk closer, the lacy white water bubbling about her waist like a ballerina's tutu. Kate pulled her bathing suit up and pushed her salt-laden hair behind her ears. Straightening her shoulders she waited, her posture resembling a gunfighter's from the Old West. Ike Clanton must have looked the same way to Wyatt Earp that day at the O.K. Corral.

When Wilma was close enough to hear her over the roaring of the surf she lifted her chin and yelled, loud and strong and clear. "God damn you, you'll never have me."

249

"You've been mine, ever since you came here," Wilma replied. "I've loved you in many ways; used many different forms. This body, this inadequate female form, is what you're running from. Not from me." She stopped bare inches away. "Do you think I'll let you go back to him? Your lover? Again?"

Kate looked directly into flat, expressionless black eyes. The thing that was Wilma, yet was not Wilma, reached out and took Kate into a lover's embrace.

"Never!" she averred. "You are mine! Mine!"

When she felt the cold, bloodless lips touch hers Kate pivoted, and grabbing Wilma's shoulders, pushed, pushed her hard and fast, directly down onto the unyielding rock. Wilma's grip relaxed. Kate did not let go. Wilma's eyes stared upward, directly into her own. Kate retched as the flat black stare began to fade, to change from inky black to a clear, hard green. Still she held her down, sobbing, as the sea rolled in.

CHAPTER TWENTY-FOUR

Daniel rolled over and stared at the ceiling. Sleep had been elusive, and little wonder, for while his body was in his bed, his mind was miles away. It had taken all his willpower to stay away from the island, from Kate, when all he wanted to do was to run to her. "Fool," he groaned, and then grinned, a wolf's grin, signifying nothing of humor. Nobility was fine in theory, but his principles were wreaking havoc on his body.

A cold shower and a mug of hot, strong coffee made him feel partially human again. He refilled the mug and wandered out to the enclosed porch. The sun had been over the horizon for at least a half hour. Smoke Island would be visible if there wasn't too much early morning fog.

He raked a big hand through his damp hair, obliterating the neat comb tracks. The pull of the telescope was irresistible. Just like a lovesick teenager who will do anything for a glimpse of his beloved, he thought disgustedly. "Right," he said aloud, and the bittersweet humor of it caused his eyes to crinkle and a genuine smile to curve his lips.

Since the inner battle for restraint was already lost, he swiftly bent down and looked through the telescope's eyepiece. His body went rigid, and then jerked in reaction, spilling hot coffee all over his hand. A single pennant was flying from Smoke Island's flagpole. It was blood red.

He made the trip in record time. Chip was waiting on the dock. He shut the engine and threw him a line. "What's happened?" he shouted, almost afraid to hear the answer.

"You sure took your own sweet time about getting here," Chip complained, then took a prudent step backward as the sheriff vaulted out of the boat and he got a good look at the expression on his face. "You'd better ask her." He indicated the stairs behind them with a nod of his head.

Daniel felt dizzy with relief when he looked up and saw Kate. Even at a distance she appeared pale and tired looking. At that moment he thought he had never seen anyone look more beautiful.

"She's got this crazy idea that Wilma's dead."

Daniel flinched. "What? How did it happen?"

"Don't ask me, Chief. I wasn't there." He flushed when the sheriff regarded him through assessing eyes. Eyes which weighed him and made no attempt to disguise that they found him wanting. "That is, uh, I'm not sure. She's been hysterical for most of the night. I can't get a straight story." He looked accusingly at the sheriff. "Perhaps if you'd been here you could have understood what she was saying."

"I came as fast as I could. I left the instant I saw the red pennant."

"We should have had flares."

"You're right. I never thought of it." He shook his head. "Okay. I'll take it from here."

He bounded up the stairs and went directly to Kate. She looked like a wounded fawn, her great dark eyes haunted with a terrible knowledge. "Hello, Kate," he said softly, and when there was no immediate response, reached out and took one of her hands. It was cold and limp. He squeezed it reassuringly. "Chip tells me there's been some trouble here. He says Wilma is dead."

She tugged on her hand and he promptly let it go. She crossed her arms in front of her chest and turned anguished eyes up to him. "I killed her."

"Kate!" Chip's shout silenced her. "It was an accident."

Daniel turned impatiently to him. "All I'm interested in right now are the simple facts. What happened. When. That sort of thing. Since by your own admission you know nothing about it, I would appreciate not hearing from you again until I get the story from Kate. Do you understand?" His voice was coldly official.

Chip nodded and looked at his wife. "Tell him what you told me. Let's see if *he* can figure it out."

Daniel ignored the sarcastic emphasis on the pronoun and focused all his attention on Kate. She looked shellshocked; he gentled his voice. "Tell me what happened. Tell me everything. Don't be afraid." He smiled encouragingly at her.

Kate began to speak, her voice a strained monotone. "It . . . it was hot yesterday, so I went for a . . . a swim. Wilma . . . Wilma was already there. In the water. I . . . I was tired," she raised her eyes to the sheriff, then quickly averted her gaze again, "and I fell a . . . asleep."

"Yes? What happened then?"

"Maybe you shouldn't say anything else now. Without a lawyer."

Daniel turned toward Chip, making no attempt to conceal the rage threatening to break free. "I told you to keep quiet," he grated. Chip was glaring at him. He struggled with his emotions, reminding himself that he was a professional. All personal thoughts and feelings would have to be shelved until the matter was resolved. "If you feel that Kate requires an attorney to be present, then by all means she should have one. But first I want to see the body. Then I'll be only too happy to take you into Puffin Landing. We can continue this discussion in my office."

"Uh, there is no body. I mean, it was, uh, too dark to search."

Daniel threw him a disgusted look just as Kate began to cry, great racking sobs which shook her thin body. He itched to take her into his arms, to stroke the dark hair back from her forehead, to kiss the brimming eyes, to reassure her that everything was all right. But everything wasn't all right. He spoke to Chip, although his eyes never left Kate. "Take her into the house. I'll be back as soon as I find Wilma. I assume I should look in the cove." He took Chip's nod for assent and turned to go.

"Wait! You . . . you'll never find her without me."

She wiped the tears from her face with the back of her hand. "She . . . she's in the water. Near . . . near the rocks."

She walked past Chip and put out her hand. Daniel immediately took possession of it. "You don't have to come. I'll find her."

"No. I . . . I should. I . . . I want to."

"Good girl." He squeezed her hand and then let it go.

"Kate." There was an implicit warning in Chip's voice.

She rounded on him, her hesitancy replaced by grim determination. "No, Chip, don't try to stop me. It's only right that I go. I'm . . . I'm the one who killed her." She leveled her gaze on the sheriff. "It was an accident. I . . . I didn't mean to hurt her. She was so strong. If . . . if it was her," she whispered.

"What do you mean by that?" Daniel asked sharply. Kate bowed her head. The two men locked gazes over it. "Well?" the sheriff demanded of Chip when it became apparent Kate was not going to answer.

He looked uneasy, then gave a patently false laugh. "She's got this insane notion that Wilma was possessed by an Indian. She's been driving me nutty all night. She's afraid to go to sleep, Chief. She claims he'll get her if she's not conscious."

"Kate?"

The soft saying of her name undid the last reserve. "It's true. It was Iye. The Shapechanger. I . . . I killed him, not Wilma. Not really." In a rush of words the story came out. Kate told it in a dispassionate voice, only omitting her surmises as to the reason for the attack, the insane jealousy that she suspected had prompted the Shapechanger into attempting sexual possession of her body through Wilma. "I woke up from a dream to find Wilma bending over me. She, 'er, touched me, here," her hand fluttered over her breast, "and I told her to stop. I . . . I wasn't interested. She laughed. She was so strong, so very strong. We, uh, fought. She, uh, he . . . it wouldn't give up. I . . . I had to do what I did." The dark eyes filled with tears again.

"What was that, Kate?" Daniel asked gently.

"We were in the water. I ran, uh, the wrong way. She chased me, over toward the rocks. I . . . I pushed her. Down. Down against them. She . . . she didn't get up."

"I see."

"Do . . . do you believe me?"

Chip snorted. "Crazy."

"Daniel?"

She looked so vulnerable. He smiled at her. "Why not?" He swiveled his attention to Chip. "Okay, let's go and see her. There's no need for you to come along," he said to Kate.

Her eyes filled with horror. "No!"

"My wife is afraid to be alone. She's scared to death she'll fall asleep."

To Kate's relief Daniel made no comment, merely motioning for her to join them. It was a quiet little procession that crossed the island to the cove.

It didn't take long to find Wilma's body. Kate pointed to the place where the struggle had ended. Daniel nod-

256

ded and then ordered her to sit and wait on the sandy beach while he and Chip made the treacherous climb over the sharp-toothed rocks. They located the body ten minutes later, floating just beneath the surface, wedged between two boulders. Chip gave a great gasping gulp and promptly lost the contents of his stomach.

Somehow Kate had hoped, had prayed, that it had all been a dream, but now she knew the nightmare was real. She lowered her head and cried, the tears coming thick and fast, although she had been crying on and off ever since the afternoon before. She was a bottomless well; her sorrow knew no bounds. The thought that she had been responsible for another's death, no matter the provocation, sickened her. Surely there had been some other way to manage? Wilma had been but a pawn, and now she was dead. Dead because of her.

"Come with me now, Kate."

She looked up to find herself sitting in Daniel's long shadow. A quick glance to the side showed her a long, limp form wrapped in a gaily-striped beach towel. Wilma's towel. Wilma. She retched.

Daniel hunkered down in front of her. "Are you going to be sick?" His voice was full of sad concern.

"No," she replied and promptly threw up, turning her head to the side barely in time. He held her forehead with one hand, steadying her, while the other gathered her long hair back behind her neck, holding it out of the way. She could hear Chip nervously pacing back and forth behind them, could feel the little spurts of warm sand he kicked up as he passed by. When her body eased out of its convulsions Daniel let her go, producing a pack of tissues and a roll of hard candy. Peppermint. She took one and word-lessly handed it back to him. He tossed the roll to Chip.

"Better?"

"Yes, thank you." She took his proffered hand and let him help her up. "Am . . . am I under arrest?"

He sighed, shook his dark head. "No. Let's find out what happened here before we do any more talking."

"What do you mean? She told you what happened. It was an accident." Belligerence was back in Chip's voice.

"She needs sleep. She's almost out on her feet. Per-haps she'll remember more after she's rested."

"No!" Kate backed away in horror.

She looked so terrified that the two men momentari-ly forgot their mutual antagonism.

"Calm down," Chip ordered impatiently, "no one's forcing you to do anything."

"You don't have to stay here," Daniel said. "You can come into Puffin Landing. You'll be perfectly safe there."

"Oh, yes. Yes." Her eyes roamed to the towel-draped figure.

Daniel read her mind. "You'll both come in with me. After you're settled I'll come back out with Doc Gully."

"The big fat tuba-playing county coroner. I remem-ber him very well," Chip said. "We had the pleasure of making his acquaintance last month after the other accidental death."

The sheriff shook his head at Chip's less-than-subtle wording. "No one's accusing Kate of anything. Now let's get going."

"You go," Chip said to Kate, "I've already wasted enough time. I'll be in the studio if you want me when you get back, Chief."

"Why you—" Daniel bunched his hands into fists.

"Callous bastard?" Chip supplied helpfully.

"The very words."

"Look, Chief, you've got your job to do and I've got mine. I suggest we both go about our business. I'm sure," he slurred the word, "that you'll see to my wife."

Kate was weeping again, quietly this time. Without another word Daniel took her arm and led her away, turning about to give her husband a last, long look. To his surprise he detected a defensive, sad expression flickering in Chip's hazel eyes. Then the distance between them fuzzed all detail. He turned his attention from the man to his wife.

Kate was still deeply asleep the second time Daniel looked in on her.

"Plumb wore herself out with all that cryin'," Maynard Gully said sagaciously after the sheriff quietly closed the door and urged him away from the room. "Don't you worry none, son. That little lady's gonna sleep until she's healed herself. Best thing in the world for her right now. Then mayhap she'll tell us what all happened out there."

"How about a preliminary report?"

"Like when?" the coroner asked suspiciously.

"Tonight."

"Now, son—" he began, only to have the sheriff cut him off with all the impatience which had been building within him since he had first seen the red pennant waving above Smoke Island.

"Cut the cornball, Doc. I'm no tourist."

"Ayuh." They grinned at each other. The doctor clapped Daniel on the shoulder, almost propelling him into the next county. "Gimme a few, maybe three or four hours. That oughta give me some ideas."

"Thanks." There was real appreciation in his deep voice.

He didn't know how long he had been sitting in the dark, waiting, when he heard her stir. Soft, sniffling sound drew him immediately across the room. She had woken up crying. He cursed when he bumped into a piece of furniture.

"Who's there?" Her voice was thin, tinged with fear.

"It's only me, Kate," he answered, and sat down on the edge of the bed.

"Where am I?"

"Don't you remember?"

"Yes. Now I do." She was in Daniel's house, in his bed. She remembered everything, but in disjointed little pieces, like one of those movies that split the screen and show you many different scenes at once.

"Daniel?"

"What, love?"

"I never meant to harm her. I . . . I just wanted to get away. I've never been so scared. I . . . I didn't care what I had to do to get away. I didn't care," she whispered, as the horror played itself out once again in her mind.

"Hush, love. Don't think about it now."

Kate fell asleep again with the tears still wet on her cheeks. Daniel tenderly wiped them away before returning to the chair where he once again took up his lonely vigil.

CHAPTER TWENTY-FIVE

Kate pulled herself out of her sleep at the urgent insistence of her bladder. The room was dark and shadowy, except for one spot of light, a standing spindle lamp illuminating Daniel, his uniform rumpled, sprawled in a chair, sound asleep in a spine-wrenching position. An open manila folder on his lap tilted at a dangerous angle, threatening to spill its contents should he shift his position ever so slightly. A mug and a plate of cookies were on the round table next to him. It looked as if he had been there for some time.

She turned on the light in the bathroom only after the door was firmly closed behind her. The mirror reflected a pale, hollow-eyed image. She used the toilet and after the barest hesitation stripped off her nightgown and stepped into the shower. Ten minutes later she emerged into the bedroom to find it empty. A lamp next to the bed was on, its glow bathing the room in soft light. The Van Gogh poster smiled down from the wall. The coffee and cookies were gone, replaced by the manila folder.

She tilted her head, listening. The house was quiet with the hush that only comes in the small hours of the morning. It was a safe haven, yet she feared being alone. Barefoot, she went into the hall. It was shadowy dark, the only light coming from the room behind her and from a thin beam streaming out from beneath the closed kitchen door. She went straight to it, hurrying through the dark parts.

Daniel was standing at the stove. When he heard the door open he put down the large wooden spoon he was using to stir a pot and turned around. His dark eyes took in everything, sweeping her from the top of her wet head down to her bare toes, peeping out beneath the hem of her nightgown. "Hello," he said, and smiled.

Kate flung herself at him. He caught her up in a close embrace, his big, hard body absorbing the tremors which wracked her slender frame.

"Easy, love. Easy," he cautioned, and tightened his arms protectively around her when she turned her face into his shoulder and started to cry. He waited patiently for the storm to pass. When she quieted he nuzzled her cheek, kissing the tears away. "You are the soggiest woman I've ever met."

She hiccuped in answer. Then her face crumpled. The tears threatened again. "I've never killed anyone before. What . . . what are you going to do with me?"

"Didn't your mother tell you never to ask a man that question? Especially not at 3 A.M. when you're in dishabille and barefoot to boot." He kissed her nose, then held her away so he could look into her eyes. They held the most wounded, hurt expression he had ever seen. He cupped her chin with one big hand, held her gaze firmly fixed to his so that she could see the truth of what he said. "You haven't killed anybody. No one." She squirmed, but he held her secure in his grasp. "Doc Gully did a preliminary report for me. You did not kill Wilma."

"But—"

"But me no buts, love. We'll talk about it after you eat. Now, blow your nose like a good girl," he produced a tissue and handed it to her, "and sit down at the table. The soup's about ready."

"I'm not hungry," she said, automatically accepting the tissue and jabbing at her eyes.

"We'll see. I've heard that from you before." He studied her face critically. "Wet cheeks, red nose, puffy eyes—and still the most beautiful woman I've ever seen." Her eyes welled up with tears again. "Uh oh." He smiled down at her tenderly. "Do you think you can cry and eat at the same time? I hope so, love, for suddenly I'm starved." His words said one thing, but his eyes spoke of an entirely different matter.

Not at all to his surprise, Kate discovered her appetite. "Ummm, good," she said about the creamy New England clam chowder and buttermilk biscuits. "Did you make it?"

"Nope. I can't take the credit. It's Ethel's. Ethel Gully, Doc's wife. Do you remember her?"

"Should I?"

"No. No reason. She came after you were asleep. Nothing mysterious," he said when she tilted her head questioningly. "She looked after you for me today. I didn't want to leave you alone."

"I wasn't going to run away."

When he saw that she was serious, he sighed. "She

was here simply as a friend, helping a friend, not as a jailor. It wasn't a matter of trust, it was a matter of peace of mind—specifically, mine. You weren't exactly in great shape this morning.''

"I know." She sounded forlorn.

"Feel better now?"

"Yes."

"Good. So do I. I got quite a scare when I saw that red pennant." He tilted his chair back until it teetered perilously on two legs. "I didn't know what to think." The chair crashed loudly back down onto all four legs. Kate jumped involuntarily. "Sorry. More soup? A sandwich? I make a wicked grilled cheese." She shook her head negatively. "Okay. Time to talk, but I think not here. Let's go where we can be comfortable."

He led her into the den and pulled the cushions from the sofa, arranging them on the floor in front of the fireplace. He gently pushed her down onto them and turned his attention to the business of starting a fire. He worked swiftly and efficiently and soon a cheery blaze was licking the wood.

"A moment," he said, and left the room. True to his word, he quickly returned with a steaming mug in each hand. "My famous tea and rum. Remember?"

She accepted the mug and took a sip. "This tastes more like rum and rum. It's so strong it'll probably knock me out."

"Doc Gully says sleep's the best thing for you," he said blandly, and settled himself on the cushions close beside her. "You've had quite a shock. Death is never pretty, especially when it's unexpected."

Kate put the mug down and twisted around to face him. The fire's glow gave her the appearance of rosy

265

good health. "I *did* kill Wilma. No matter what the report says." His expression was noncommittal. "You don't believe me, do you?"

He looked at her thoughtfully, at the wide open black eyes, the stiff posture, the hands tensely clutching the knees of her crossed legs. He ignored the question. "How did it happen? How did Wilma die? Tell me everything. Don't leave anything out, the way you did this morning. It's just the two of us here. You can't shock me," he said matter-of-factly, reading her expressive face. "Now. Start from where I left you yesterday morning and tell me everything you did. Everything. Take your time, love. Remember, I want to know *absolutely* everything."

At some point during her recitation he reached out and enclosed her in his arms, settling her between his legs, her back snugged securely up against his chest. Whether he did it for her, to ease the painful narration, or whether he did it for himself, because his need to hold her close was overpowering, was a moot point. Her voice got stronger, surer, after that, as if the protection of his embrace imbued her with courage.

He had to force himself to show restraint as the tale unfolded, for he wanted nothing more than to roll her under him, to stop the dreadful tale with a deep, healing kiss; at the very least to take the horrible words into his own mouth, to swallow them whole so they never again would sound in the air.

Kate held nothing back, finding release in the cathartic telling. When she finished she bowed her head, only stirring when she felt his lips moving in her hair. She swiveled about and faced him. "Do you believe me now?" she asked, voicing the question yet again.

"I think you believe it," he said slowly, "but the facts just don't support your story." He shifted her around, so they could face each other more comfortably. "Doc Gully says she didn't drown."

"That's impossible. I . . . I held her down. Him down. Iye. Deliberately. I . . . I didn't even think of her. Of Wilma, I mean. It was him. He was jealous. Of you. Us. I only wanted him to stop. He . . . he can do anything he wants to me. I . . . I can't seem to prevent it. Maybe I don't want to stop him," she whispered in a forlorn little voice. A convulsive shudder rocked her slender frame. "Have I shocked you?"

"Oh, love," he said, and kissed her softly on the lips.

Her eyes filled with tears. "Her head hit the . . . the rocks. I . . . I held her. Under the water. Her eyes were staring up at me. Flat. Black. Awful."

"Kate, I seem to remember that Wilma's eyes were green."

"What?"

"Green. Wilma had green eyes, didn't she?"

"Yes. Like emeralds. Shrewd eyes."

"You just said they were black."

"They were. When she was Iye. They . . . uh, changed. After . . . after I killed her." She shuddered and the stinging, hurtful tears overflowed. "Oh God, I'm sorry. I . . . I can't seem to stop."

"You will." Calmly he produced a tissue and mopped her face. "She didn't drown and there was no contusion severe enough to have caused death. She had scrapes and bruises from the rocks, from being in the water, but there was nothing lethal."

Kate stared at him, momentarily forgetting to cry.

"That's impossible!" She narrowed her eyes consideringly. "What does he say killed her?"

"A bee. Or bees. There were several puncture marks. It's, uh, a little difficult to tell just how many. She must have had the same allergic reaction as Natty Bumppo. Doc says we should know for sure when all the tests are concluded."

She was shaking her head vehemently, her long hair swishing silkily over her shoulders. He threaded a hand through it and clasped the back of her head.

"Yes, Kate. The facts are unbendable."

"There was no bee."

"You were upset. With good cause. Accept what I'm telling you. For now, do it because I ask you; later, well, I hope the facts will convince you. Okay?"

"Yes." It was given grudgingly, but she had no choice. "Daniel—"

"What, love?"

"I didn't imagine it."

"No one is saying you did."

"You're thinking it." She lowered her head, unwilling to meet his gaze.

He tugged gently with the hand twined in her hair, forcing her head back up. "I'm thinking how very much I want to make love to you."

"How can you want to? Doesn't it disgust you?"

"I think you'd better explain that." He had a good idea what was tumbling through her brain, but he wanted to discover if she understood it herself. He gave her rigid body a gentle shake. "Doesn't what disgust me?"

Her hands fluttered toward her face, as if to hide it, and then fell limply back down onto her legs. "The dream. It was so real. I was sore when I woke up. It . . . it must have been Wilma . . . Wilma's hand. Oh God," she cried, "a woman, touching me. It's . . . it's . . ."

"Hush, love. Hush." He soothed her with meaningless murmurs, with calming strokes down the long, gleaming hair.

"Don't you see? Even if I thought I was stopping Iye, it was really Wilma. It was her body. I couldn't separate her from what was happening."

"You're afraid that you wanted to kill Wilma. Because she touched you intimately. Isn't that right?"

"Yes. Yes, yes, yes," she sobbed.

"But you didn't kill her." He put a finger on her lips, prevented her from interrupting. "You struggled with her. You were upset. Shocked. Confused. You never noticed the bees. It was all over very fast, Doc said. Listen to me, Kate. You did not kill Wilma."

He tightened his arms about her and sank down until they were lying full length on the cushions. He held her, rocking her slightly, until he felt some of the tension seep out of her body. The fire hissed and crackled, spreading its warming light like a blanket over them. He propped himself up on an elbow and smiled down at her, speaking to her wordlessly.

Kate softened under the infinitely tender, loving gaze. Despite everything he still desired her.

"You're so very beautiful." The deep voice was husky, intimate. "I want you. Let me make love to you, Kate, my love."

She heard and understood that it was the truth. When he bent his dark head and started to nibble on her lips she gave a soft little welcoming cry, and when his mouth took hers in a kiss at first slow and then increasingly demanding, she forgot all her self-imposed strictures and relaxed into the joyful world of pure sensation. Her lips tingled, burned hot under the ardent assault. He demanded nothing more from her than that she take from him.

He kissed her for long, slow minutes, his tongue sweeping her lips, searching for a relaxation, an invitation to venture inside. He took advantage of the smallest of sighs, introducing his tongue into the hot moist cavern, sliding it past her lips with her indrawn breath. She let him rove at will, his play against her teeth, around the mysterious, sensitive walls of her mouth going unanswered, until she met one thrust with one of her own. He groaned and pulled her closer still.

It was impossible for her to remain impassive. The confusion and the terror receded, chased to the back of her mind by the stimulating duel of their tongues. When he finally dragged his lips from hers she was shivering.

"Kate, my beautiful Kate," he whispered.

She shivered even more when his tongue probed the intricate whorls of her ear. She moved closer to him, instinctively seeking the reassurance of his rock-hard body. She was like a little furry animal, wordlessly communicating her trust in him.

He understood the silent language of her body. "Ah, Kate, love," he groaned, and rolled her onto her back.

She lay quietly looking up at him, her great dark eyes fixed trustingly on his face. The look almost undid him.

"You are safe, Kate, nothing is going to harm you. Nothing. It's all over. All over, love. For both of us."

His voice held a slight tremor when he spoke again. "You can't know how I felt, what awful thoughts went through my head when I saw that damn red flag. Oh God, if anything had happened to you . . ." He bent and kissed the corners of her lips. "You're safe. Safe from everything and everyone. Do you hear me?"

He had to be satisfied with a nod, for Kate was struggling for composure, a great lump in her throat preventing speech. Slowly he caressed the slender column of her neck, the long, sensitive fingers relaxing the tightness as they stroked. His eyes held her, speaking directly, silently, of his desire. As she gradually relaxed under the almost hypnotic cadence of his touch he grew more bold. His hand drifted, brushed her collarbone, investigated the rounded neckline of her nightgown. "My beautiful Kate," he sighed, "I want you so." With infinite lovingness he placed his hand on her breast.

Kate stiffened and turned her head to one side. "I'm sorry. I . . . I can't." Her eyes were clamped tightly shut; all she could see was Wilma, leering at her, ogling her naked breasts.

"Look at me." The hand left her breast and moved to her chin, forcing it around. "Open your eyes and look at me, love. I won't force you to do anything you don't want to do." He placed his hand under hers. "Take my hand. Go ahead, take it," he urged.

"Why?"

"Because you want me," he said simply, "and this will make it easier for you."

Her hand curled around his. "Tell me what to do."

"Just move my hand. Show me where you want me

271

to touch you. Remember, you control it. Let me touch you. Move my hand, love.''

"Unfair," Kate groaned.

His head came down and captured her mouth in a deep, drugging kiss. Despite her fears she responded to him, her body knowing who played it, even if her mind yet did not. Very soon the kiss was not enough. She moved his hand up her body, slowly, gliding it over her hip, into the dip of her waist, adjusting to the knowledge of a male hand on her flesh. Daniel, it's Daniel, she told herself, and placed his hand on the underside of her breast.

She could feel the tension in his body and felt shame. He was so patient, so understanding; he deserved better from her. But the memories would not go away. Although the room was shadowed, with the low-burning fire the only source of light, she could still feel the heat of the blazing sun; Iye the Shapechanger, possessed of Wilma's body, wanted her. She felt unclean.

"Help me," she moaned.

"What do you want, love?"

"I want it to be two nights ago," she said sadly.

"I can make you feel like that again. Trust me, Kate."

For answer she moved his hand fully onto her breast. He kissed her deeply while he kneaded the soft flesh, her hand still holding his. Her heated skin pushed achingly against the thin cotton of her nightgown. She urged him to the other breast, her body slowly overriding her mind. The tempo of her breathing quickened, and with a sharply indrawn breath she arched upward, offering herself to him.

As his mouth closed over her breast his hand sought

272

the hem of her gown, pushing it up until her legs and hips were bare, bathed in the red-gold glow of the flames. He raised his head and studied her, marveling at the contrast of his deeply bronzed skin against her paler flesh.

"Let's get rid of this," he said, and swiftly stripped the gown over her head.

Kate closed her eyes and waited for the inevitable. His reaction was swift, a sharply indrawn breath which hissed out explosively into the night quiet.

"What happened here?" he demanded, and she knew without raising her lids where his gaze rested.

"It happened in the struggle," she said quietly. "I told you."

The rage which gripped him was fast and furious. He could not tear his gaze from her lacerated breasts. The scratches and abrasions were not deep, but each one was like a slash through his heart.

"God damn her. God damn her to hell."

It was Kate's turn to soothe. "It's all right. Truly it is. It will heal and the marks will fade." There was an atavistic gleam in his eyes. Suddenly she was afraid. "Daniel?"

The tentative, pleading note helped him to curb the primitive wildness which was flooding him, the insane urge to retaliate for the injury done. He wished to inflict like pain as punishment.

"Daniel, please."

The soft plea entered his chaotic thoughts. Wilma was dead. There would be, could be, no vengeance. Slowly his mind cleared, let go of the savage thoughts. "Love," he breathed, "I'll erase her from your mind. I'm going to touch you. All over." Not waiting for an answer, needing the symbolic act as much for himself as for her, he turned her over onto her stomach and lightly glided his lips and hands over every inch of her.

It worked like a charm, a potent healing for both of them. With every silken caress he obliterated the memory of an alien touch, expunging it methodically, replacing it with a quivering arousal. By the time he turned her to face him she was moaning her desire. He worked his way down her body, his tongue following the path of his fingers, imprinting himself deep into her consciousness, continuing until nothing was left untouched. He knelt at her feet and studied the slim body. There was still one thing to do, one place he must make whole.

Kate gasped as she felt him part her thighs. "No," she said weakly, and struggled up onto her elbows.

He ignored her feeble protest and slid his hands up the inside of her legs. His dark eyes held hers as he slipped his hands beneath her, firmly grasped her buttocks and raised her hips. Then he lowered his head.

Kate surrendered to the passion he had awakened in her. Her body was aflame, burning with a bright, shining awareness. Desire inflamed her senses, obliterating everything else, everything that had come before. All she knew was she wanted him, this man who was miraculously making her whole. As he elicited sensations she had not even dreamed existed, she reached down and tangled her fingers in his hair, pressing him ever closer to her, telling him by the urgent demand how very much she needed him. It was torture, this loving; it was unbearable; she feared it would end.

Her world was swirling color; it was sound; it was light. Her hips danced; he held her, moving to her rhythm. A hot kernel of molten desire tightened in her belly, drawing her essence into its knot. She screamed as it burst, shattering her, fragmenting the Kate she was into a new being, a Kate forged in the flames of love.

He took her in his arms, held her tightly as she reformed herself from the scattered fragments of her being. His lips took hers, and regaining some semblance of sanity, she plucked at his clothing, her fingers fumbling awkwardly with the buttons.

"I want you in me," she said, her voice husky, hoarse with the need to give him such pleasure as he had given to her.

He kissed her again and with the grace of a large, dark cat, rose to his feet. She held up her arms and he bent down, scooping her up in one sweeping, easy motion. His lips captured hers in a wild, demanding kiss, and then he was striding out of the light into the darkness, down the long hall into his bedroom, where he lowered her to the bed. Perched on the edge she watched him through passion-hazed eyes as he quickly shed his clothes and came to stand before her, magnificent in arousal.

Without a word she leaned back on her elbows and slowly, tantalizingly, opened herself to him. She was offering herself to him in the most elemental way possible. He grew more aroused, just looking at her; at her elegant, supple body; at her small, firm breasts.

He wanted to tell her how beautiful she was, but words need air to sound, and she had stolen his breath away. He put his hands on her legs and raised them until they were on a level with his waist. She understood what he wanted and wrapped them tightly about him, enclosing him in the loving circle of her body. He could wait no longer. With one lithe movement he leaned forward and covered her mouth with his, his tongue thrusting boldly inside the dark cavern as his hips surged forward and he plunged deeply into her. That one, sure stroke brought him to a blinding, shuddering completion.

He felt her smile against his lips, a female affirmation of power as old as time. He took the smile and shaped it to his lips, kissing her with a deep intensity, trying desperately to satisfy his consuming hunger for her.

Kate moved her hips, delicately, exploringly. "Love me again," she demanded.

His laughter flowed over them. Withdrawing from her he moved her more fully onto the bed, coming immediately to stretch his long length beside her. "Your wish is my desire, my love," he said, and gladly proceeded to do her bidding. He loved her slowly, thoroughly, savoring each precious moment, for he knew the night was magical, out of the stream of time.

CHAPTER TWENTY-SIX

The insistent ringing of the telephone along with the pealing of the front doorbell pulled Kate out of a deep sleep.

"Damn," Daniel mumbled, and then favored Kate with an angelic smile. "Morning, love. How's my girl?"

Kate rolled over.

"Not a morning person, I see. I'll make a note. Sorry, it's on your side," he apologized, lunging over her and groping for the telephone, which he kept on the floor under the bed. "This better be important," he growled into the receiver.

The voice on the other end was shrill and perfectly audible to Kate. It demanded to know what the sheriff was doing to protect the good citizens of Puffin Landing, one Mildred Sparrow in particular, from the Curse of Smoke Island. That the lady spoke in capitals was perfectly obvious to Kate, who was unashamedly eavesdropping. Daniel gave the standard stonewall of officialdom: everything-is-under-control-no-cause-for-alarm-thank-you-for-calling routine.

He replaced the receiver and grinned. "That was Mildred Sparrow. She's usually the first. Beats the other two by at least ten minutes, every time. I'd better get the door. Whoever it is doesn't sound like a quitter," he grumbled as he threw the covers back and got out of bed.

"What other two? Daniel! You can't answer the door like that." To her surprise she blushed a fiery red.

He grinned a wide, wolfish, devil's grin. "Right. I just wanted to see if you were watching. Don't move, I'll be right back." He retrieved his pants from the floor and was into them and out the door after treating her to a broad wink.

Kate strained to hear what was happening, but could only hear the door opening and then closing again, decisively, the sound echoing through the house. The phone rang. She automatically reached for it.

"I think I'd better answer that."

She snatched her hand back, as if from something with very sharp teeth. Something venomous. He kissed her bare shoulder and whispered in her ear. "Rosemary Gillespie, right on schedule."

It was a rerun of the conversation with Mildred Sparrow. "That's two," he said when the receiver was once again cradled, "only Jane Porter to go."

Kate hitched herself up against the brass headboard, the comforter snugged securely under her arms. "Is it always like this? Who was at the door?"

"No to the first, a reporter, sleazy variety, from some national rag, to the second. He won't be back. At least not soon," he amended judiciously.

"It's because of me, isn't it?"

"It's because people have long memories. It's also because they're titillated by the proximity to something out of the ordinary. Bizarre. It's very exciting, as long as it doesn't touch you." He glanced at the clock, held up a finger in anticipation. "Any moment now. Jane Porter," he said, and smiled smugly when the telephone rang on cue. She received the same treatment as her predecessors. When he finished the call he lifted the receiver off the hook. "That's enough of that. The others'll have to wait until I'm in the office."

He leaned over and took Kate in his arms, bestowing a very thorough kiss upon her. "Mmmmn. Nice. Any dreams? Since you've been here, I mean."

She looked startled for a moment, confused by the rapid change of subject, then slowly shook her head. "No."

"Good." He kissed her again, lingeringly. When he pulled away there was a mischievous gleam in his dark eyes. "The way I see it, love, you have three choices now. You can shower first, or I can shower first, or we can shower together." He kissed her neck invitingly. "I vote for the third option," he volunteered.

"There's a fourth choice," Kate said, struggling to keep a quaver out of her voice. The mere touch of his lips to her skin sent waves of longing through her. It was a heady feeling, one she had not experienced before. She smiled saucily. "I could go back to sleep, now that you've disabled the telephone. Who are the Misses Sparrow, Gillespie and Porter?"

"The Three Fates. Don't think you can change the subject." He nibbled on her earlobe. "If you choose to stay in bed I can guarantee it won't be to sleep."

279

She shuddered, the bold statement sending a frisson of anticipation skittering down her spine.

Sensitive to her slightest move, he raised his eyes to her face. "What's the matter, love? Are you too sore?"

Kate turned her face away to hide the hot color which flooded her cheeks. She was acting like a silly, inexperienced, recently deflowered virgin, when what she really wanted to do was to fling back the covers and drag his body onto hers.

Daniel regarded the delicate stain of color suffusing the slender column of her neck with great interest. She was a delight; fiery passion at night, shy demureness with the light of day.

Kate proved him wrong almost immediately he had the thought. "I'm a bit sore," she said, biting her lip consideringly, "but, I think I'm about to get a lot sorer." She took his face in both her hands and brought him down to her lips, her kiss telling him explicitly of her desire.

Daniel whispered into her mouth. "Which shall it be, love, the bed or the bath?"

"Both," she answered, sliding down and pulling him onto her eager body.

"What happens today?" They were finishing breakfast, blueberry pancakes and sausage for Daniel, coffee for Kate.

"I go to work and you stay here, probably to waste away from malnutrition by midmorning." Daniel looked at Kate and shook his head. "Seriously, I want you to keep a low profile. At least until Doc Gully gives me the final report."

"So you do have your doubts about how Wilma died."

"That's not it," he said sharply. "Some of the people here are very superstitious. The Sparrow-Gillespie-Porter trio is just one small example. The ladies are harmless, but others are not."

"What do you mean by that?" she asked in a small voice.

Daniel sighed. "Think, Kate, you haven't led a sheltered life. That reporter on the doorstep before sunup is just one example of the hell life can become for you if you're not careful. Once those creatures smell blood they never give up. Look," he said, moderating his voice, "Smoke Island isn't popular. The decision to open it again after all these years met with a good deal of grumbling, but there was nothing anyone could do to stop it. The people around here have very long memories. There were some accidents. There are those who say that things happen only when there are people on the island."

"Maybe they're right."

He tilted his head back disbelievingly.

"No, listen to me, Daniel. Maybe there's truth in their fears. You know," she said thoughtfully, "I'm not the only one who felt something. Paul and Melinda did, too. Something happened the night we all had dinner in town and Wilma was alone on the island with them. They never could say exactly what it was, but Melly did say something strange. Something about together, if they were together, touching, he wasn't strong enough." She hunched forward, her body tense with excitement. "You know, she must have meant

281

lye. Oh, don't you see, I'm not the only one who knows he's there.''

He hated to debunk her argument, especially since it had put some sparkle back in her eyes. ''They're city kids. It's easy to imagine all sorts of things in an unfamiliar setting.''

''Does that apply to me also?'' she asked stiffly.

He raked a hand through his hair. ''Damnit. I'm not going to sit here and argue with you.'' He leaned toward her and brushed her cheek with the back of his knuckles. ''Kate, beautiful Kate, just trust me that it's better for you not to be seen in town today. For your sake, love, that's all. I swear.''

''Okay. But Daniel—'' She stopped and stared off into space for long moments.

He remained silent, watching her. The risen sun was a warm swath of pale yellow across the table. The brightness of its illumination contrasted sharply with the shadowed parts, making them appear faded, like sepia photographs in an old album.

''I know what I saw. Wilma was possessed. You can't make me believe otherwise.''

He was gallant enough to let her have the last word. After he left she tried to read, choosing a mystery from one of the piles in the den, but the frequent references to death and dying made her think of Wilma. The television held her interest for even less time. At first it was a novelty, after three months without it, but the game shows and soap operas seemed juvenile.

Daniel called twice, the first time just to say hello, the second time to tell her that he would be able to get away for lunch.

He took her to a roadside restaurant several miles

from Puffin Landing. It was crowded with vacationers and the odd long-haul trucker. The menu was all cute Colonial, with verbose descriptions of each item.

"The food is good, despite appearances," he said.

Kate picked at her tuna-stuffed tomato with little appetite. Daniel wolfed down a cheeseburger deluxe and then tucked into hot apple pie with a thick wedge of cheddar cheese on top.

"You eat like a crabby kid," he said conversationally.

Kate sipped iced tea and pointed an accusing finger at his dessert. "You, sir, eat like calories don't exist."

"I know all the waitresses here. They take 'em out in the kitchen."

"I just bet you do," Kate said. She had noticed the admiring looks thrown his way.

He winked and the last piece of pie disappeared. "That was good." He pushed the empty plate away and became the sheriff. "I released Wilma's body this morning."

It took several moments for her to realize what he said. She leaned forward, her shoulders hunched, her body tense. "Then you have a final report?"

"Doc's satisfied the cause of death was bee venom."

There was a silence while Kate digested the information. "I see," she said quietly.

He thought she would argue the findings. "He's good, Kate. Doc Gully's been coroner for a long time."

"Will you take me back to Smoke Island today?" she asked, surprising him with the question.

It was his turn for silence. He reached across the table to capture her hand. It felt cold. "Why? Are you going back to Chip?" Her hand jumped in his; he clasped it more firmly. "I won't let you go easily. I'm more than prepared to fight for you."

She lowered her head, but not before he glimpsed the sadness in her eyes.

"I mean what I say."

She tugged her hand free and slipped out of the booth. "I'll meet you outside."

Daniel stared after her retreating figure with pain-filled eyes.

"How're we doin'?"

"Just fine. Check, please," he said, not even looking at the waitress.

She was leaning against the car when he emerged from the restaurant. He was relieved, since part of him had feared she would fly, leaving him alone with misery and only the memory of a bright shining love. He took a deep breath and mentally told himself not to be a fool, not to push her too fast. She straightened when his shadow touched her.

"I'll take you anywhere you want to go," he said simply.

The island was the same; yet it was not. Kate thought maybe it was her. Eve changed by the apple; knowledge was bitter fruit.

"He's probably at the studio," she said when the house proved empty.

"C'mon, let's go." He got no argument. It was obvious she did not want to be alone.

They crossed the island in silence; he was talking to her without using words, telling her how much he wanted her, how much he needed her, letting his dark eyes plead his case. As the studio came into view he slowed his steps, then stopped altogether when they were still a short distance away.

"I'll wait here to make sure you're all right. Go on. I'll be back for you in a little while."

"Where are you going?" Her voice was high and thin.

She looked very vulnerable with her eyes large and round and fixed on him with a suspicious brightness. "To the flagpole. I've got those flares Chip requested. I also thought I'd pile some wood for a signal bonfire." He reached into his pocket and handed her a tissue. "Here. I don't expect you've got one. I'll be back soon." He gave her an encouraging nod.

Kate turned once, at the door. He was standing under a tall evergreen. It could have been Great Bear standing there; only the clothes were different. She blinked and shook her head. Less than an hour on the island and fantasy again seemed real.

"Chip," she called, and quickly went inside when he answered.

The studio was flooded with clear northern light. It was an untidy mess except for the space around the easel. Chip carefully placed his palette and the brush he was using on a cluttered table.

"Hello, Kate, I'm glad you're here." He came to meet her, kissing her lightly on the lips in greeting. "Come and see what I've done so far." He led her to the huge canvas and stepped aside to let her have an unobstructed view.

She had expected surliness, perhaps outright hostility. Nonplussed by his mildness, by his apparent hap-

285

piness to see her, she blurted out the reason she had come. "We've got to talk."

"What do you think of it?"

"About Wilma, Chip."

"What about her?"

Kate relaxed when she heard the testiness creep into his voice. This was a Chip she recognized. "Her funeral."

It was a short, brutal statement. Chip's shoulders slumped. "What about it?"

"It's tomorrow. Her brother made all the arrangements. We should be there."

"I can't leave now. Good God, Kate, just look in front of you. See what I've done. How can you even ask me to go?"

Kate actually saw red. "Are you truly this selfish? Answer me. I don't recognize you anymore."

"Kate. I can't . . ." He reached a hand toward her, palm up, then dropped it to his side when she made no move to take it.

"I'm going now. To New York."

He said nothing, made no move to stop her.

Outside she leaned against the wall while she tried to regain control of her emotions.

"Kate."

Chip was standing in the doorway. He thrust his hands into his paint-speckled pockets and leaned against the doorjamb. It was quiet, except for the usual island noises: the sough of the wind through the trees; the cries of the gulls overhead; the buzzing of a bee in a clump of purple wildflowers.

"What is it?" Her voice was leaden, leeched of all expression.

"I never meant for this to happen. Any of it." He kicked the doorjamb, looked at the sky, the trees, the room behind him before looking again at her. "Even the thing with Wilma."

Puzzled, Kate stared at him. Surely he could not mean her death.

Chip fidgeted, started to reach for her again, then apparently thought better of it. "It just happened, you know. One of those things. It didn't mean anything."

At last Kate understood what he was confessing. "Oh no," she whispered, "she had both of us." Then, as the true horror of it penetrated her mind, she started to laugh.

"Stop it, you're hysterical."

Kate sobered at once. "No, I'm not, but I'm beginning to wish I were. It would be easier."

When Daniel returned he found her alone, tears running down her cheeks.

CHAPTER TWENTY-SEVEN

New York was hot and humid, filled with the unlovely odors of an urban summer. Their small apartment, on a less-than-romantic street in fabled Greenwich Village, was stifling. The phone rang before she had secured the three locks on the front door.

"Hello," she said, breathless.

"Kate! I've been calling every hour since I heard. Where have you been? The funeral's tomorrow." Anita's excited voice exploded into her ear.

"Hold it a second. I just got in and the apartment's unbearable." She turned on the air-conditioner and reluctantly returned to the telephone. Life had been simpler without it. "Hi, I'm back," she said, producing a cheery voice for her sister-in-law.

"Where's Chip? You said 'I.' " Trust Anita to zero in on the one word that interested her.

Kate launched into the explanation she had formulated during the plane ride. She had not wanted to test it so soon. Anita listened in silence; a bad omen. Kate's voice dwindled, came to a stop. There was a sniff from Anita. In the background Kate could hear Gus yelling at one of the kids.

"How are the kids?" she asked brightly, shamelessly stabbing at maternal pride to avert an unwelcome discussion. It failed.

"Cut the crap, Kate. We'll wait dinner for you."

"Anita—"

"Call a cab," she said and hung up.

"Terrific," Kate told the dead receiver.

One hour and thirty-seven minutes later she was sitting in the Barths' living room on the upper West Side, a vodka and tonic in hand. Her long hair was still damp from the shower she had treated herself to before answering Anita's less-than-gracious invitation.

"You're looking well," her brother-in-law said conversationally into the little well of silence that descended after the bustle of first greetings was over.

Anita gave him a scornful look. "She looks terrible."

"Thank you both." Kate took a long swallow and leaned back into the cushions. Anita looked militant. Kate was too tired, too wrung out emotionally, to be polite. "How did you hear about it?"

"It was on television!" Melinda squealed excitedly.

"There was a picture of Uncle Chip," Paul contributed. Kate groaned and her nephew looked at her curiously. "It was the picture you like, Aunt Kate. The one where he's wearing the striped tie."

Chip's press photo. Kate remembered the day he went to have it taken, how many different ties they had tried until finally choosing the burgundy and navy

289

stripe. "Serious young artist dedicated to his craft," Kate had teased, holding out a muted red and blue paisley.

"Needy young artist seeking rich patron." Chip had grinned, and caught her in a tight embrace. "Stripes are for up-and-comers, hon, paisleys are for established fat cat types."

The memory hurt.

Kate resurfaced in the green and white living room to find four faces staring at her. "I'm . . . I'm sorry. I must have been daydreaming."

"You've been through a rough experience."

Kate smiled at Gus, grateful for his steadying presence. "It's been a rough summer all around."

Anita's sensitive antennae picked up the nuance in her voice. She shooed the children into the den to eat their dinner in front of the television set before Kate could make a protest, then adeptly maneuvered Gus and Kate into the dining room. She had the entire story from Kate before they reached dessert.

"*Wilma?* That's incredible!" Anita's hazel eyes grew round. "Did you get the impression she swung both ways?" she demanded of her husband.

Kate interjected before Gus had a chance to answer. "How are you so sure she wasn't just oriented toward women?"

Anita's eyes slid over her, fixed intently on the wilting lettuce surrounding the remains of the seafood salad.

Awareness flooded Kate, tensing her body instantly. "You knew."

Anita shrugged. "I did try to warn you."

"You told me to have a baby, for crying out loud. Some warning." Gus was looking bewilderedly from one to the other. Kate leaned toward him. "Don't feel too bad about being confused. I didn't know myself until yesterday that Wilma and Chip were having an affair. Not until he told me. It was nothing personal, he said. It was all done for art's sake."

"Uh. Maybe I'd better leave you two alone."

"No, don't go, Gus. I'm not going to make a scene."

"Kate—" Anita began defensively.

"I mean it, Anita. All that doesn't much matter anymore. No," she held up a hand to forestall her sister-in-law from breaking into speech, "I'm not going to discuss it. Not now."

"All right, Kate. Whatever you say." Gus sent his wife a significant look.

"Wilma wasn't interested in women; most especially not in me. I think I would have had some hint if that had been the case."

"What are you saying?" Gus asked.

"She was possessed."

"Be serious," Anita snorted, sounding exactly like her brother.

"I am," Kate said quietly. "It wasn't Wilma who wanted me. It was Iye, the one called the Shape-changer." Anita looked blank. Kate explained, careful to keep her tone even. "Iye was the shaman who was left on the island. As punishment. The . . . the sheriff told us about him. Remember?"

Anita shrugged, looked uncomfortable. "It was a story. Something to amuse the kids."

"No, it's more than that," Kate said doggedly. "It actually happened, and now it's legend. Please, you've got to believe me. Iye used Wilma. I'm positive that's what it was. Not the other thing." She turned to Gus. "You remember how the kids acted the week you were on the island. Ask them why. What they felt. I'm willing to bet the Shapechanger tried to get to them. Remember the night they were with Wilma?"

"No!" It was almost a shriek. "I mean, I don't want them questioned." Anita looked at her husband pleadingly. "Gus?"

He patted her hand. "Relax."

"I don't want them to know about this, 'er, lesbian thing." A look passed between husband and wife.

"She wasn't a lesbian," Kate said stubbornly.

"You just don't want her to be one, that's all," Anita said. "The other thing is just too crazy."

"Maybe you're right," Kate said, recognizing that Anita needed her capitulation more than she herself needed her support.

Back downtown in the quiet apartment Kate realized how very alone she was. If Anita and Gus did not believe her, would not even discuss it, then no one would. Only the fringe loonies, the people who called late night radio shows with reports of aliens landing in their backyards would show a keen interest in the story. They would just love it.

The ringing of the telephone intruded into the bitter thought.

"I miss you."

Kate sucked in her breath in an attempt to keep from crying.

"Go ahead. Cry. I can afford it. Rates are cheaper at this hour," Daniel said. He waited and his reward moments later was a loud sniff. "That's it? You can do better."

The lightly teasing tone helped her to pull herself together. "I'm glad you called," she said in a voice which only quavered slightly. "I could use some support."

He was quick to guess the reason. "Anita?"

"She thinks I'm crazy."

"No she doesn't," he said sharply. "I would imagine you just shocked her, if you told her about Wilma's . . . ah, assault."

A short silence ensued, during which only the sounds of their breathing and the small mechanical clicks and whirs of the open line between Maine and New York was audible. When Kate finally spoke it was in a very small, contained voice. "Maybe I am, Daniel."

"Don't do this to yourself, love." His sigh reached down through the miles, evoking his frustration at not being able to take her in his arms, if necessary to shake her until the dark thought was expunged.

She ignored the tender remonstration. "It's the one explanation that fits, isn't it? If you're crazy nobody thinks it the least bit odd if you spout impossible theories. It's what Anita thinks, I'm sure. Oh God, can you imagine what she'd say if she knew about the dreams?" she asked, her voice rising precipitously.

"Stop it, Kate! There's nothing wrong with you. You've had a stressful summer. It's natural for you to protect yourself." He paused, softened his voice so that she had to press the receiver close to her ear to hear him. "God knows I haven't helped. The last thing you needed was the kind of pressure I've exerted."

It was her turn to reassure him. Her sense of humor pushed through, lightening her tone. "I don't know about that, Daniel," she said roguishly. "Some of the pressure you've applied has been, um, most delightful."

A warm chuckle traveled the line. "That's my girl," he said approvingly.

His loving concern sustained her through the long night. But as the bright hot sun rose, slanting aggressively through the cracks in the blinds, all trace of well-being fled. Only one emotion remained. It was with dread that Kate got up to face the day.

The small cemetery in Queens was very old, some tombstones dating back over two hundred years. The grass looked like hay, sere and brown. It was tough underfoot. The mourners clustered around the grave, incongruously green, the gaping hole concealed under a temporary mantle of artificial grass.

Kate kept to the back of the crowd after noticing several people with cameras. Press coverage of so private a ceremony, the idea of grief served up for public consumption, was abhorrent to her. She said as much to Anita, who had insisted on accompanying her.

"Wilma would have loved it. I keep expecting her to pop up and start directing things." Kate's slender form jerked at the harsh words. Anita shrugged unapologetically. "Wilma was the epitome of brashness. That's the way she was, there's no use glossing over it just because she's dead."

Kate turned slightly away as one of the camera-toting people stared curiously in her direction. Anita was right, but it was still an offensive thought. It was over eighty degrees and the air was visibly unhealthy with a grayish-yellowish haze obscuring the sun. She felt queasy and disoriented. Everything seemed unreal, dreamlike. Wilma was not dead, lying coiffed and painted and beautifully gowned in a highly varnished mahogany box. Wilma was not having an affair with Chip. Wilma was not a lesbian.

The graveside service was mercifully short. Kate heaved a sigh of relief and was about to urge Anita to leave when a soberly dressed young man approached.

"Mrs. Windsor? I thought I recognized you. I'm Pete. Peter Warren. Wilma's brother." He took her hand, the one holding a clumped tissue, and squeezed it. "I heard from the sheriff up in Maine that you were there when my sister died."

"I, 'er—" Anita shifted her weight from one foot to the other, making Kate conscious of her presence. "I . . . I—"

"That's all right. I understand." Peter Warren bobbed his head, dropped her hand. He was at least five years younger than Wilma, and the only resemblance between them was his green eyes and a certain way he angled his chin when he talked. "I just wanted to tell you how grateful I am that . . . that she wasn't alone, that there was a friend with her when she . . . when she died." His voice cracked. He tugged self-consciously at his collar.

Wilma was dead. She had an affair with Chip. She had not been a lesbian.

A petite brunette came and linked her arm through Peter Warren's. "My wife, Linda," he said, and the small woman smiled politely.

Linda Warren looked fragile and old-fashionedly

feminine, with tendrils of dark hair wisping damply about her forehead and neck, where they had escaped from the twisted bun piled high on her head. Her dress was white cotton, demurely appropriate mourning for a summer funeral. Kate wondered how she and Wilma had gotten along.

With distaste written plainly on her face, Linda Warren looked around at the milling people. "Did Wilma cook up this curse thing? It would have been just like her. She'd do anything to get publicity for your husband."

Kate stared. The prim little wife was able to take care of herself. Someone called Kate's name before she could think of a reply. A flashbulb went off in her face. Quickly she turned away.

"Hey! One more, Mrs. Windsor. Look over here."

Someone thrust a tape recorder in front of her. "Where's your husband, Kate? Shouldn't he be here?"

A second reporter jostled the first one for space. His foot scraped along a gravestone. He seemed not to notice. "Is he afraid?"

"Afraid?" The pushing, shoving reporters were closing her in, leeching away the thick air. She had to strain to breathe; she felt faint.

The reporter was short and overweight. He was perspiring heavily. "Afraid," he repeated.

"My husband is working very hard. Wilma . . . Wilma would have understood why . . . why he isn't here." The reporter faithfully recorded her stumbling statement in his notebook. Over his bent head Kate caught Linda Warren's cynical gaze.

The reporter raised his head, persisted in his questioning. "But is he afraid? Are you? Look," he said, and held up a pudgy hand, started counting on his fingers. "People die on that island. In 1932 it was Lothar Voss, his son—"

Kate stiffened. "His son?"

The reporters sensed something. They crowded closer. The first one spoke. "Yeah. The kid was struck by lightning."

"Oh no," Kate moaned. Another flashbulb went off in her face.

Anita grabbed her arm, started to edge her away. "We're leaving," she said tartly.

Safely in the car, insulated by the tinted glass from the reporters and Linda Warren, Kate swiveled about so that she was facing Anita. "You heard," she said, "it couldn't be coincidence."

"Accidents happen," Anita returned prosaically.

"The same one? Over and over again?"

"Let's get out of here." Anita switched on the engine. "Those reporters look like they're coming for you again. How about lunch?" she asked as she steered them through the cemetery gates.

Wilma and Natty Bumppo dead of bee venom. Two boys dead of lightning. So what if the deaths were separated by more than fifty years. Who else? How?

"There's a new restaurant near Lincoln Center. Salad and quiche. All right?"

"What?"

Anita braked for a red light. "Do you want to try it? It's too hot to eat anything heavy."

"How did Lothar Voss die?"

"Damn," Anita swore as the light changed and the driver behind her leaned on the horn.

"Do you know how Lothar Voss died?" Kate asked again when she gained Anita's attention.

"No. Why should I?" Anita responded. "It's ancient history. Come on, Kate. Forget about it. Let's go have a nice long lunch. You'll feel better after you eat."

They stopped for another light. Kate stared out the window. A traffic sign caught her eye. She narrowed her eyes, an idea taking shape in her brain. "Could you drop me at the airport?"

"La Guardia or Kennedy?" Anita blurted out, startled by the question.

Kate pointed to the sign. "La Guardia."

"You're going back to Chip." Anita heaved what could only be described as a textbook sigh of relief.

Kate saw no reason to disabuse her of the mistaken assumption. It was a natural thought coming from Chip's sister. Before long she stepped out into sticky wet heat in front of the departure terminal. Anita stayed in front of the building, despite the warning signs to move on. At the entrance doors Kate yielded to impulse and returned to the car, motioning for Anita to roll the window down. She stuck her head inside the coolness and looked squarely into hazel eyes. Chip's eyes.

"I'm not crazy," she said, then quickly withdrew, leaving her sister-in-law to stare after her.

Inside the terminal Kate hurried to the nearest car rental counter. Twenty minutes later she was headed for the Throgs Neck Bridge and Connecticut. Margaret Voss lived in Connecticut; that had been the return address on the proper little note Chip had received congratulating him on winning the Voss Grant.

Kate put her foot down on the accelerator. Suddenly it was very important to find out how Lothar Voss died.

CHAPTER TWENTY-EIGHT

Kate took Interstate 95 to Route 7 where she headed north, following the map she got at the car rental agency. On the outskirts of Danbury she stopped at a small mall to stretch her legs. The air was no better than New York's soupy mix. Within seconds after leaving the car her skirt and blouse, so cool and elegant looking when she had put them on in the morning, were clinging damply to the small of her back.

"Wonderful," she mumbled under her breath, and headed for the telephone booth she had spied from the road.

For once all the telephone books were still attached. She found the listing she was looking for under "Voss, M.," and scribbled the address on the map, then folded it neatly and placed it in her purse. Despite her desire to see Margaret Voss as soon as possible, she forced herself to have a cup of coffee and a donut. She was back on the road in ten minutes.

Traffic thinned out as she traveled north over gently

rolling hills, past small towns and villages that appeared little changed during the two hundred years of their incorporation. Relieved of the need to concentrate on her driving to the exclusion of all else, Kate tried to organize her thoughts. Now that she knew Margaret and Lothar had lost a son, by lightning—surely not a coincidence—she suspected that other, less tangible similarities existed between the two summers. It was no longer just the question of how Lothar had died. Margaret possessed knowledge; she must be persuaded to share it.

The widow of Lothar Voss lived in a charming 18th century farmhouse just south of Cornwall. A thin woman with wispy blue-tinted white hair opened the door. Her expression when she saw Kate, rumpled and travel worn, was less than inviting.

"I'm sorry to barge in on you like this," Kate apologized, "but I must talk to you. I'm Kate Windsor. Mrs. Charles Windsor." The woman continued to scrutinize her closely, making Kate even more aware of her disheveled state. "It's very important, Mrs. Voss. Please, may I come in?"

The woman moved back and held the door open. Relieved, Kate stepped over the threshold into cool dimness.

"I'm the housekeeper. Edna Trask." She sniffed and turned her back on Kate. "Wait here. I'll see if she's feeling well enough for company."

Kate's first instinct was to follow her, to insure that she got to see Margaret Voss, but she was unable to break the ingrained rules of politeness that bound her firmly in place. Time enough to be rude and force her

301

presence on Lothar's widow if the housekeeper denied her admittance.

Curiously she looked around, admiring the simple Colonial furnishings and the stenciled wallpaper in warm tones of old gold and blue. Catching sight of herself in an oval wall mirror, she quickly ran a comb through her hair and put on some lipstick. Then she unsuccessfully tried to smooth the worst of the wrinkles out of her skirt, using the palms of her hands. A sniff behind her announced the return of the housekeeper.

"She'll see you." Edna Trask sniffed again, making her own feelings quite plain. Kate followed her upright body along the hall and through the kitchen. "She's out back in the garden. Old bones don't like cold."

The garden was a delightful sweet-smelling hodge-podge of flowers and bushes, apparently set out with no formal plan. The housekeeper led her to the back, where shade trees cast long shadows over a grouping of lounge chairs.

"She's dropped off to sleep," Edna Trask said, stopping short.

Fearing she would be denied the interview, Kate brushed past the housekeeper. Margaret Voss must have sensed her presence for she raised her head.

"Mrs. Voss," Kate said softly, stepping out of the sunshine into the shadow, "I apologize for intruding, but . . ." Her voice trailed away as the elderly woman shrank back against the chintz-covered upholstery in an attitude of alarm.

"Ooooh," she moaned.

Edna Trask elbowed Kate aside. "Do you have pain?" she asked sharply. "Do you want your pill?"

Margaret Voss was clutching the housekeeper's arm,

trying to lever herself out of the chair. Kate bit her lower lip anxiously, helpless, unable to do anything, even to say anything, since apparently she had triggered Margaret's fright.

"Leave us," Margaret said clearly.

"Mrs. Voss," Kate said pleadingly, only to be interrupted by the officious housekeeper.

"Go," she ordered. "Can't you see what you've done?"

Kate started to back away as the housekeeper turned her attention wholly to her employer, trying to ease her back against the cushions.

Margaret Voss was proving intractable. "No. You go away, Edna," she said impatiently, "I want to talk to the girl. Alone." Gone was the frail manner, the shrinking fear.

A by-now-familiar sniff punctuated the air. Kate reclaimed the three steps. After a long look, which would have withered a less determined person than Kate, the housekeeper marched off, her head held high.

"Come closer, girl. Sit next to me. It hurts my neck for me to have to look up at you."

Kate hurried to comply with Margaret's wishes as faded blue eyes studied her closely. Kate grew uncomfortable under the prolonged scrutiny. Her hands were sticky damp with perspiration; she could feel moisture trickling down between her breasts. A bee buzzed a nearby flower; inevitably, she thought of Wilma.

"Mrs. Voss," she said into the silence, "I apologize for disturbing you this way, but—"

"I thought I recognized you, that you were someone I knew long ago," Margaret interrupted, "but of course you're not." She was sitting up straight, her eyes dancing with life, with suppressed excitement. She reached out a brown-spotted hand and lifted a strand of Kate's hair. "Beautiful," she said. "Glossy, like the feathers of a raven." She laughed at the expression on Kate's face. "No dear, I'm not senile. I'm just an old woman who thought she'd go to her grave without seeing this day." She sighed and released Kate's hair. "It was a long time ago, but I'll never forget how she looked."

"Mrs. Voss, I'm Kate. Kate Windsor. My husband Chip, 'er, Charles, won the Voss Grant. I'd like to talk to you about, 'er—"

"Oh, I know who you are, dear. Edna made that clear. As to *why* you're here, I knew that the second I saw you. I'll never forget how she looked, the way she moved, even if I only saw her in my dreams. She was so happy. So was I, until . . . until—"

Kate felt the blood rush from her head. Her hands grew icy cold; little dots of yellow danced before her eyes. She closed them, felt her hands enfolded in a warm, dry clasp. *Dreams*. Margaret had said dreams.

"Isn't that why you're here?" Margaret whispered close to Kate's ear. "Didn't you suspect that I had seen her too? Little Sparrow. You resemble her so closely." Gently she patted Kate's cheek. It was wet. "Oh dear."

"I'm sorry. I seem to be doing a lot of crying lately." Kate fumbled through her handbag, searching for a tissue.

"Here, dear, take this. Edna keeps me well supplied."

"Oh, thank you." Kate accepted Margaret's tissue

304

and after drying her eyes and blowing her nose, returned Margaret's smile. Margaret had a very pleasing smile, warm and kind and—understanding. "Daniel would laugh. He always has to give me tissues."

"Who is Daniel, dear?" Margaret asked.

To her embarrassment, Kate blushed. "The uh, sheriff. Of Puffin Landing. Daniel Sheridan. He . . . he takes care of Smoke Island for the trustees of the grant."

Margaret looked thoughtful for several moments, then her face cleared. "Oh, yes. I remember the name now. I get letters, reports of the management of the funds from Lothar's estate. The grant is one part of it, and, I must tell you, something I didn't completely want. You see, I never could be quite sure that it was safe to let anyone live on that island. I never told a soul what happened. I wouldn't have been believed, you know." She frowned. "I had almost convinced myself I had imagined it, everything that happened that summer, because—because of my son."

"I just learned that he died on the island. I . . . I was so sorry to hear it."

Margaret shook her head sadly. "It was a very long time ago. Over fifty years. He was little more than a baby that summer. He'd be a middle-aged man today." She fixed Kate with a shrewd blue gaze. "Then that's what brought you here, isn't it?"

"Yes." She could be nothing but honest with Margaret. "That was one thing. You see, two boys were struck by lightning last July, the night of the fourth. One died. His . . . his body washed up on the island. It . . . it was awful."

Billy Sproul lying dead beneath the dock. White skin, splotched with bleeding freckles of brown. Seaweed snaking over him. She shuddered, saw again the rumpled bed, the dented pillow, the dark, sea-wet plant on the snow-white sheet. The dream that night had been real. Too real. *Oh God, what I suspect happened didn't really happen. Did it? Did it?*

"Kate? Are you all right?"

Kate gulped, nodded. "Something else happened that night. Something disgusting, unholy. A dream. I think. I . . ."

"You know, dear, it's very hard to shock me. I've lived a long time, seen a lot of things." She patted Kate's hand, then, incongruously, winked. "Women who married artists, back when I married Lothar, in the twenties, were considered no better than they ought to be." She chuckled, a rich sound of remembered wickedness. "Of course today, with what goes on, what I did, or what people *thought* I did—well, it all seems rather tame now. Pity. I think my generation had more fun; it's better when it's forbidden."

Kate was digesting this interesting viewpoint when the housekeeper effected an unsubtle interruption. She placed a tray with a pitcher of lemonade, the ice tinkling musically against the glass, on a small round table next to Margaret's chair. A heavenly aroma of freshly baked biscuits and muffins wafted from a linen-covered wicker basket.

"You need your strength," Edna Trask proclaimed.

"How very thoughtful," Margaret said blandly. "Edna bakes the best muffins in Connecticut. She spoils me shamelessly. Thank you, Edna, we won't be needing anything else right now."

Kate hid her amusement at Margaret's adept manipulation of the severe housekeeper. She refused a muffin, but accepted a glass of the lemonade and gratefully sipped the refreshingly cool liquid while Margaret helped herself to the contents of the basket.

"Um, zucchini squash muffins. They really are good. Are you sure you don't want one? I can't resist. Why should I? I have few enough pleasures left."

There was nothing Kate could say to that. Margaret ate the muffin with gusto and poured a second glass of lemonade for both of them before taking up the thread of the conversation. "So you see, Kate dear, there is nothing you can tell me that I won't understand," she said as if they had not been interrupted. "Perhaps I'm the only person on the face of the earth who will. That's really why you came to me, isn't it?" She needed no answer. "Tell me everything," she demanded, "including those things that are none of my business. They may turn out to be important. You may begin by telling me why the name Daniel Sheridan brings red to your cheeks." She smiled a mischievous smile which sent wrinkles cascading through her clear skin.

Kate talked, unburdening herself. Margaret proved a wonderful listener, raptly attending, an expression of deep understanding on her face. Compassion warmed her eyes. They were sisters in an exclusive sorority; bound by mutual experience—of the real, the imagined, the impossible. The minutes ticked by. Kate left nothing out. Old Nate warned her again not to go to the island. Natty Bumppo frolicked in her memory; died alone and presumably afraid.

"Poor dear," Margaret interjected.

Kate wondered briefly which of them she meant, then decided it was not significant. She described her feelings, her perceptions of Smoke Island, how she came to think of it as alive, imbued with a distinct personality all its own. Margaret nodded encouragingly as she related the dreams, told how they started, unclear, teasing, growing ever more vivid, more addictive— more erotic.

"Yes, I know," Margaret commented.

Heartened, Kate continued. The events surrounding the Fourth of July were especially painful to relate. The near-drowning of Melinda, the burning hail that attacked Paul right after they heard the legend of Iye, the Shapechanger, recited by Daniel Sheridan as they sat around the campfire: all described as unemotionally as possible.

Margaret made her repeat the legend; she had never heard it before. Blue-veined lids closed over the blue eyes as Kate patiently repeated the story. Iye's dark longing for Little Sparrow, his treachery, the final punishment; it all came pouring out, its impact not one whit lessened by the repetition. When she finished, the elderly woman nodded once, as if agreeing with something, then opened her eyes. It was the signal to proceed.

"That night I had another dream." Kate's voice fell to a barely heard whisper. Margaret leaned close to catch the words. "Two things happened in that dream. Two new things. I finally saw the face of Great Bear. It . . . it was Daniel, and—"

"Yes." It was the gentlest of prods.

"It was Daniel's face I saw, and in the very second I recognized him, I . . . I *felt* him, felt him inside me."

She raised pain-filled dark eyes to blue eyes which never wavered, never lost the kindness they expressed. "It was wild and wonderful, the loving in the dream that night. I had never felt like that before."

"What happened next?" Margaret was seemingly unfazed by the revelation.

Once again Kate awoke the next morning to the sound of her niece's screams. She described the bed, the dampness, the seaweed, the horror of the drowned Billy Sproul, the hysteria when she learned her husband had not been in their bed the night before.

"You think it was the boy?"

Kate felt nausea rise, swallowed convulsively, finally managed a thin whisper. "Yes."

"Go on," Margaret said calmly.

Kate described Chip's aloofness, his growing alienation from her, from everything that did not concern his work to Margaret in a flat, noncommittal voice.

The widow of an artist, Margaret was not fooled. "So you took a lover," she said.

"Not right away. I still had hope."

Margaret shook her head in the first negative gesture of the afternoon. Sadly, Kate understood it only too well.

"I had hope," she said again, "until Wilma came back. Wilma Thompson, Chip's agent," she explained.

"The girl who was buried today," Margaret said. "It was on the news, dear, but even if it hadn't been of sufficiently lurid interest for the media I would have known. The trustees are in a twitter. She died on my property, you know."

"I hadn't thought about that."

309

"No reason that you should. It was an accident, wasn't it?"

Kate locked eyes with Margaret Voss; black to blue; youth to age. "It was murder."

The ugly word brought the first gasp to Margaret's almost translucent lips. "Murder?"

The changing dreams, Little Sparrow's increasing apprehension, her puzzlement over the difference in Great Bear, his altered performance as a lover—the words tumbled from Kate in a torrential spate. The day—was it only two days ago?—in the cove, the dream which turned to nightmare, the metamorphosis of Great Bear to Iye, from considerate tenderness, from exhilarating passion to cruel disillusionment, to downright hurtful, punishing meanness. She told it all. Wilma lusted for her in the heat of an August afternoon. They fought again, the struggle described in vivid detail. She didn't omit she deliberately held Wilma under the water.

When Kate finished there were tears on her cheeks again. Automatically she accepted another tissue.

"Blow your nose," Margaret ordered and Kate complied. "What did the coroner say?"

"Bee venom."

"Bees. Again?"

"That's the other reason I came to you." Kate was feeling better, drained, but nevertheless better.

"You want to know how Lothar died." Margaret held up a hand, palm forward, in the universal gesture meaning "stop." "It wasn't bees."

"Oh."

Margaret continued as if she had not heard the defeat in Kate's voice. "It's time for me to talk, dear.

310

Listen," she admonished, and in a strong, clear voice, carried them both back over half a century to a summer that differed little from the present one. "Your experiences are almost a mirror image of mine," she began. "Lothar was not an easy man, mind you. Never easy, but always interesting, vital, exciting—until that summer."

Margaret sat back and told her story. It was an eerie parallel to Kate's, save for the obvious difference that Margaret had lost a son. Lothar had increasingly withdrawn, not because of the tragedy, Margaret supposed, but because of his work. "Nothing else was important," she stated, "not even me and my grief. It was as if I wasn't there. Oh, I think he would have noticed eventually if there was no food on the table, but only because it would have slowed his work." She said it without bitterness. The old hurts had lost their power.

"I lost myself in dreams," Margaret continued, "wonderful, exciting dreams. I never stopped to question them, I was only grateful they came. They diverted me, made life bearable. The girl, Little Sparrow, was so young, so hopeful, so happy with her virile husband. She was a joy to watch. I suppose I was just the tiniest bit envious," Margaret said primly.

Kate smiled. She understood perfectly.

"The summer was almost over," Margaret went on, "and I began to think that nothing would ever be the same again. I started to think of leaving Lothar. He didn't care for me, I thought. How could he? He was in love with his mistress. No, dear," she said, forestalling Kate's question, "not a thing of flesh and blood. Art was his mistress. He cared more for her than he ever did for me. But I think you've had similar thoughts.''

"Yes."

Margaret took a sip of lemonade. "It's one of the pitfalls in a marriage to an artist." She shrugged. "I think that one loves more than the other in any marriage. It's just more obvious in some. Anyway, I was close to despair. I had lost my son and, in a way, my husband too, and then one day everything changed. I was dozing in the little clearing by the side of the house when Lothar appeared. He was like the old Lothar; charming, considerate," she raised her chin, *"importunate,* if you get my meaning."

Kate did. How happy Margaret must have been to have her husband back. Husband, lover—no longer father to a son—but in time that too could change. Yes, Margaret must have welcomed him joyously back into her embrace on that summer's day.

"We started to make love. Right there in the clearing. It was wonderfully exciting, like never before. He was rough." The faded cheeks tinted a delicate shade of rose. "I liked it that way."

Kate carefully kept her face neutral. Margaret was her mother, her sister, her daughter. They were twins separated only by time.

"Then *he* came, stood over us, watching."

Iye? Had Margaret seen Iye on that long ago afternoon?

"It was over," Margaret said, the animation leaving her features, "over and never completed. For how could it be, with him there?"

"Who? Who was there?"

"Why, Lothar, of course!" Margaret seemed surprised at Kate's confusion. She frowned, then her face cleared. "I forgot to tell you. There were two of them. Two Lothars."

"Two?"

"I'm no more crazy than you are, dear." It was said slyly. It worked.

"Two of them," Margaret said firmly. "I never told this to another soul, Kate Windsor, but I'm telling you now today because—Why, bless my soul, I do believe I'm telling you because I finally know it's true. It really happened. Thank you, dear, you've made an old lady very happy."

"Mrs. Voss—"

"Margaret, dear. After all we've been through together."

"Margaret," Kate began again, "what happened? After . . . after Lothar appeared?"

The elderly woman's face froze, the remembered events stiffening her features into a wooden mask. "There was an accident. He died. He fell off the cliff."

Disappointment flooded Kate. So close. One look at Margaret's ravaged face and she knew she would never question her, no matter her burning curiosity. If Margaret held the answers, and Kate was sure she did, then they would remain her secret, her responsibility, forever.

Margaret broke into her thoughts. "That's not quite cricket of me, is it, dear? No, don't answer, we both know it isn't. You're entitled to the truth. As unbelievable as it is."

Kate felt miserable. "I've brought you enough pain."

"Pain purges."

"Iye said pain is pleasure. There . . . there is no difference."

"How astute of him." The tartness was back in Margaret's voice. "I can almost wish he had favored me with that insight all those years ago. But never mind, I shouldn't be facetious. You want to know what happened. How Lothar died. Well, dear, it's just as I said. He fell off a cliff. They *both* fell off the cliff, locked together, like Siamese twins. Gone, in the blink of an eye."

"How?"

Margaret did not even pretend to misunderstand. "One minute we were making love, when suddenly there were two Lothars, one standing over us, watching, his face changing with the speed of a cloud on a windy day, and the other . . . the other still loving me with a ferocity, an *intentness* which was all-consuming. Then he saw Lothar, the one standing, and he stopped, stopped loving me. It may seem strange to you, but at first I was furious," Margaret said defiantly. "I lay there forgotten, aching, thinking only of how empty I was. Then the shock of what I was seeing paralyzed me. I could do nothing." She trembled, remembering. "He disengaged himself from me. Slowly. I could see he was enjoying enraging the other Lothar. Then he got up. They faced each other; one dressed in smelly, paint-spattered clothes; the other naked, covered in sweat, from loving me."

"Margaret—"

"It's all right, dear. I have to say it. Perhaps now it'll stop haunting me. I . . . I couldn't tell them apart. It was awful. One of them laughed, I don't know which one. The laugh snapped me out of the shock. I knew then."

"How?"

Margaret looked faintly surprised by the question. "The smell, dear, it was the smell. I'm sure it's the same with Chip. No matter how thoroughly he bathed, or what cologne he used, Lothar always, *always* smelled faintly of turpentine." A strange expression crossed her wrinkled face; the faded blue eyes darkened until they looked like two sapphires, bright and hard. "I think I knew something was different that afternoon, right from the first. But I didn't care. I didn't care." She gave herself a little shake. "My, this is a day for truths, isn't it?"

Kate remained silent. After a pause Margaret continued. "Lothar grabbed the other one, the naked Lothar, and shook him. He . . . he was shaking smoke, then flesh, then smoke again. They struggled and fought, shouting, cursing, damning each other. I . . . I found myself crawling . . . crawling after them, because . . . because I couldn't get up. My legs wouldn't hold me. It seemed to go on forever, yet I guess it didn't take long at all. The struggle ended at the cliff. He . . . they fell."

Kate found herself twisting the soggy tissue. She could picture the spot, see the two men grappling, writhing, falling.

"I'll never know if he did it on purpose."

"What?" Kate thought she had missed something. "Did what on purpose?"

Margaret sat up straight. The young girl she had been peeked out of the faded blue eyes. "Why, dear,

I'll never know if he fell, or if he chose to go over the cliff, taking that other one with him."

"Which one?" Kate whispered.

"That's a question that maybe you'll be able to answer. You are going back, aren't you, dear?"

CHAPTER TWENTY-NINE

The first time Norman Day saw Kate drive through Puffin Landing he was on his way to Guido's Down East Pizza Parlor. Maybe one of his friends would be there. They could pass the time, rapping, bragging, lying, the way they always did. Things were different now, now that he and Joe didn't seem to be friends anymore. It wasn't that they didn't like each other. *He* still liked Joe. It was more— "Hell," he mumbled to himself, "we're both scared shit every time we see each other."

This piece of honesty was before him when he saw the rented car brake for the village's red light. Norman slipped into the shadow of Ye Olde Collectible Shoppe's darkened storefront and watched. When the light changed the car went a block and then turned off, toward the sea route.

She was back from New York and making straight for the sheriff's house. The rumors must be true. Norman slipped out of the shadows and went on his way.

No one would ever hear this from him. He liked Kate. She had always been kind to him.

Daniel's house was dark. Kate bumped the rented car over the rutted driveway at a speed guaranteed not to prolong the life of the tires. She was out of the car and ringing the doorbell before the sound of the engine completely died. "Damn," she said as she realized there was no one home. She had tried the office in town first, but it had been locked for the night. She had been sure he would be home. She had two choices. She could wait or she could find another way to get to Smoke Island. She got back in the car. There really had never been a choice.

The second time Norman Day saw Kate drive through Puffin Landing she was exceeding the village's conservative speed limit. He was just coming out of Guido's where there had been pizza but no companionship. Just a few old guys, friends of his father's, killing some time before they went home to their wives.

There were only a few cars abroad. Guido's was on a hill; Norman had a good view. He watched Kate's rented car go down three blocks and make a left, heading for the docks. He began to run.

She had parked the car right in front of the public dock. Smack inside the wide double yellow lines that edged Puffin Landing's only tow-away zone. Norman snorted to himself. They'd have to wake up Walt Perkins if they wanted a tow. The crusty old bastard sure would blister your ass if you disturbed his sleep.

Tourists, night owls, and the few permanent residents of Puffin Landing who preferred the dark for their activities were the only people still about. Norman knew all about them; he had flirted with some of them the year his grades had dropped, when he was thinking of making it big on the street. The sheriff had put an end to those plans. He had taken him on a tour of a big-time jail. The lesson had been learned. He guessed he owed the sheriff. Since in his mind the connection between Daniel Sheridan and Kate was now firmly established, he felt obliged to see what she was up to.

Kate was poking around the boats. She was halfway down the dock, moving slowly, ignoring the smaller boats in favor of those with sleeping accommodations. It was obvious what she was after. Norman slowed his forward progress, fearing interference on his part could prove inimical to his best interests.

The night sounds of the waterfront were magnified by a stiff breeze. Boats creaked at their mooring lines, buffeted by waves that slapped against their hulls before swooshing under the pier in choppy foaming curls. He could hear Kate, farther away now, the distinct sound of her footsteps echoing hollowly across the water.

It took several seconds for him to realize that she had cried out. "Holy shit," he said under his breath as the sounds of a scuffle reached him. In a split second he chose bravery over cowardice, action over prudence, and set off down the dimly lit dock at a dead run. He was yelling at the top of his lungs, a long, drawn-out ululation, which would have scared himself had his ears been tuned to it. Two startled faces materialized out of the murk. Norman skidded to a halt in front of them.

"What th'hell d'ya think yer doin', sonny?" Old Nate yelled. "Yer goin' t'wake th'dead with all yer hollerin'."

Norman felt hot color flooding his face and was glad for the obscuring dark. So much for Sir Galahad. He felt like a fool. Kate put her hand on his arm, on the bare skin, right beneath the sleeve of his T-shirt. A strand of her long dark hair was caught by the breeze, blew up to tickle across the base of his throat; he could smell her perfume, light and flowery. His face flamed even redder.

"Thank God you're here. You've got to take me out to the island. There isn't anyone else to do it. You've got to take me."

"Miss Kate, ma'am—"

"I wouldn't ask if I weren't desperate. Please, Norman. Please."

"Crazy. Yer crazy iffin yer do it."

For once Norman and Old Nate agreed. "Why don't you have the sheriff take you?" It was a stall, since he had a strong suspicion that she had already tried.

"He's not home."

They were both looking at him; Old Nate with the half-focused but somehow piercing stare which had earned him no little fear from Puffin Landing's young and old alike; and Kate, with a wild, pleading gaze which found his soul and laid it bare for his own inspection. The last thing on earth he wanted to do was to go back to Smoke Island, in the dark. He gave it one more try. "It's dangerous. At night," he said.

"I know. Otherwise I'd just ask to borrow your boat,

but I'm afraid I'd never reach the island and I *must* get there. I *must.*"

She had forgotten her hand was on his arm, if she had ever known it at all. Norman hadn't forgotten it, not for one second. It tightened when she spoke, conveying her anguish in a language more potent than any spoken word.

"Please, Norman. I have no other choice."

Norman found he too had no choice.

Daniel hung up the telephone and stared off into space. It was late and he was tired and where the hell was Kate at this hour? He would have a cup of tea and read the report one more time, hoping he was wrong. Then he would call again.

He picked up the thin folder containing Dr. Maynard Gully's final autopsy report on Wilma Thompson and went into the kitchen. The tea grew cold while he read. It was there; the same as the first time he read it; the same as the twelfth time he read it: Wilma Thompson had been dead for roughly eighteen hours before Kate said she had died.

Nothing made sense. He raked a hand nervously through his hair, picked up the mug and took a sip of tea. It was awful. He poured it down the drain and turned on the kettle again. The clocked ticked five minutes away. He would wait ten minutes more before calling her again.

He took the fresh mug of tea and the folder into the den. The room felt empty. He could sense Kate's presence everywhere: on the sofa, looking up at him with wounded eyes the first time he brought her here; on

321

the pillows in front of the fire, her body flushed with desire, painted in hues of rose, by passion and firelight both. He wrenched his thoughts away and stared off into space, trying to think.

There was no arguing with the report. Doc Gully stood firmly behind it. "What do you mean error?" he had roared not an hour ago. They were in Doc's living room, his wife Ethel hovering anxiously in the doorway, pulled away from the television set by the sound of their raised voices.

"What do you think?" Doc bellowed at her. "Daniel here says the time is wrong. He says the girl died eighteen hours later. Eighteen hours, Ethel. *Three-quarters of a day.* What do you think of that?"

Ethel *tsk tsked* and left them alone. The draw of the nighttime soap obviously far stronger than any real-life drama.

"Stop shouting, your audience just left. Tell me why you couldn't be mistaken."

Doc Gully went on for a long time, growing more technical by the minute, detailing exactly why his report was accurate.

Daniel drew a long, shaky breath. "I was afraid of that."

"You aren't questioning me?"

"No."

"It's Kate's statement you're worried about, isn't it?" Maynard Gully held out his hand. "Give it here, son. Maybe you've missed something."

He knew it was hopeless when he handed it over. If there was a mistake, it had to be with the autopsy report. He had been with Kate, loving her, at about the stated time of Wilma's death. He could never forget that time.

"Doc," he said, "put down the papers. I've got to tell you something."

The coroner listened without interrupting. "I see." He steepled his fingers, fixed the sheriff with a penetrating stare. "You couldn't be wrong about the time? The day?"

"Not likely."

"Mayhap Kate got herself a mite confused. She's been a lonely little lady out there all summer. A day more or less wouldn't much matter, now would it? Not to her, and certainly not to the other one. Wilma. Especially not when you and she were going to, 'er—"

"No!" A cold rage swept through him.

"Easy, son. No offense meant. I had to ask."

"Okay." He let a silence build while he worked consciously at diminishing the anger which had arisen at the merest hint that Kate was somehow implicated in a cold-blooded cover-up. "It's impossible, what you thought. Kate was telling the truth. As she saw it. I believe her."

"For what it's worth, so do I. I heard her myself. The little lady wasn't lying. I've had too much experience not to know."

Daniel shook his head. "Kate's telling the truth. Your report's factual. The two are mutually exclusive. There must be an answer somewhere."

"Hmph. Son, you've got yourself a little mystery, all right."

He had come home then. Home to an empty house, a silent telephone and very uncomfortable thoughts. There was an explanation, one that fit the facts, but it was too fantastic, too outright off-the-wall crazy to even entertain. At least not while he was sober.

What if Kate was right? What if Iye still lived? Had he taken Wilma's shape, used her to get to Kate? Was it possible?

"No, it's not possible, damn it!" he roared into the empty room, every bit as loudly as Maynard Gully at his most impressive. He went to the telephone and punched angrily at the buttons. "Come on Kate, answer," he said as someone started to bang on the back door.

He slammed the receiver down in midring and stalked through the house into the glassed-in porch. Old Nate stood on the top step, a peculiar expression on his wizened face.

"It's late, Nate. What do you want?" His anxiety over Kate was so great that he almost growled the question.

"You'd better go out right away to Smoke Island and see what's going on. That fool kid Norman Day took Kate out there a while ago. I tried to stop her but she had her mind set. I can't like it, Daniel. Not after what happened."

It took Daniel several moments to realize what was different about Puffin Landing's town character. Gone was the thick accent. Nathaniel Elwell Smith had surfaced within the shell of Old Nate. Daniel felt a chill skitter down his spine. Suddenly his own incredible thoughts didn't seem so ludicrous. He took off at a dead run, hoping it wasn't already too late.

CHAPTER THIRTY

Smoke Island appeared deserted, looming dark and forbidding looking out of the night. In the sudden silence after Norman cut the engine, Kate sat, unmoving, wondering just what she was doing there. Chip probably would not thank her.

"Uh, Miss Kate. Ma'am? We're here."

Kate shut her mind to the gloomy thoughts. It would all be over in a little while. Everything. Perhaps even her marriage.

"Miss Kate! *Please.*"

The urgency in the teen's voice roused her from the inertia which threatened to paralyze her. Too much, much too much was happening to her.

"Ma'am?"

Only one more thing to do. She got up and smiled at the alacrity with which Norman rushed to help her out of the boat. The smile faded almost immediately, leaving her features sober. She knew what it had taken for him to come to the island again—and at night.

"Thank you, Norman," she said gratefully when

she was standing on the dock. "I don't know what I would have done without you. I shouldn't be too long. If Chip isn't at the house then the only other place he could be at this hour is the studio, and—"

"Miss Kate!" Norman's eyes were so big and round they looked like two saucers. Orphan Annie's eyes filled with stark horror. "I . . . I can't *stay*. I . . . I—"

"You must, Norman, there's no other way," Kate said firmly. He was the only way off the island, and it was imperative she leave tonight—with Chip. Margaret had supplied the initial urgency, but it had escalated during the long drive from Connecticut, gnawing like a corrosive in her belly.

"Wait here. I won't be long," she promised, and hurried toward the granite steps, knowing that in another moment she would tell him to go, cut off her only avenue of escape to see the fear leave his eyes.

The steps were hard to negotiate, forcing her to go slowly since her leather-soled sandals had an alarming tendency to slip. Thank God they were fashionably flat; it would be murder trying it in heels. It seemed forever until she was at the top. The path before her was dark, strange, like the first night on the island. She should have brought a flashlight. She was about to call down to Norman to see if he had one when the sound of the boat's engine ripped the night quiet.

"Norman," she screamed, heedlessly running down several steps. "Normaaaaaan!"

Stupid. She should have known, would have known if she were thinking clearer. The boy had been tested to his limit. His bravery, in light of his fear, had been monumental.

She was on her own.

"You should have known the damn kid wasn't dependable."

"Chip!" Kate jumped at the suddenness of his appearance. The old protective feelings for the teenager filled her. Chip had been hard on him, right from the first. Hot words tumbled out. "He's very brave. After what's been happening here, to come back—"

"He left you flat," Chip interposed rudely. He came closer, held out his hand. "Here, you'd better get off those steps before you break your neck." He drew her up to the safety of the dirt-packed path. "Let's go. I don't want to stand here all night," he said impatiently.

"We've got to leave. Now. Tonight. There's no time for explanations."

He had retained her hand in his and now his grip tightened, became almost painful. "Is that why you came back?"

"Yes." She tugged at her hand. "You're hurting me." He started to walk, taking her with him, forcing her into a half-run in order to keep up. "Stop! You've got to listen to me! We've got to get off this island tonight. It's not safe."

He released her in front of the house. It was totally dark save for the rising moon. Chip's sandy hair looked silvery; his face was a chiaroscuro, pure light and shadow, bleached of color. His eyes bored into her, intense and dark.

"You must believe me. Margaret said—"

"Margaret?"

He was standing very close. She looked up, searched his face, seeking the reassurance of the familiar, some indication that he would listen. "Margaret Voss. I . . .

327

I went to see her, after Wilma's funeral. We had a very long talk."

"That bitch! She was amusing, but only for a little while." He ran a finger down Kate's cheek, laughed harshly when she shrank back. "Not like you." He hooked the finger under her chin, tilted her face up. "My dark beauty."

She jerked her face away, but not before he had a chance to see the expression of disgust which passed over her features. He laughed again, a sound totally devoid of warmth.

Kate got angry. Wilma had been agent, friend, hand-holder and lover to him. She deserved better. She shivered as she thought of the shrewd, brassy, honey-blond agent lying in her grave. Her memory deserved better. "You're a cold bastard," she spit at Chip. "You'll never find another person like Wilma."

"Ah, the green-eyed one."

A cold, numbing thrill of fear raced down her spine. Her heart began to thud heavily in her chest as suspicion entered her mind; a long, thin, snaky filament of doubt. Impossible.

He grinned at her. "I thought we were talking about Margaret."

He made no move to touch her again, yet Kate took another step backward. "How do you know Margaret?"

"Kate. My lovely, dark Kate. Don't worry. You're perfectly safe with me."

She extended her hand, whether in a gesture of repudiation or in order to symbolically ward him off, she did not know. Her breath caught in her throat, then issued reedily out through her barely parted lips. She had to know. "Who are you?"

For answer he moved close and touched his fingertips to the hollow at the base of her throat. She could feel her own pulse, pounding in a fearful arrhythmic beat. His fingers pressed down. Desolation swept through her, a loneliness, an isolation complete, chilling. Her eyes flew to his. They were twin pools of black, as dark and infinite as the sky above.

"You know who I am," he said, and pressed his lips to hers.

Nooooooo, she screamed in her head, as her body responded to the subtle, questing pressure of familiar lips and tongue. She relaxed, softened against him as he skillfully built desire, replaced desolation. He had done this before, only now it was real, not a dark dream of frustrated longing.

"I want you so," he breathed in her ear when they finally broke apart. "I've waited a long time." He closed her into his arms.

Kate sensed the leashed power, the barely restrained need emanating from him. She did not require the evidence of her senses, the absence of the faintest trace of the odor of turpentine, to know who held her. He had come to her in dreams, reached out through time and space to make her his own. His power over her was absolute. She was lost.

He felt her surrender. His body stiffened in triumph. He threw back his head, the stars above mirrored in his eyes as glittering cold points of light, and shouted his exultation into the night.

The primitive outpouring of emotion jarred Kate out of her fatalistic acceptance. She shoved him away, throwing him off balance by the sudden violent movement. Without close physical proximity her head cleared; she could think again.

"Where's Chip?" she demanded, warily keeping out of his reach. Danger lay with him; his very touch was a seduction she could not resist.

He knew it. It amused him to indulge her. He negligently waved a hand, encompassing the island. "He's here."

Kate started to inch away, alert to any sudden movement he might make. He was grinning at her, a wide, confident, infuriating display of total assuredness. Let him gloat, she thought. All she had to do was keep him busy, let him think her trapped. She would break away and locate Chip and together they would find a way off the island.

"Why would you want him?" he asked in a conversational tone.

The question stopped her cold.

"Ah, I see that got your attention." He chuckled, shook his head.

The voice, the intonation, the familiar movement of the sandy head sent chaotic thoughts racing through her brain. She must be crazy. This was Chip. It *had* to be him. He was punishing her, playing a mad, vindictive game because of what she had done.

"He doesn't love you, you know. Not the way I do. You were right. He's a cold bastard."

Kate stood frozen to the spot, like a fox speared by a headlight's beam. Was he doing this, scaring her, because she had left him, gone to New York, to Wilma's funeral? Did he feel abandoned? Was he so petty? Or was it because of Daniel, because she had given him her body, her love? No, not that. Chip might suspect, but he did not know for sure.

"He'd never forgive you, not if he lived forever." He had managed to come closer. "I have already forgiven you. All I want is for you to be with me. Forever."

He had forgiven her? "Oh no, Daniel." That was who he forgave her—and the he who was doing the forgiving was not Chip. The realization she was not insane, was not imagining this, was borne home to her.

"I see you finally understand. I forgive you even him, because I'm so alone." His voice was a low-pitched whisper, but so close was he that his breath moved her hair.

Her mind groped to encompass the terrifying truth. "You're Iye, the Shapechanger."

"Yes."

The flat admission released her from thrall. Rage filled her, a red misty curtain in front of her eyes. "Monster," she hissed. "Murdering monster. You killed Wilma, didn't you?"

"I did what was necessary."

"Necessary?" Billy Sproul, Wilma, Lothar Voss and his son—who knew how many others—all dead because . . . Why? She drew herself up, faced him squarely. "Necessary for what?"

"For you. For the strength to love you."

He made no move to touch her, yet she sensed his control, the same leashed power she had experienced before—in dreams. The abject loneliness, the waves of frustrated longing, had been very real. He had been her shadow lover, promising, ever promising, without the ability to take what he wanted. The reason was obvious.

"You needed a body."

His eyes burned with an unholy light. "My own has long since gone to dust, but I survived, survived even that! I live because I am whatever I choose to be. I am the wind, the earth, the grass, the trees, the fog that blankets the sea. I have traveled the years, the long, lonely, empty years, drifting and dreaming, waiting, always waiting."

Kate clung to the idea that there was still time—time for her, for Chip—to escape. Margaret had seen two Lothars. Kate knew she must find the other Chip. The real Chip. She knew she must keep Iye talking, distract him.

"What did you wait for?"

He seemed surprised by the question. "How can you ask? I've shared my dream with you. *You* are the one I've waited for, through the minutes, the hours, the years, the centuries of time. It's you with your hair like the darkest night, your eyes which brighten with desire, your body, so soft, so firm, so eager for love."

She took a small careful step back. "I'm not in your dream. It's Little Sparrow you want, not me."

"She is dead, dead to me forever. Her body is gone, her spirit also. I had to make do with pale substitutes. They never were enough, never came close to what I lost."

He was referring to Margaret Voss, and probably to others before her. Kate spoke without thinking. "So you just killed, without purpose, to relieve your . . . your boredom?"

He looked at her coldly, but she was beyond caring.

She had seen the result of his work. Margaret Voss had nothing but memories too. Only she had been blameless.

"Did you kill Lothar Voss?"

He laughed. "That vain, petty man? Just like your husband. Selfish." He laughed again. "He didn't much care about his wife until I did, then it was too late. He thought to destroy me, instead he destroyed himself. But he taught me a lesson. I learned. Just as I always have." His hands clenched, his entire body went rigid with emotion. "They tricked me, lured me here, to this place, this *prison*. They thought I would die. They left me to die. Alone. Alone."

He looked at Kate, his body relaxing its tenseness. "No longer. I'm no longer alone. I've waited, dreamed, drifted through time, and now I have you. You, my dark Kate, my vibrant beauty. You shall be my mate, my life, my companion. Forever." He held out his arms. "Come to me. Let me touch you, love you. Remember how it was. Remember. Think of the dream. Come to me." He took a step forward.

His voice was like black velvet, dark, sensuous, compelling. Kate felt her body soften, could not control the tingling of her skin, the feeling she could not breathe unless he held her, stroked her, relieved the ache in her breasts, her belly, with his body.

"Come to me," he said, his voice a caress. His influence was subtle, insidious. His yearning, his wanting her so desperately drugged her mind. "Come to me. I will make you mine. Forever. I have chosen you. Only you. I will make you immortal."

The moon was now overhead, very bright, very revealing. Kate could see every detail, every line, the very texture of his skin, the little pulsing vein in his temple. She looked up into his eyes. They were ink black, blazing with a cold light.

He was very close. "Perhaps it's this body which offends you." Chip's image trembled, dissolved, became a thick cloud of gray smoke which shimmered, coalesced into a tall, broad-shouldered figure. Great Bear held out his arms to her. "Come to me."

The horror of it released her from his spell. She turned and ran. She raced around the corner of the house, expecting at any moment to hear him coming close, feel a hand on her shoulder. She fled into the woods, sped down the path leading to the studio. It was dark under the umbrella of the trees, dark and treacherous underfoot in her leather-soled sandals. She must reach Chip. She concentrated on that, blocking her mind of everything else, of the night sounds, the rustlings in the underbrush, the low-lying branches that caught her hair, her clothes, the tender exposed skin of her arms, her face. She developed a stitch in her side, making it awkward to run. She held her side and went on.

She was panting now, panting from the exertion and from the fear, the overwhelming fear of what was behind her, coming for her. Her skin prickled. All at once she slipped and went down on her side, jarring the breath from her body with the force of the fall.

Where was Iye?

She rolled over onto all fours, pushed herself up onto her knees. She had to get up, get moving, find Chip. She used a big fir as purchase, walked her hands up its rough bark, pulling her body up inch by slow inch, until she stood leaning against it, her forehead pressed against her crossed hands while she waited for a sudden dizziness to pass. *I live because I am whatever I choose to be. I am the wind, the earth, the grass, the trees, the fog that blankets the sea.* Was this tree Iye? Was she leaning on him?

The woods were suddenly silent; she could hear her own breathing, but nothing else. She looked behind her. Nothing; at least nothing she recognized. She pushed away from the tree, turned to go. Something caught her eye; something moving, swaying, knocking against the other side of the tree. She saw it, identified it, and then the night was no longer silent as she opened her mouth and screamed—screamed and screamed and screamed again, until her throat was raw and her body was no longer capable of producing sound.

She was unable to take her eyes from it, from the body of her husband, swinging high above her, garroted by a branch, sharp needles embedded in his neck like an obscene ruff. A deadly boa. His face was dark, his tongue protruded. She reached up, grasped his foot, tried to stop his slow, twisting turn. As if it mattered. But it did, to her. It was the only thing she could ever do for him again. Something dripped on her arm. Thick black drops. Blood.

Twigs snapped behind her. She whirled about. He made no effort to conceal himself. He had no reason to. He had won.

CHAPTER THIRTY-ONE

He stopped in front of her, where she stood, shocked, beneath Chip's slowly twisting body. "I told you I learned. Lothar Voss was a valuable lesson." She stared at him with wide, vacant eyes. "There is nothing to stop us now. I will make you forget. You will be mine."

Panic flooded her as he reached out. Automatically she jumped back. Something poked her between the shoulder blades. A strangled cry choked out of her throat as she realized it was Chip's foot, dangling four feet off the ground. "Nooooooo," she moaned.

"Forget him. Come with me. I've waited long enough." He closed his hands around her upper arms.

The rational part of her retreated to a small protected place in her brain. "Let me go! Let me go. Letmego. Letmegoletmegoletmegooooo," she screamed, and balled her hands into fists which pounded him, pummeled the familiar/alien body with frenzied strength.

He shook her until her head snapped back. Wild,

grief-maddened eyes rolled up into her head. He slipped one arm behind her and was bending to place the other beneath her knees when she twisted and shoved him hard in the chest with the heels of her hands. He staggered off balance and she went racing away.

It was a mad flight, a run through densely growing trees, through choked underbrush that hid pitfalls even from the wary. Kate ran heedlessly, instinctively trying to put distance between herself and the terror behind. A gnarled root was her undoing. She tripped and fell flat. She lay still, her body bruised and sore, tingling from scrapes which were oozing blood, inhaling the smell of the damp needle-strewn earth. Everything became clear to her fear-maddened brain. All bodies return to clay. Her fingers began to scrabble in the dirt. There was a strange new sound in the forest. Intent on digging her grave, she tried to identify it, finally placed it as her own voice, keening an eerie tuneless song.

"Oh God," she moaned and collapsed with her face pressed against the ground. Hot stinging tears flowed from beneath her closed lids. A warm, rough tongue licked the trail of tears on her cheek. She opened her eyes to long, silky auburn hair, graceful, floppy ears, an inquiring muzzle from which the tip of a pink tongue escaped. "Natty Bumppo!" she cried, for one glad moment forgetting he had to be a sham, a dog of no substance. The setter yipped a low greeting, stretched his head up, exposing his neck for the oft-sought greeting, soliciting the love pats she always bestowed. She reached toward him, her fingers already tingling from the electric charge on his glossy coat, when she remembered. She snatched her hand back, as if from something fanged.

"Not fair," she screamed at the Shapechanger, who regarded her through well-remembered, beloved dog eyes. Hot, bright anger blazed within her, superseding the paralyzing fear. Her hand closed over a stout branch.

"Beast! Killer! Freak!"

She swung, putting her entire body into it. She swung for the setter, who had given her nothing but love; for Billy Sproul, victim of time and place; for Wilma, dead before her time; for Margaret Voss, sad relic; for Chip, whose swollen dark face with its fat, obscene-looking tongue bulging out of the dead mouth would not leave her mind; and, finally, for herself. Her aim was accurate, the blow should have landed the weapon solidly against his head. Instead, it sliced through smoke. The last she saw of Natty Bumppo was the proud, plumy tail, waving as if in farewell.

Great Bear regarded her with sorrowing dark eyes. He scooped her into his arms, went striding surefooted through the dense trees. He stopped in a clearing and put her on her feet. "It's time, my love. I will wait no more."

It was the clearing where she and Daniel had made love on a magical night that now seemed an eternity away. With a sinking sensation she knew her subjugation was to be total. Iye was jealously destroying even her memories. Her soul shriveled into a painful knot.

She felt him fumbling with her clothes, his fingers clumsy, unaccustomed to the concept of buttons, zippers. His borrowed shape was trembling with his need. Impatient, he hooked his fingers into the soft cotton material of her blouse, pulled sharply. The fabric tore, the buttons popping free. His eager hands spread the material wide, then swiftly moved to cup her breasts.

"Ah, so good." He groaned and lowered his head, his lips fastening on one breast with all the hunger of his love-starved soul.

Kate's head fell back, her eyes closing. His tongue was sweeping her tender flesh and it was responding, as if his attentions were welcome. Her breasts swelled, pushing more firmly into the shape of his hands. He slid an arm around her, drew her close to him.

"Look at me. Look into my eyes and remember, remember the long nights, the dreams, the pleasure that we shared." There was exultation in his voice as he moved his hips suggestively against her, letting her feel him.

A last, desperate plan formed in her brain, born of his assurance that her conquest was imminent. She forced herself to limpness, hoping he would misread it for the soft yielding which precedes love. Slowly she opened her eyes.

"Yes, yes, soon. Soon, my love," he breathed, mistaking her glazed, unfocused gaze for an escalating passion. She ground her hips against him, causing him to inhale sharply. He grabbed her hands when they strayed to the breech clout of doeskin that was the only garment he wore. "Patience." His hands moved to her waist.

"Let me, it'll be faster." She brushed his hands away, giving every appearance of trembling eagerness.

He looked at her glazed eyes and searched her face. Apparently he was satisfied with what he saw, for he tugged the material that covered him out of its confining band and knelt to spread it on the ground.

Kate forced herself to wait, one heartbeat, two heartbeats, then kicked him on the side and whirled away to go running through the haunted woods. She broke out of darkness into the bright beam of the moon's light where it illuminated the whitely gleaming flagpole on the windswept cliff. She entertained little hope of rescue, surely not in time to save her from the ancient lust of Iye, yet she must try to do something, anything, to delay the moment. One last gesture of defiance.

The bonfire Daniel had prepared needed only a touch of gasoline and a match. Kate got both from the metal box under the flagpole and went to work. The wood flamed instantly, the fire licking its way up the pyre, sending the urgent message roaring up into the night-dark sky. She waited until the entire pile was aflame.

It was a fatal mistake.

With a cry of rage Iye rushed past her, Great Bear's shape dissolving into thick gray smoke that settled over the leaping flames, choking them, depriving them of oxygen, of life. The fire began to die.

"No!" Kate ran to the signal fire, plucking a burning branch out and flinging it as far as she could into the trees. She reached for another, ignoring the searing pain as vulnerable flesh encountered live flame.

She had thrown two more branches when Iye stopped her. His strong arms lifted her up and flung her to the ground. She landed with a thud that jarred the breath from her body. The Shapechanger was again a thick cloud of smoke, busy trying to extinguish the new fires burning in the dry, scrubby underbrush. Kate turned her head and saw the can of gasoline and the box of matches. She curled around, got up so that she hid the can and slipped the matches into her pocket. She picked up the can and backed toward the trees, sloshing gasoline with every step.

"Stop!" It was Chip, in voice and inflection; the voice of command.

Kate put down the can. He nodded, approvingly. She fumbled in the pocket of her skirt. He was coming for her, coming to take her, to possess her, to steal her soul for his own. Her hand closed over the box of matches. She brought it out, opened the box. The scratch it made on the side of the box sent a shiver skittering down her spine. She held the burning match in front of her, shielded by her other hand. Chip disappeared; Great Bear looked at her with pleading, love-filled eyes.

"No. No, no, no, no, no."

She dropped the match. The woods ignited with a mighty whoosh. Flame raced in a molten river of fire, consuming everything in its path. The resinous trees crackled and spit golden sparks as they exploded under the pressure of the heat. Kate was in a race with time, barely two steps ahead of the conflagration. She took the path, flew down the dark treacherous way. She passed the body of her husband, lost precious seconds while she watched it catch, turn white-gold as fire embraced it in a blazing cocoon. Gone forever was the horrible face, the stiffly swaying corpse.

There was no time to mourn. Kate fled toward the dock, but the fire was greedy, feasting on the timber. She was cut off from the dock, from any hope of rescue there. Behind her she heard a great explosion and looking up saw the night turn to day as the studio, with its flammable materials, contributed to the destruction of the island. Thick smoke choked her, put tears in her eyes. Her heart labored, beat an erratic tattoo as it strained the tainted air from her lungs.

The night wind was pushing the fire toward the south. It herded her like a frightened doe. She came at last to the cliffs on the wild side of the island, the smooth, inaccessible cliffs that rose straight from the sea. Behind her the inferno raged. She knew it would be her final resting place.

"Kate." Iye as Great Bear stepped out of the raging conflagration. Naked, his bronze body gleamed red-gold in the fire's light. He took her in his arms and she let him, looking up into eyes which held sadness, pain and hurt. "I can make you immortal," he said and brought his lips down on hers.

Kate was transported back to a dark dream, to a time and place where she lay with him, his identity yet unknown. Then, he had shown her his longing, his loneliness—deep, cold, profound. Now, his dark longing filled her soul. She understood, responding to him on an elemental level. His need was so great, but so was hers. She held aloof, reserving the reasoning part of herself for the only life she had known. She wanted to go into eternity as what she had always been.

"No. I can't."

Respect tinged with a great sorrow painted his face. "There is little time left to us. Let me make it easy for you then."

Kate shivered in his hot embrace. He was fire and he was offering to take her with him, deep into the heart of the flame. It would be over quickly.

"Kate!"

She thought she would never hear that beloved voice again. With a glad cry she wrenched herself from Iye's arms, never stopping to wonder why he let her go. She looked out to sea, from where the shout had come, and saw a boat rocking on the waves. A shower of sparks singed her hair. Daniel would see her die.

"Come with me." Iye's voice was soft, yet she heard him clearly above the roaring of the fire. He made no move to touch her.

She tore her gaze from Daniel, so like yet so unlike the tall figure by her side. He was watching the sheriff with gleaming eyes; covetous eyes. Realization flooded her. Helpless, waiting to die, there was still one thing she could do: she could save the man she loved.

"Go away. Go away, Daniel. Go back. He's strong. Very strong. He'll take your body."

He ignored her. "Get down. Stay low. I'm coming to get you."

It was too late. A tongue of flame leaped out, touched her back. She stepped forward, near to the edge, looked down to the waiting rocks, like sharks' teeth, promising a quick, painful death. It was obvious to them, the two men who looked like twins, what she meant to do.

"Kate! Don't!" Daniel's voice tore through her. She imprinted its timbre on her brain.

"Come with me. Come to forever. I'll take you beyond pain." Iye wooed her with silken words, with unholy promises that only he could make.

Fire nibbled at her skirt. It was time. Kate took her life into her hands and commanded her own death. She took several steps back and then ran, ran straight for the edge of the cliff. There was no hesitation, not even a moment's pause. When she reached the edge she leaped, her body arcing up and over, out into space, on her way to oblivion.

Kate saw the heavens, said good-bye to the stars, like diamonds spilled across black velvet. She turned, looked down, saw the rocks, the sharp rows of death, beyond them the face of the man she loved. His was the image she wanted to take into eternity, but not the way he looked now, not with that haunted, horrified, helpless look. She spoke to him in her mind, using pure thought, hoping somehow he would hear, would understand. *I love you,* she said, over and over again, then wondered why she had the time, why she was not dead, why the look on her lover's face had turned from terror to stark disbelief.

She felt strangely light, buoyant. She seemed to glide through the air. She turned her head, saw gray feathers, the beautiful shape of a wing. Up, up she soared, catching the current, leaving the foaming sea and the terrible rocks far below. It was glorious, this freedom, this flight to forever. Into her mind came the flash of a dream, a dreadful feeling of longing, dark and sorrowful. Iye. He was in her thoughts; he was the air beneath her, above her, around her; he was the current which lifted her, supported her; he was the one who kept her safe. His need, his dark longing, poured into her, chilling her soul.

She circled, winging high. He was giving her a choice. His voice filled her head, offered immortality, exhilarating her by this taste of what could be. He whispered in her mind. "It's not too late. Say yes. You want to say yes to me."

She did. God help her, she did. He sensed her

344

thought, joyfully reached into the core of her being to make her his own.

Her heart said no.

"Wait!" It was a silent scream in her mind.

She folded the sleek gray wings, in close to the pure white breast, and streamlined, aimed for the sea. Like a silver bullet she streaked earthward, slicing through the path of the moon, relinquishing immortality with elegant grace. As she plunged into the dark-blue water he bade her farewell; she felt it as a sigh, a soft letting go as the cold waves embraced her form. She said his name in her mind. *Iye*. It was her way of saying goodbye.

Death was cold and dark, but the expected pain from the dousing of the light of life was absent. She felt something grab her arm, lift her up. She found herself, unbelievably, in the tight hold of Daniel's arms.

He climbed into the boat and pulled her up after him, wrapping her shivering body in his jacket. "Kate, my love, my life," he whispered in her ear as she stirred, opened dazed dark eyes to meet his tender gaze. He bent his head and kissed her, the hard, demanding kiss reaffirming her being, her right to life.

They finally broke apart and turned as one toward the blazing land. Smoke Island was being totally consumed, but before, where the flames had spread greedily, randomly, there was now an order, a gathering in, a solidness. With a sound like rolling thunder a great column of flame shot up, high into the night-black sky. Immense, awesome in his grandeur, Iye rose above the island, his body born of flame. He towered over them, a magnificent conqueror of time. They saw him as he once had been, in the true splendor of his earthly form.

Daniel kicked the engine into life. He steered the boat out, away, then changed direction, set them to circle the island, following his ancestors' path in a primitive reaction to the displayed might of Iye. Round and round they went, circling the island, repeating the ritual of long ago. He felt Kate's hand on his sleeve, turned to look where she pointed. A thrill of superstitious awe raced through him: they were not alone. Canoes paced them; sounds of chanting filled the night. They reinforced the boundaries of the prison: *the heavens above, the earth below and the sea, to the circumference of the circle made by their canoes.*

It could be an illusion, born of exhilaration, of euphoria. It could be nothing more than the flying surf, the sound of the waves as they slapped the rocks, but Daniel doubted it. Deep inside he knew the truth. The shamans had come from the past to protect the future.

He brought Kate close into his arms, held her so that he could feel the beat of her heart. "It's over, love. Nothing will survive. Iye is gone forever." He felt her shiver as she turned for a last, long look.

"God help me, Daniel, part of me loved him."

"I know." He tightened his embrace possessively. "It doesn't matter anymore." He could afford to be generous. He had what he wanted; everything else was ashes.

EPILOGUE

SEPTEMBER

While the first fingers of autumn blazed in patches of red across the northern land, Smoke Island lay charred and barren, a drear landscape of rock and scorched, blackened trees. Ash lay thick and gray, swirled by the wind. Nothing of the house or studio remained; the fire had leveled everything, without prejudice, consuming the creations of man and the magnificent, centuries-old products of nature with the same impartiality.

Nothing remained. Nothing alive. Nothing the eye could see.

Near the cove, in a crevice beneath a rock, a tiny microscopic spot of green was growing. The fire had covered the rock, had heated its surface, had searched beneath, in its quest for fuel, but somehow, some way, had missed this tiny, insignificant particle. Day by day, cell by cell, it increased in size.

* * *

He was small; weak. He must rest.

Patience.

He was drifting, dreaming, traveling the river of time. It was good, the dream, vivid, filled with exciting images; with her. She had come again, his dark, vibrant beauty; she would come again.

Patience.

He drifted, dreaming.

BLOCKBUSTER FICTION FROM PINNACLE BOOKS!

THE FINAL VOYAGE OF THE S.S.N. SKATE   (17-157, $3.95)
by Stephen Cassell
The "leper" of the U.S. Pacific Fleet, SSN 578 nuclear attack sub
SKATE, has one final mission to perform—an impossible act of
piracy that will pit the underwater deathtrap and its inexperienced
crew against the combined might of the Soviet Navy's finest!

QUEENS GATE RECKONING   (17-164, $3.95)
by Lewis Purdue
Only a wounded CIA operative and a defecting Soviet ballerina
stand in the way of a vast consortium of treason that speeds toward the hour of mankind's ultimate reckoning! From the best-
selling author of THE LINZ TESTAMENT.

FAREWELL TO RUSSIA   (17-165, $4.50)
by Richard Hugo
A KGB agent must race against time to infiltrate the confines of
U.S. nuclear technology after a terrifying accident threatens to
unleash unmitigated devastation!

THE NICODEMUS CODE   (17-133, $3.95)
by Graham N. Smith and Donna Smith
A two-thousand-year-old parchment has been unearthed, un-
leashing a terrifying conspiracy unlike any the world has previously known, one that threatens the life of the Pope himself, and
the ultimate destruction of Christianity!

*Available wherever paperbacks are sold, or order direct from the
Publisher. Send cover price plus 50¢ per copy for mailing and
handling to Pinnacle Books, Dept.17-213, 475 Park Avenue
South, New York, N.Y. 10016. Residents of New York, New Jer-
sey and Pennsylvania must include sales tax. DO NOT SEND
CASH.*

CRITICALLY ACCLAIMED MYSTERIES
FROM ED MCBAIN AND PINNACLE BOOKS!

BEAUTY AND THE BEAST   (17-134, $3.95)
When a voluptuous beauty is found dead, her body bound with
coat hangers and burned to a crisp, it is up to lawyer Matthew
Hope to wade through the morass of lies, corruption and sexual
perversion to get to the shocking truth! The world-renowned author of over fifty acclaimed mystery novels is back—with a
vengeance.

"A REAL CORKER . . . A DEFINITE PAGE-TURNER."
— USA TODAY
"HIS BEST YET."
— THE DETROIT NEWS
"A TIGHTLY STRUCTURED, ABSORBING MYSTERY"
— THE NEW YORK TIMES

JACK & THE BEANSTALK   (17-083, $3.95)
Jack McKinney is dead, stabbed fourteen times, and thirty-six
thousand dollars in cash is missing. West Florida attorney Matthew Hope's questions are unearthing some long-buried pasts, a
second dead body, and some gorgeous suspects. Florida's getting
hotter by deadly degrees—as Hope bets it all against a scared
killer with nothing left to lose!

"ED MCBAIN HAS ANOTHER WINNER."
— THE SAN DIEGO UNION
"A CRACKING GOOD READ . . . SOLID, SUSPENSEFUL,
SWIFTLY-PACED"
— PITTSBURGH POST-GAZETTE

*Available wherever paperbacks are sold, or order direct from the
Publisher. Send cover price plus 50¢ per copy for mailing and
handling to Pinnacle Books, Dept. 17-213, 475 Park Avenue
South, New York, N.Y. 10016. Residents of New York, New Jer-
sey and Pennsylvania must include sales tax. DO NOT SEND
CASH.*